CAPTAINS

&

CONSPIRACIES

THE INTELLIGENCERS ⚓ BOOK FIVE

BY
JANE GLATT

Books by Jane Glatt

The Mage Guild Trilogy
Unguilded
Unmagic
The Unmage

The Conjurers Duology
The Bookbinder's Daughter
The Shaman's Son

The Intelligencers
Pirates & Privateers
Traits & Traitors
Sailors & Spies
Dinghies & Deceit
Captains & Conspiracies

CAPTAINS

&

CONSPIRACIES

THE INTELLIGENCERS  BOOK FIVE

BY
JANE GLATT

TYCHE BOOKS LTD.

Captains & Conspiracies
Copyright © 2022 Jane Glatt

Published by Tyche Books Ltd.
Calgary, Alberta, Canada
www.TycheBooks.com

Cover Design by Indigo Chick Designs
Interior Layout by Ryah Deines
Editorial by Karley Hauser

First Tyche Books Ltd Edition 2022
Print ISBN: 978-1-989407-42-4
Ebook ISBN: 978-1-989407-43-1

Author photograph: Eugene Choi
Echo1 Photography

This book was funded in part by a grant from the Alberta Media Fund.

Thanks to all the hard working, essential workers who have been keeping the world running

CHAPTER 1

"WHAT'S GOING on?" Pia stood on her tiptoes in an attempt to see past Gustav's mother, Venne Falk.

"Someone just came in from Nurmi," Venne said over her shoulder. "Seems there's trouble there."

"That's no surprise," Pia replied. She should probably make her way through the crowd that had gathered in front of the ship building office. It was still called that even though during the winter Berna Strauskas—as the representative of her mother, the Interim Grand Freeholder—had been using it for official Fair Seas Treaty business. "There was trouble when Gustav and I were there two months ago." That was when they'd delivered the message to Clan Freeholder Timonis that the shipyards—his shipyards—were being commandeered by the Interim Grand Freeholder on behalf of the Three. Because they had proof that he'd committed treason.

Within a week they had delivered the same message to the other Swyford Clan Freeholders, and neither Liina Nowack nor Koit Kozlow had seemed surprised by what they'd been told.

With a sigh, Pia ducked past Venne and squeezed through the crowd. Someone noticed her and called out. "Intelligencer coming through, let her pass."

Half of the people stepped aside, and the other half turned to look at her.

"Thanks," she said over her shoulder. When she reached the

door, she knocked. "It's Pia."

The door opened, and Gustav grinned at her. "About time, get in here."

She stepped past him into the warm hallway.

"There are no reports of anyone hurt or sick," Gustav called out to the crowd. "Go on home. We'll give an update a little later."

He closed the door and turned to her. "Come on, you need to hear this." He led the way down the hall.

The sudden heat was stifling, and Pia yanked off her hat and undid the buttons on her coat as she followed Gustav through the door to Berna's office.

Berna sat behind her desk. Jarri and Janni Breck were off to one side, Jarri standing behind Janni, who was in her chair. A couple of shipbuilders, including Gustav's father Gunnar, ranged along one wall. Kaja, her eyes on Pia, leaned down and spoke to Berna.

Even from the back, the man who sat in front of Berna looked familiar. Pia Concentrated and then nodded.

"I knew you'd recognize him," Gustav said into her ear. "It's the man who chased me when I delivered the message to Timonis. The one you tripped up with the wood pile."

"What's he want?" she asked, her question louder than she'd planned.

"That's what we need to find out," Berna said. "Pia, I'm glad you're here, and I would very much like you to listen to what Freeholder Reenberg has to say and then give me your opinion."

"Of course," Pia replied. She shivered as her Trait triggered. She'd discovered that her Trait was really good for determining how unrelated information was connected. She'd been doing her best to practice, but there wasn't much to test it on other than the weather. She was confident that she could predict when a storm would hit and how long it would last, but she had no idea if she'd be able to figure out anything based on what Timonis's man said.

"It's the pirates," Freeholder Reenberg said. "For most of the winter we've been able to keep them secluded in a freehold, but now they've gotten out and they're tearing Nurmi apart looking for food and drink."

"Secluded," Berna repeated. "I thought that they were imprisoned in Leif Stendhal's freehold?"

"They were there," Reenberg agreed. "And now they're not."

"I would expect Clan Freeholder Timonis to take care of this situation," Berna said. "Not only is it his responsibility, but I believe you work directly for him as a guard. Is he the one asking for help?"

Reenberg shifted in his chair, and something about that caught Pia's attention. What did she know about the pirates? Ah, of course.

"The Clan Freeholder is part of the problem," Pia said. "The pirate captain has convinced Timonis to do something that the rest of them don't like."

"Is that true?" Berna asked Reenberg.

The man fidgeted in his chair again and then sighed loudly. "It's true. I don't know what he's promised them, but they're walking around town like they own it and everything in it. The town's food supplies have all been moved out of the common warehouses, and people are worried about starving. Clan Freeholder Timonis won't listen to reason. He just doesn't seem to care about the rest of us."

"You want me to intervene on behalf of the Interim Grand Freeholder," Berna said. "Do the rest of Timonis's freeholders want that? I will not act against a Clan Freeholder without the support of the majority of his freeholders."

Reenberg pulled a sheet of paper from his pocket. "A few signatures are missing," he said. "Mostly because the weather was closing in, and I needed to get here before a storm hit." He handed the paper to Berna, who unfolded it. She held it out to Kaja.

"I'll need to confer with my Intelligencers," Berna said. "I hope you understand that I can't have you wandering around town by yourself." She nodded at Gunnar Falk, who stepped away from the wall.

"I'll see to him," Gunnar said. Reenberg stood up and, with a hesitant nod at Berna, followed Gunnar out of the room.

"What can you tell us about the ones on the list?" Berna asked Kaja.

"It seems to be most of Timonis's minor freeholders," Kaja said. "People who would normally be loyal to him. I recognize a couple of the signatures: they seem valid."

"So, it's a real request," Berna said. "Pia, take a look at the names and tell me how you knew Timonis was working with the pirates. Again."

Pia took the list from Kaja and scanned it. She didn't know most of them, so she couldn't make any connections. She handed the list to Gustav and turned back to Berna.

"The new pirate captain is Ursa Ozlinch," Pia said. "Dagrun Lund thinks she has a Keeper Trait. That Ursa can bind people to her."

"I can confirm that," Kaja said. "According to Dagrun, Ursa's Trait is fairly strong. She used her Trait on Dagrun's sister Inger, and Dagrun was unable to counter it."

"You think the new pirate captain has bound Timonis to her with a Trait." Berna nodded. "Can we unbind him?"

"Maybe." Pia looked at Gustav. "But Timonis is stubborn."

"Stubborn is an understatement," Gustav said. "Ursa Ozlinch has had two months to get him on her side. I doubt we can change Timonis's mind in less than that."

"We don't have two months." Berna said. "That food must be found or people could starve. There must be another, more immediate, option."

"If Ursa died, the hold she has on Timonis would die too," Kaja said. "At least that's what seems to have happened when Margit Ansdottir died."

"Are you suggesting we kill her?" Berna asked.

"It won't come to that," Gustav said. "I'll use my Trait on Ursa."

"If you think it will work," Berna said. "You had no success with Timonis."

"Dagrun Lund thought Margit Ansdottir's Traits affected Ursa Ozlinch," Kaja said. "There is no reason to think Gustav's won't."

"It's worth a try," Pia said. "I'm coming with you, of course." She was not going to let him go to Nurmi alone.

"Thank you, Pia," Berna said. "I will count on the two of you to make sure that the threat the new pirate captain poses is resolved, one way or another. Before you leave, Kaja will tell you which of these freeholders," she gestured to the list of names, "you can ask for help if Gustav's Trait doesn't work."

Pia closed her eyes for a moment before nodding. She met Gustav's solemn gaze. She hoped his Trait worked on the pirate because otherwise it sounded like she and Gustav were expected to figure out how to kill her.

THE *ATLAINE* CUT through the waves, and the wind whipped past Calder as he stared out across the sea. They'd heard a rumour that Pinho had come south, but so far, he hadn't spotted any ships. Not Pinho and what was left of his fleet, nor the pirates in the *Vassan*.

"Take us back home," he said to Darya.

"Yes, Sir."

Calder nodded, strode away from the wheel, and went forward to the bow, worried that they'd somehow been misled. That the rumour had been a deliberate falsehood in order to lure the ship away from Zelesso and leave the city vulnerable.

He had to remind himself that Dag hadn't seen any hidden threats in the rumour. Besides, she was in the city and should be able to make sure it was safe. A watch had been set up to look for obvious threats, and Dag would see any hidden ones.

Before they confronted the Arressan council they wanted to know where Pinho was, but so far Luck had not helped him.

He sighed. Charis was in contact with some influential people in Messanos, including council member Nilus. The news he'd sent was that without Pinho to back her, Floros was quickly losing the confidence of her allies. Her main advantage was that she still had control over Pinho's shipbuilding facilities, which employed dozens of people and was the path to wealth for many others.

At this time of year, the shipyard was quiet. It was the usual lull in work that happened a few months after midwinter when the stockpile of timber had been depleted. Shipbuilding in Arressa relied on Fair Seas Treaty timber, much of which was supplied by his mother's freehold.

Calder was going to threaten to make the work stoppage permanent. Charis thought that would be enough to ensure that Floros lost the little support she still had, but only if Pinho—along with his resources and alliances—was no longer a factor.

The Pilalian captain hadn't been seen in weeks. Neither had Rahm or the pirates.

Calder thought it possible that the pirates had fled back to Strongrock. There were reports of them pillaging along the coast of Pilalia, so if they were able to gather enough supplies, they might stay away from Arressa long enough for Charis to join the council. One more vote could keep Floros from making all of the decisions.

If Rahm had gone to Strongrock with the pirates, that would be even better.

Calder frowned. His father held his token. With the compulsion gone, would he stay in Zelesso? Or had his new target—selected by the head of the suicide assassins—been enough to cause him to disappear without saying goodbye to his wife and children.

With the Frozen Pass closed, there was no way for Rahm to get to Tarklee by ship right now. He might have decided that Strongrock was a safe place for him to wait for the pass to open.

The other option, one he didn't think his father would attempt in winter, was to cross the Teeth in a small sailboat.

NADEZ KNOCKED BUT didn't wait for an answer before entering Lauma's office.

"A third warehouse has been emptied," Nadez said. "It happened last night."

"*Skit*," Lauma swore. "Did anyone see anything? I thought we doubled the guards?"

"We did." Nadez sat down heavily across from Lauma. "But the four of them are nowhere to be found."

"Deserted or murdered?"

"I don't know yet," Nadez said. "But if they're not dead, they might wish they were." They'd been keeping close watch on their dwindling food stores, and the only people at these warehouses had been guards. Someone was stealing the last of the food, and it wasn't a mob of hungry people: this was an organized theft. "I'll be visiting all of the Freeholds again starting today. I'm not going to pretend I'm doing anything other than looking for the stolen food."

"You're taking guards with you?" Lauma asked.

"Yes," Nadez replied. "The ice is starting to recede near the dock, so I will take the ones who were helping keep the *Tazeyar* free." Keeping the ice away from the hull of the ship had been a constant task for the past few months. "I'll make sure there are plenty of guards for overnight shifts in case it gets cold enough to freeze again."

"Good. Let me know what you find," Lauma said. "You think Ottosen is behind the thefts?"

"Who else has as much to gain?" Nadez replied. "And is willing to let people die for his plans? But he's too smart to hide the stolen food on his own freehold. I'll have guards search in unlikely places while I am visiting the Clan Freeholders."

"Can you trust the guards?"

"Most of them are dependable," Nadez replied. "Many are furious at the thought that some of their own may have been complicit and disloyal. No one—especially the guards—wants to see food riots."

"Very well," Lauma said. "The ice farther out in the harbour is getting trickier for ice fishing. I'll need to be out there to monitor for safety. I'll continue organizing the storage and distribution of whatever they catch, as well. People need to see us working to ensure that everyone eats."

"No matter how small a meal," Nadez said. Like everyone, she was thinner than she'd been at the start of this. Lauma had made sure that food distribution had been fair, and so far, that had been enough to prevent people from getting too angry or desperate and rioting.

There had been a few souls in the beginning who had contested Lauma's actions, but now, so many months had passed that the citizens of Tarklee seemed resigned to their hunger. But if they didn't at least stop further thefts, Nadez wasn't sure people would continue to be calm when rations had to be reduced, yet again.

"It's still at least a month before we can expect to see the *Atlaine*?" Lauma asked.

"Probably," Nadez said. "As long as they can find something to fill their hold with and don't have to wait for new crops." From her study of shipments out of the Sapphire Sea, she knew that food didn't usually start arriving until mid-spring, still almost three months away. But she'd spoken to some of the Merchant Adventurers, and they'd assured her that was partly due to travel time from Tarklee, through the Frozen Gap, and then back home. A ship already in the Sapphire Sea that could sail through the Teeth should have a much earlier arrival date. Something they were all counting on.

Nadez got to her feet. "Shall we meet here later?"

"Yes." Lauma frowned. "We could use some of my son's Luck right now."

"And Dagrun's Unseen Trait," Nadez replied. She nodded and left the office, heading towards the barracks. On the way she hoped to have some inspiration about exactly where to have the guards search.

"Do you want me to shorten the sail?" Gustav asked. He rubbed his mittened hands together, trying to keep his fingers nimble. It wasn't quite spring, but at least this far south the sea was mostly clear of ice. Over the winter, Pia had insisted that he teach her how to sail an ice boat. Now that they were on open water, there were different pitfalls she had to learn to deal with.

"Since you're asking me, I assume that I do," Pia said. She stared up at the sky, and he could practically see her Concentrate in order to make a decision. "Half sail," she said finally.

He nodded. "That's what I would do." He rose and untied the sheet and shortened the sail. They were about half way to Nurmi, and the sun was high in the sky. Pia had chosen today to travel because she'd said they would have a steady wind and clear skies. So far, she was right.

"I *know* that's what you would do. If I ever get sailing lessons from someone else, I might learn about other options," Pia said. "Hold on, the wind is going to pick up."

Gustav sat down and grabbed the mast. Pia hadn't been wrong about the weather in weeks, and he had no reason to think she'd be wrong now. She'd spent most of the winter talking to people with weather knowledge, and she didn't remember everything they said, not the way Kaja did with her Memory Trait. But somehow when Pia Concentrated, she was able to access the relevant points of what she'd been told, put it all together, and figure out what was going to happen in the next few hours and—increasingly—for the next few days.

It was extremely impressive, and valuable, but he had to remember that Pia's use of her Trait depended on her having enough useful information.

The wind picked up, and the path ahead of the little boat was soon dotted with whitecaps. "Is it going to get any rougher?" he asked.

Pia shook her head. "No, but it will be like this until late afternoon."

A wave hit the prow of the sailboat, and spray washed over

him. It didn't soak him, but much more of this and he would be completely wet, and it was still cold enough for that to be dangerous.

"We need to get out of this rough water." He crab-walked to the stern. "Either by landing or heading away from shore and hoping it's calmer farther out." He scanned the shoreline. "If we can make it, we could set ashore in Setberg." The tiny logging village had been all but abandoned when the pirates had raided and burned the warehouses and docks. "And then walk to Nurmi," he finished.

They had their own food with them, and the Elorelle River would provide them with water. Even if a few people had returned to the village, they could probably find an abandoned house or workshop to stay in. Anything was better than a night spent huddling in the boat.

"Let's do that," Pia said. "I'll take us in closer to shore. Hopefully it won't be much rougher than what we're sailing through."

The waves had more force and direction closer to land, and Gustav had to take over the tiller. He struggled to stay far enough out from shore to keep the sailboat from being pushed onto the rocks by the strong wind. Pia adjusted the sail so that they tacked out towards the open sea.

"There's the mouth of the Elorelle," Pia called out.

Gustav looked past her, and a moment later a huddle of burnt-out buildings came into view. "I smell smoke," he said. "I think someone is here."

"I guess someone returned from Nurmi," Pia replied. "Look, there's a sailboat tied up to what's left of the dock."

Gustav turned the tiller and pointed the prow towards the dock. If the dock was already in use that meant it should be safe for them to use too. Pia untied the sail, rolled it up, and lashed it to the spar before grabbing an oar from the bottom of the boat and paddling.

Once they were close enough to a relatively undamaged stretch of dock, he pulled up the tiller, untangled the painter, and climbed up onto scorched wood. He tied the little boat up, and Pia joined him.

"It seems solid enough here," she said. "Oh look, someone's come out to meet us."

He followed her gaze to a single figure standing on shore watching them. Gustav raised a hand in greeting, and after a moment the figure raised one in reply.

"Let's go see who's living in Setberg," Pia said. "And see if they have any news of Nurmi."

She set off along the dock, and Gustav followed her. As they got closer, their host became clearer. Gustav paused. It was unusual, but not unheard of, for a Pilalian to be so far from Tarklee.

DAG ABSENTLY POURED herself more tea as she stared at the map.

"I wish we knew for sure that the pirates had gone back to Strongrock," she said, voicing something they all had said before. "And no, we should not send the *Atlaine* to check." It had been three days since Calder had returned after chasing the rumour about Pinho. Three days without any other whispers of sightings. They had no more days to wait. The Three had no more days to wait. Even now the path through the Teeth might be open.

All they needed to do was buy food in Messanos. The worry, besides not finding anything to purchase, was that the Arressan Council would not allow them to. She looked across the table and met Calder's eyes. "It's time to go."

"I agree," he replied. "Charis, how soon can you be ready?"

"I'm ready now," Charis replied. "My contacts have been waiting for my arrival for days."

"I'm ready too," Inger said.

They planned on sending the council a signed notice from Calder, representing his mother, stating that no timber from the Strauskas Freehold would be sold to Arressa while Pinho and Floros were in charge. The note would advise the council that the Merchant Adventurers were aware of—and would enforce—this decision.

Dag, Calder, Inger, and Charis would travel into the city and wait at the Merchant Adventurers office for the council's reply.

Dag blew out a big breath. "That's it then. Darya, when can we sail?"

"We can be ready in an hour," Darya replied. "But I suggest we wait until dark, in case Pinho has someone watching us."

"All right," Calder said. "We'll leave just after dark and arrive in Messanos in the morning."

Dag remained seated while everyone except Calder filed out. It was his family's home, after all. Well, it was his father's home, along with his second family.

"Esma will want to come," she said. "And I think she should."

Calder sighed and held his hands out over the map, and Dag put hers into them. "She's been begging me to come," he said. "She talked to you?"

"Yes, but she didn't have to. She knows Messanos better than anyone other than Charis. I want them both there so that one of them can always be with Inger."

"I thought you were certain that Inger's Trait no longer makes her an obvious target?"

"I am," Dag replied. "But her position does. Esma was working with her before, so it won't seem odd if she's at the Merchant Adventurers again. Besides," she paused. "I think enough people know who Esma's father is, and that could help keep them both safe. And remember, Rahm previously told merchants to sell to us. We want them to sell to us again."

"Esma comes," Calder said. "And Rahm is useful even when he's not here."

"He did supply your mother with enough coin over the years to allow her to buy most of Byholt," Dag said. "Without that we'd have nothing to threaten the council with. I just hope it's enough to turn everyone away from Floros."

"It has to be," Calder replied.

"Yes, it does," Dag agreed. They didn't have enough information to produce a backup plan, and this one assumed that Pinho wasn't in Messanos. So, this had to work.

NADEZ STRODE UP to the door of Saulia Holt's Tarklee home and knocked on the door. It was late, but she didn't think this could wait until morning.

One of the missing guards had recently been seen here, and she needed to confirm it. Guards flanked her because if it was true, Saulia Holt was potentially working against the Fair Seas Treaty Alliance.

"Open up in the name of the Three," she called. "It's the Master Intelligencer. I must speak with Clan Freeholder Holt."

Lights flickered in a couple of upstairs windows, and she knocked on the door again before taking a step back.

"You're certain it was him?" she said to Bendiks, who stood on the step below her.

"It were him," Bendiks replied. "I bunked beside Fricis for four years. I know how he moves and how he skulks." He spat. "Traitor."

"All right." She stepped back up to the door. "We have a report that you are harbouring a deserter from the Guard," she called out. "Open this door now."

Finally, there was sound from the other side of the door. It opened, and Nadez squinted against the lamplight that spilled out.

"Come in, Master Intelligencer," Saulia Holt said as she tied her robe. Her assistant, Mykol, stood behind her, holding the lamp.

Nadez strode past her, Bendiks and half a dozen guards following her inside, crowding the entrance hall.

"Do you really need all these guards?" Saulia asked.

"I don't know yet," Nadez said. "It depends on what answers you give me and whether we need to do a full search of your estate. Where is Guardsman Fricis?"

"I have no idea who that is," Saulia replied. She walked past Nadez and through a doorway. Nadez stared at Mykol, who looked away, before following Saulia into a large sitting room. The housekeeper scurried away from the fireplace, a small fire crackling in it.

"Mykol knows," she said. "Bendiks, bring him." She paused to watch the housekeeper sidle towards a door at the far end of the room. "Your housekeeper stays too."

"Maeve?" Saulia asked. "What does she have to do with any of this?"

"I didn't think it would do any harm. I'm so sorry," Maeve said. "Just a couple of nights, that's all he needed. He's my nephew, you see, so I had to help on account of my poor sister."

Saulia turned her gaze onto her assistant. "Mykol? Did you know about this?"

Not for the first or probably the last time, Nadez wished for an Unseen Trait. Had Saulia really not known, or was her household saving her at their own expense?

"I'm truly sorry, Clan Freeholder," Mykol said. "I found out late today, after the guardsmen had been here for hours. I should have told you right away."

"Where is Fricis right now?" Nadez asked. Whatever else was going on within the Holt Clan Freehold, she needed to question the deserter. Finding out who had stolen the food and trying to locate it was more important than treason. Something she'd challenged Lauma on months ago but now, sadly, understood.

"Yes," Saulia said. "Of course. Mykol, you are to fetch him at once. At least two of Nadez's guards will join you."

Nadez nodded at Bendiks and the guard behind him. When Mykol left the room, they both followed him.

"Master Intelligencer," Saulia said. "I want to apologize for the behaviour of my household. I assure you that I had no knowledge of this, but of course, it happened under my roof, so I take full responsibility. What exactly is this man accused of doing?"

"He had guard duty the night all the food was stolen from a warehouse," Nadez said.

Saulia frowned at her housekeeper. "Maeve! How could you be party to this?"

"I'm sorry, Clan Freeholder," Maeve said. "I'm sure my nephew didn't take any food."

"But he knows something," Nadez said. "Why else would he desert and come here to hide?"

"I heard rumours that food stores were getting low," Saulia said. "But no one has said anything about thefts."

"We don't want anyone to panic," Nadez said. "I've had guards scouring the city looking for either the food or someone who knows where it is."

"Panic," Saulia repeated. "Are things really that dire?"

"We hope not," Nadez said. "But if the thefts continue, we *will* face starvation before we make it to spring."

"I see." Saulia shook her head. "Maeve, you need to tell us what you know."

"I don't know anything about stolen food." Maeve hung her head. "Just that my nephew was in danger and needed a safe place for a few days."

Nadez frowned. Had Maeve really not known? Although, whatever the maid had known was less important than what her nephew knew.

"Here he is, Master Intelligencer," Bendiks said from the doorway. "Shall we take him to the jail?"

"Yes. I'll deal with him there. Bring Mykol and Maeve along as well." The housekeeper whimpered, and Saulia sighed.

"I am very sorry about this Master Intelligencer," Saulia said. "My household will cooperate completely. Isn't that right, Maeve?"

"Yes, I will tell you what I know."

"Good," Nadez said. "I will let you know what decision I make in regards to your staff: whether they will be free to return here, if you want them, or if they will face any charges."

"I would like them back," Saulia replied. "If that's allowed. I would not turn out anyone when the city is still at such risk."

"Very well," Nadez said. She hadn't expected Saulia to abandon either Mykol or her housekeeper since they'd both been trusted members of her parents' household.

"Thank you, Clan Freeholder," Maeve said. "I am ever so grateful." Head bowed, she walked out the door.

Nadez nodded to Saulia Holt on her way out of the house.

Lights were visible in a few other houses when she stepped outside.

Nadez sighed. She'd been up for almost twenty hours: interrogating the prisoners would have to wait. There were still two warehouses to check before she could grab a few hours of much needed sleep. After giving instructions to Bendiks, she took a couple of guards and headed out into the city.

CHAPTER 2

PIA DID HER best to make her smile seem natural. The truth was, her Trait was screaming that nothing this man had told them made sense. He called himself Hakon, but she was certain that was not his name, nor was he a logger from Setberg. She flashed a hand signal to Gustav telling him to be careful about what he said.

"Oh sure, my da taught me to sail one of these little boats before I could walk," Gustav said. Without looking at her, he nodded once, acknowledging that he understood that this Pilalian was a threat.

Pia looked from Gustav to Hakon, and her breath caught in her throat. He was looking at her hands. She shoved them behind her back, hardly daring to breathe. His eyes narrowed for a moment, and she knew that he'd seen her hand signal and worse, he knew what it was.

"I think we can help each other," Hakon said, abruptly interrupting Gustav.

"Do you need a sail?" Gustav asked. "We don't have a spare but . . ." He trailed off when Hakon crossed his arms and frowned.

"Help each other how?" Pia asked.

"I've a mind to do a favour for Intelligencers," Hakon said. "If you promise to do a favour for me in return. And don't insult me by pretending you're not Intelligencers."

"We should talk somewhere warmer then," Pia replied. Hakon

smiled, but it didn't make her feel safer. "I smell wood smoke."

"All right," Hakon replied. "Follow your nose. I'll be right behind you so don't try anything. And I know my share of dangerous girls, so don't think I'll drop my guard around you."

Pia sighed and blinked at Gustav as she passed him on her way to a small huddle of buildings. She heard his steps behind her as she walked along a path, following the smell of smoke. The door to the little hut was closed, and she paused in front of it.

"Go on in," Hakon called out from behind. "There's just me so don't worry about startling anyone inside."

She pushed the door open, and a blast of heat hit her as she stepped into a one room cabin. By the time she, Gustav, and their host were all inside, there was little free floor space.

"If I'd known I was going to have company, I'd have picked a bigger cabin," Hakon said as he closed the door. "Sit."

Pia and Gustav did as they were told, sitting at a small table in the only two chairs she could see.

"No, you wouldn't have," Pia said.

Hakon leaned against the closed door. "I wouldn't have what?"

"You wouldn't have picked a bigger cabin," Pia said. "You don't care about our comfort and heating a bigger cabin would take so much more time and effort."

"True." The Pilalian stared at each of them for a few moments. "What are your Traits?" he asked. "And don't say you don't know what I'm talking about. You," he motioned to Gustav. "I like you, and I don't usually like anyone which means you're what, likeable? Is it useful?"

Pia met Gustav's eyes and shrugged. She didn't see any harm in telling him what he wanted to know, especially when not telling him might make him angry. She had a feeling that would make things much worse.

"Charisma," Gustav said. "And yes, it can be useful. Though I'm not that good at using it."

"What about you?" Hakon said to Pia. "You seem to be in charge in some way. Is that your Trait?"

"I'm not in charge," Pia said. "We're a team. My Trait is Concentration. It's useful to block out any distractions."

"Ah. And what do you Concentrate on when you block out those distractions?"

"So far it's mostly weather," Pia replied. "If I learn enough about snowstorms, for instance, I can usually tell when one is about to hit and how long it will last."

Hakon laughed. "You predict the weather? I can think of half a dozen people who would want that ability. I could sell you to any one of them for a tidy sum."

"But you want something from Intelligencers," Pia replied, staring at him. Now that the threat was out in the open, she was calm. She'd endured captivity once; she would not allow anyone to do that to her again. She'd rather be dead. Hakon's eyes narrowed, and he gave her a solemn nod, making her think that he understood that about her.

"I do want something," Hakon agreed. "And I offer my services in exchange."

"What do you want?" Gustav asked. "That only Intelligencers can supply?"

"I have heard that there is an Intelligencer who can Unmake anything. Is that true?"

Pia and Gustav exchanged a look. This was not what she had been expecting.

"It is true that there is an Intelligencer with an Unmaking Trait," she said carefully. "But just because they have been able to Unmake every object they've been assigned so far, does not mean that we can guarantee that they can Unmake *anything*."

"So, it *is* true," Hakon said. "And it's a fair point that success up until now does not mean continued success. I will accept an honest attempt to Unmake something of mine. What would you like in exchange?"

"We need to discuss our options," Pia said. "In private."

"I'll give you half an hour. Don't try to escape. You won't like what happens if you do." Hakon opened the door and backed out.

Once the door was closed, Pia held up a hand. "I need to Concentrate," she said. "And see if I can figure out who this is and what he's doing here."

"All right," Gustav said. "I see the makings for tea. We might as well be comfortable."

Pia nodded and closed her eyes. A shiver ran up her spine as her Trait kicked in.

A moment later, she opened her eyes. She was always surprised at how much she had tucked away in her head.

17

Snatches of conversations she'd overheard, things she read, even what people wore.

And from what Hakon wore and how hot he'd kept the cabin, she *knew* he wasn't from here; *knew* that he hadn't spent the winter in Nurmi. Somehow Hakon had travelled here from the Sapphire Sea. And the only people on the Sapphire Sea who knew about Jarri's Trait were Calder Rahmson and Dagrun Lund.

This Pilalian had a connection to them, somehow.

Gustav set a mug of tea down on the table in front of her.

"How much do you know about Berna Strauskas's brother, Calder Rahmson?" she asked him.

DAG WATCHED THE street from the doorway of the office of the Merchant Adventurers.

"I don't see anything unusual," she said over her shoulder. "Other than it's too quiet."

"Jaak should have been back by now." Calder stood behind her and looked out over her shoulder.

"How long before we go after him?" She'd worried about sending Jaak to give the message to the Arressan council instead of Inger, but in the end, they hadn't had a better option. They all trusted Jaak, and because he so clearly was a simple sailor, they thought he'd be safe enough. Safer than Inger would be, anyway. Dag sighed. She did not want to be wrong.

"Give it another few hours," Charis said.

Dag turned to look at him. He was nervously pacing the room. Her sister sat at the desk with Esma across from her as they sorted through papers.

Inger was hoping to find records of food stores that had been offered for sale before she and Charis had fled Messanos. The hope was that some of it was still available. Dag would buy anything edible: grain, beans, dried fish, although that was not very common on the Sapphire Sea. And they wanted to do that before the council had a chance to forbid it.

She ran her hand through her hair and looked back out at the street. Something about this wait made her uneasy. Her Trait hadn't activated, so nothing Unseen was at work. She hoped.

"I have some names," Inger said.

Dag stepped away from the door. Inger stood up, waving a couple pieces of paper.

"I need to see these people," Inger continued. "In case they still have some of these goods to sell."

"What is it?" Dag asked. She held out her hand, and Inger passed the sheets to her. "Preserved olives, barley." She flipped to the next paper. "Beans. Barrels and barrels of dried beans. If it's all still there, it might fill half the hold!" Beans were the hope. They were stable and lasted a long time when dried and kept a belly full longer than bread. "We will take everything they have," she said. "As soon as they can deliver it."

"I need to see what they still have and negotiate a price first," Inger said. "And they have to be willing to sell to us."

"I'll come with you," Esma said. "And remind them that Rahm authorized them to sell to us before. Charis should come too."

"Who are we visiting?" Charis asked. Dag handed him the papers, and he nodded. "It should be safe enough for me to meet with these merchants. It's possible they'll have some useful information."

"We'll be back soon," Inger said. "Hopefully with some of these goods secured."

"We still don't know if Pinho is in the city," Dag replied. "Be careful."

"We will," Inger replied.

Once the three had left, Dag closed the door until there was just a sliver of space to watch the street.

"I'll keep watch from the window," Calder said. A few minutes later he called softly. "Jaak's here. He's at the window."

Dag scanned the street. Jaak coming in through the window meant that there was trouble. Satisfied that she wasn't stranding Inger out there, she closed the door and set the bar into place.

"They'll be here soon," Jaak said as he poked his head through the window. "Looking for Calder and Inger."

He was about to climb in when Calder shook his head. "I think it's best if that's all they find." Calder looked over his shoulder. "Think you can convince whoever is coming that you're Inger?"

"Unless they know her well," Dag said, joining him at the window. "What happened, Jaak?"

"Floros was there," he said. "And still seems to be in charge of the council. There were four people, as Charis expected."

"So Nilus was there?" Dag asked.

"Yes, at least I saw an older man who I think was him," Jaak said. "I didn't hear anyone called by name except for Councilwoman Floros. There was a second woman and a younger, as well."

"Did they have guards?" Dag asked. Messanos guards held the city, and word was that they were neutral, but the Arressan council had their own security.

"Half a dozen guards in two different uniforms," Jaak said. "Not sure if they were working together or at cross purposes."

"Were you able to tell them about our threat?" Calder asked.

"Yep. I gave them the letter and told them that Clan Freeholder Strauskas will not sell timber to anyone in Arressa and that the Merchant Adventurers have been advised. The other woman, she got really angry and started shouting at Floros. How she only did anything because of the guarantee of timber for ships and how her partners were counting on new ships to replace ones lost to pirates." Jaak grinned. "Floros looked worried and kept saying it wasn't possible that anyone with that kind of authority was in Messanos. Calder, I said your name and Nilus laughed, but the other man, he stared at me and got all quiet." Jaak's grin faltered. "I didn't much like that quiet, so I left and came back here to warn you."

There was a knock on the door.

"They're here," Dag said. She grabbed a coat that Inger had left draped across a chair and pulled it on; her twin apparently hadn't gotten any tidier since they'd shared rooms at the Hall.

"You head to the ship," Calder said. "Let Darya and Rafael know where we're going, then come back here and wait for Inger, Charis, and Esma. They've gone to see about food shipments."

"You sure?" Jaak asked.

"Yes," Dag replied at the same time as Calder.

"We need to resolve the issue with the council," he continued. "They could ban merchants from selling food to us."

"This could be our best chance to make sure they don't," Dag said.

There was a second knock on the door, and then it rattled as someone tried to open it.

Jaak's head disappeared from the window, and with a nod to Calder, Dag headed to the door.

"Coming," she called out. She lifted the bar and opened the door. Two guards stood outside, one in grey and one in blue.

"Inger Lund, Merchant Adventurers," she said. "What can I help you with?"

NADEZ PAUSED IN front of the main door to the jail. She'd spent more time down here in the past few months than in all the rest of her years as an Intelligencer.

And it wasn't simply because she was now Master Intelligencer: she was quite certain that Joosep Sepp hadn't spent much time in the jail, talking to prisoners. Though, if he'd been more proactive as Master Intelligencer, then perhaps she wouldn't need to be down here quite so often.

She sighed. No sense blaming Joosep, especially since he'd eventually understood his mistakes and had died because of them.

She'd spoken to both Maeve and Mykol already. Neither of them had more to add to what they'd told her last night, so she'd sent them back to Saulia Holt. Let the Clan Freeholder decide what their punishment should be for lying to her.

She knocked on the door and nodded to the guard when it opened a crack.

"He's not said a word since he arrived," the guard said as she opened the door wider, allowing Nadez room to enter the jail.

The door thudded shut, and the guard locked it.

"He's had food and water?" Nadez asked.

"Aye, same rations as us." The guard frowned. "Which means he's as hungry as we are."

"It's the same as what he'd get in the barracks," Nadez replied. She headed down the hallway towards the cells. The next door she came across was open and the guard nodded and stepped aside.

Nadez stared at the prisoner for a moment. He was lying on the small cot with a blanket wrapped around him. She cleared her throat, and the man sat up on the bed and looked at her with wide eyes.

"Fricis," she said. "You know why I'm here." His family's Clan Freeholder was Ottosen, which tied the thefts to him, but right now she had no solid proof.

Fricis looked down at the floor. "I know."

"Your family is safe," she said. He looked up at her again. "Your aunt has been released and sent back to Clan Freeholder

Holt, and everyone in your mother's household has been brought to the Hall. They are not prisoners and will be free to visit you once you tell me what I need to know."

Fricis sighed. "I want to believe you," he said. "But I can't risk it. I can't risk their lives if you're lying to me."

Nadez took the note from her pocket and held it out. "I trust you will recognize your sister's handwriting?"

Fricis grabbed the note and read it. "This is Fanni's hand all right. But why? Why help my family?"

"Almost anyone can be forced to do things they don't want to do," Nadez said. "You ran to your aunt, to family, for help, and she did what family does. She helped you even though she knew it was the wrong thing to do. Which is what you did for your family. You did something that you knew was wrong in order to help your family, to keep them safe. Now I need you to tell me, in your own words, what happened."

"You already know," Fricis said. He sighed and carefully folded the note. "But I want to see my ma and Fanni." He faced her. "Clan Freeholder Ottosen sent a message with Fanni two weeks ago. Nothing in writing of course, and the wording was gentle, just a simple *wait for my instructions*, but Fanni was scared so I knew it was serious."

"I'll confirm that with your sister," Nadez said. "Then what happened?"

"That day, when I was on guard duty at the warehouse, one of the other guards took me aside and told me that he had my instructions. He and I would pair up for rounds and leave the door open. He didn't say, but I figured that the other guards were either in on it too or wouldn't live until morning. As soon as we left the door open, I said I had to use the privy. I ran as fast as I could to Aunt Maeve."

"You thought that you'd be safe in the house of another Clan Freeholder."

"Clan Freeholder Holt has her own guards," Fricis replied. "I planned on staying a day, maybe two just until I could figure out what to do about my ma and sister. I didn't want my aunt to get into trouble."

"The other two guards," Nadez asked. "We found no trace of them or any evidence that they were killed."

"I don't know where they are," Fricis said. "As I said, I left as soon as the door was open. They must have been part of it. Or maybe they ran, like me."

"That's possible," she replied. She doubted that so many guards were compromised at the same time, but just in case, she'd ask Lauma to rearrange the guard schedule to make sure they were from a mix of Freeholds.

"And the guard who told you to leave the door open," she asked. "Who is he?"

"Never met him before," Fricis said. "Which is why I knew he was from Ottosen. Said his name was Joosep."

"All right." It wasn't an exceptionally unusual name, so when she'd seen a Joosep listed as one of the missing guards, she hadn't thought anything odd about it. But they hadn't been able to track down anything about him, and now she had to wonder if Ottosen was mocking her.

"I'll tell your family that they can visit," Nadez said. "After I speak with your sister."

"Thank you," Fricis said. "I know I have no right to anything, so I thank you."

"If you remember any other details, let the guard on duty know and I'll come back." Nadez turned and headed back the way she'd come.

If Ottosen thought to prod her into making any rash moves against him, he was mistaken. Recovering as much of the stolen food was her only goal right now. She'd deal with Ottosen later, once they were past this crisis. As long as they made it past the crisis. As long as they made it to spring, and beyond.

GUSTAV EYED THE abandoned warehouse. There were no tracks in the snow, nor could he smell smoke. He didn't think anyone had been here since he and Pia had been chased away by the pirates two months ago.

He eased back through the trees to where *Hakon*, who Pia figured was Berna and Calder's father Rahm, stood holding a rope that was tied to Pia's bound wrists.

"No sign of anyone," he said. "We should be able to make a fire. At least last time we did, and no one noticed us."

"Good," Rahm said. "Gather wood. I want a big fire. I'm tired of freezing my ass off." He pushed Pia forward. She'd already braced for it and was able to stay on her feet as she stepped into

Gustav's footprints.

Rahm glared at him as he went past, and Gustav fought to keep his response neutral.

He hated how rough Rahm was with Pia, and he did his best to pretend it didn't bother him, but he was pretty sure the man knew.

He sighed and headed under a tree, looking for firewood. Rahm would take it out on Pia if he was late, or didn't bring enough, or if Gustav did anything other than exactly what he was told.

Pia didn't complain, but he thought that was because she was using her Trait to block out everything.

To be fair, Rahm didn't physically hurt Pia. At least not more than tight ropes hurt her. But he had kept food from her, which he knew, given her past, made her furious; although, she'd been hiding that from Rahm.

Arms piled with branches, he followed the footprints in the snow to the entrance he and Pia had used before. Once inside, he headed to the alcove.

Pia stood in the corner. The rope that bound her hands was tied to a crossbeam. Rahm waited beside the old fire pit.

Gustav dropped the wood beside the fire pit and set about making a fire. Once the kindling was ablaze, he carefully added small sticks and then some larger pieces of wood. Once the fire was big enough, he stood up.

"I need to go find some bigger logs," he said.

"There's lots of wood right here," Rahm replied. "You are not to leave my sight."

"The last time we were here we burned everything that we could find," Gustav said. "I'd need an axe to take the doors apart."

"Then she'll need to use her Trait," he gestured to Pia, "and Concentrate and find something. You are not leaving this building."

Pia frowned. "We already agreed to your terms," she said. "We're not going to run away."

"But you might go back on our deal," Rahm said. "Unmaking traded for me getting rid of these pirates." He grinned. "Although I almost want to thank you. Ursa Ozlinch! This will be fun for me."

"We know who you are, *Hakon*," Pia said. "Or should I call you

Rahm?"

Rahm's eyes narrowed. "Even if you know my name, you *don't* know who I am."

"We know Calder," Gustav said. "He's one of us."

"Yes, and my son knows exactly who I am," Rahm replied. "Just because you know him doesn't mean I will treat you lightly."

"What about Berna?" Pia asked, and Rahm's head snapped up. "Does she know the type of man you are?"

"What do you know about her?"

"We don't just know about her," Pia said. "We *know* her. I'm not sure she would be surprised that you have taken people her own age hostage, but she would still be disappointed."

"Ah well, she wouldn't be the first child of mine that I've disappointed."

"Like you disappointed her mother," Pia said. "And Yakop."

Gustav shook his head at Pia. Rahm looked angry now, and he didn't think an angry Rahm would make mistakes. No, he thought an angry Rahm would just be more dangerous.

"You need to stop talking," Rahm said. He strode over to her and glared at her.

"Then make me," Pia said. "I will not be held captive any longer. Not by you, not by anyone. Release me or kill me."

Gustav sucked in a breath. He didn't think Pia was pretending. He thought she meant what she'd said: she would rather die than remain a prisoner. Why had she waited until now?

And then it dawned on him. She was giving him a chance to escape.

He shook his head. He would not abandon her.

"Untie her," Gustav said.

Rahm looked over his shoulder at him.

"You know she means what she said," Gustav continued.

Rahm laughed and then visibly relaxed. "I do know," he said. "I knew from the moment I met her that she would rather be dead than captive." He shrugged. "Now I know that she also knows it to be true." He walked over to Pia and untied her. "I also know that you won't leave her to die." He tossed the rope into the fire. "Now go get more wood. It's still too cold in here for me."

Gustav hesitated, and Rahm grinned.

"Go on," he said. "We'll be fine. Now that I know what you're made of we can work together and produce a plan to rid this village of pirates. I'll even throw in a threat to the Clan Freeholder."

"What?" Gustav was stunned. What had just happened?

"Sure," Rahm said. "Timonis has caused me trouble in the past. Putting him in his place will be another unexpected pleasure."

"It's all right," Pia said. "We can trust him. At least in this." She made a hand signal confirming what she'd said out loud.

"If you say so." He turned and headed outside. He wasn't sure what had happened, but he trusted Pia.

CALDER FOLLOWED DAG into the room and stopped half a step behind her.

A large table stretched across the far end, but only four of the ten seats were filled. Interestingly, only the two women in the middle were sitting beside each other. The other two councillors, both men, were at opposite ends of the table. He wondered if that was simply their old seats or if it was a visible sign of where they stood on issues.

Then he noticed the guards at the backs of the two men and he revised his opinion. The men were sitting at the ends because they didn't trust the two women. Or each other.

"Inger Lund," the older of the two women said. "We have been advised that the Fair Seas Treaty countries will not supply the timber for new ships. Ships that were destroyed while in your waters, I might add. What do you say to this?"

"Councillor Floros," Dag said. "As you know, the Three also lost many ships: even more than Arressa. We will need much of the timber ourselves. As well, one of our largest Freeholds has decided not to sell to Arressa."

"Why is that?" the other woman asked. "And who speaks for them?"

"I speak for them," Calder said, stepping forward. "I am the son of Lauma Strauskas, Clan Freeholder and the largest supplier of timber in Byholt."

"I do not recognize you," Floros said. "Who vouches that you are who you say you are?"

"I vouch for him," Dag said. "On behalf of the Fair Seas Treaty Alliance."

"You didn't give us your name," the younger of the two men

said. "Who are you?"

"Intelligencer Calder Rahmson," Calder replied. The man who had asked the question frowned. "I am an agent of the Alliance and my mother, Lauma Strauskas, is currently the Interim Grand Freeholder." He paused. "And yes, you have dealt with my father Rahm."

"I believe him," the older man said. "He has the colouring of that dangerous scoundrel we hired."

"Be quiet, Nilus," Floros said. "Your opinion doesn't matter."

"It does if I agree with him," the younger man said.

"Jurgus, don't be ridiculous. He could be lying about everything."

"Here's my patch." Calder held it up. "Anyone who knows Rahm would understand that lying about a connection to him would not be appreciated."

"Floros," the woman beside her said. "Fix this! I need that timber."

"It looks like you'll get no timber, Audra," Nilus said. "No matter that you betrayed your own house in order to acquire it."

"Shut up, old man," Floros replied. She turned back to Dag and Calder. "Name your price. I hear you need food. This council can arrange that for you."

Calder looked at each councillor. Nilus was clearly enjoying this, Audra looked stunned, Floros was outwardly calm, but he sensed that she was seething with anger, and Jurgus. Well, he wasn't getting a read from him. What did Jurgus want?

In front of him Dag made a hand signal. He nodded even though she couldn't see it. It was time to tell Floros what they wanted. He was grateful that they had started looking for food before speaking to the council.

"My price," Calder said, "is for something that I, as an agent of the Three, cannot demand. I will tell you that Clan Strauskas will not sell to an Arressan council we do not trust. We do not trust Thekla Floros, who is a close ally of Fihaldo Pinho and so will not sell while she is a councillor."

"How dare you!" Floros said. "I should have you thrown in jail for that."

Calder shrugged. "Neither of my parents would see that as sound negotiating."

"Even if Floros is no longer on the council," Jurgus said. "It does not mean you will trust us."

"True," Calder replied. "But I trust the judgement of the agent for the Merchant Adventurers. She has much more experience with this council. Inger?"

"I have always found Councillor Nilus to be fair," Dag said. "And I insist that Charis Diakos, who has advised you in the past, be formally added to the council."

"Of course, you would," Floros said. "He's your lover."

"And therefore trusted," Calder said.

"I agree to this," Jurgus replied. "Nilus, I assume that this suits you?" Nilus nodded. "That leaves you, Audra. The only way to get what you already betrayed your house for is to now betray Floros. What do you say?"

"She says no!" Floros shouted. "It's a tie vote. And as head of this council, I have the right to make the decision."

"I say yes," Audra replied. She turned to Floros, who looked furious. "I've been very clear on what I need. And what I'm willing to do for it. If you cannot deliver, I must make a different alliance."

"How dare you!" Floros said. "I will see you ruined!"

"Guards," Jurgus said. "Please escort Thekla Floros out of the room so that she has time to reflect on her behaviour. Threats against a sitting councillor cannot be tolerated, even by one of our own."

Jurgus turned to Dag and Calder. "On behalf of the council, I will send an official request to Charis Diakos, asking him to join us for our next meeting. Shall I have it delivered to the Merchant Adventurers office?"

"Thank you," Dag said. "I will let him know to expect it."

Three guards hovered behind Floros, who looked like she had no intention of leaving quietly, so Dag and Calder left before having to watch her being dragged from the council room.

"That's one thing accomplished," he said once they were out of the building. "Did you figure out anything about Jurgus?"

"Not yet," Dag replied. "I'll need to talk to Inger and Charis about him. About Nilus and Audra as well. They both seem transparent—Audra is desperate for timber—but simple people with simple wants don't tend to rise to power."

"They do not." He sighed. "We didn't get a chance to ask where Pinho was."

"I know," Dag replied. "He clearly has a hold over Floros."

"Yes. We'll need to decide what to do about that." He knew that Dag had to leave, that delivering food to Tarklee was the priority. Perhaps he could stay here and try to find out where Pinho was. He looked at her as they walked through the streets. She wouldn't like being separated. Neither would he.

CHAPTER 3

"THE SISTER IS not the solid link to Ottosen we were hoping for?" Lauma asked.

Nadez shook her head. "No. She didn't get instructions directly from the Clan Freeholder or anyone with a formal connection to him." They were in Lauma's office, and Nadez was beginning to think that there was no hope of recovering any of the stolen food. "Her message was from a man *people just know* does odd, mostly unsavoury, tasks for the Clan Freeholder. But nothing concrete that ties him to Ottosen."

Lauma frowned. "Of course he has people like that he can call on."

"I'll keep looking for the stolen food," Nadez said.

"But you don't have much hope of finding it," Lauma finished.

"No, I don't," she agreed. "It's been three days. That food could be anywhere by now. Most likely it's been broken up into smaller parcels and distributed. Even if we found some of it, it would be hard to prove where it came from."

"You're probably right," Lauma said. "The only good news is that there have been no new thefts and every single guardsman has been assessed. The food we still have should be safe."

"The bad news is that it won't be enough," Nadez said.

"Not even with the reduced rationing," Lauma said. "I've doubled the number of people ice fishing and have seasoned fishermen inspecting the safety of the ice twice a day. If we had more ice boats, we could safely send them across the ice and out of the harbour."

"But we don't," Nadez said. It was a familiar complaint of Lauma's. Tarklee Harbour tended to have barges and larger fishing boats that were too big and heavy to be fitted with ice runners. And since the harbour rarely froze, the few smaller boats that existed were not constructed to bear the runners. They'd tried to add runners to a couple of boats but had ended up destroying them so had given up. Once the ice cleared from the harbour, everything that floated would be needed for fishing.

"We will next year," Lauma promised.

Someone knocked on the outer office door.

"I wouldn't have locked that door if I'd known you were expecting someone," Nadez said.

"I'm not expecting anyone."

"I'll see who it is." Hoping it wasn't more unwelcome news, Nadez headed past the empty desk for Lauma's non-existent assistant to the door to the outer office. She unlocked the door and stared in surprise at Clan Freeholder Henrik Ottosen.

"Clan Freeholder," Nadez said. "What can I do for you?"

"You?" he replied. "Nothing. If I'd wanted to talk to you, I would have gone to your office. Instead, I am here, at the Grand Freeholder's office. Are you acting as her assistant these days?"

Nadez ignored the jibe and stepped aside to allow Ottosen to enter.

"Clan Freeholder," Lauma said from the door to her office. "Come in."

Ottosen smirked at Nadez as he entered Lauma's office. Nadez closed the door and relocked it before following him. She sat down in the remaining chair and, keeping her expression neutral, nodded to the Clan Freeholder.

"I don't see why your *assistant* has to be here," Ottosen said. "This is a conversation for Freeholders."

"The Master Intelligencer does whatever tasks are required to keep the Three and all of our people safe," Lauma said. "As do I. I could ask what you have done in that regard, Clan Freeholder."

"That is why I am here," Ottosen replied. "To do my part in safeguarding the Three." He leaned back in his chair. "I understand that you two have lost a significant amount of the food we have all been counting on to get us to spring."

"It wasn't *lost*," Nadez replied. "It was *stolen*. In well-planned and very well executed thefts by someone who understood all of our security measures and found weaknesses that they exploited."

Was Ottosen here to gloat? How much of her investigation did he know about?

"Call it what you want," Ottosen said. "The result is that food went missing on your watch."

"As did four guards," Lauma said. "Who we believe were either hired by someone or were killed. Or a combination of the two."

Nadez was watching Ottosen when Lauma lied about all four guards being missing. She thought he'd relaxed ever so slightly. Was he here to find out if they had Fricis?

"Four guards are unaccounted for?" Ottosen replied. "It's even worse than I expected."

"Four guards," Lauma repeated. "We have found no trace of any of them."

"Well. That says much about you as a leader, does it not?" Ottosen asked.

"Or the desperate times we live in," Lauma replied. She sighed. "You said that you were here to do your part. What is it that you can do?"

"It's what I have already done," Ottosen said. The look he gave Nadez was smug. "Which is find the food your *assistant* could not. Even now I have wagons bringing it here."

"You are delivering food?" Lauma asked. "How did you find it?"

"How do you know that it's the food that was stolen?" Nadez asked. What was Ottosen doing? He must know that *they* knew he had stolen this food. So why return it?

"Someone told me about it," Ottosen said. "And I assume it's the stolen food because no one else should have this much."

"We'll need a secure place to put it," Lauma said. "Nadez?"

She sent Nadez a warning look, and she nodded. Getting the food back was more important than proving that Ottosen had stolen it.

"We have a warehouse close by that should have enough room," Nadez said. "I'll go and let them know to expect it." She stood up. "Thank you, Clan Freeholder." She caught Lauma's grateful nod before she left the office.

There was plenty of time to figure out what Ottosen was up to once they had the food safely stored and tallied. Let the man think he'd won, let him think he was superior. None of that mattered right now when they were so desperate.

PIA PACED IN front of the fire. Rahm had been gone since dawn, leaving her and Gustav in the old warehouse. It was dark now, and she desperately wanted to know what had happened although they didn't dare leave. Rahm had told them to stay, and it had definitely sounded like a threat.

"Maybe the pirates killed him," Gustav said.

She snorted. "People like that don't kill a man like Rahm. Neither does a self-important *skit* like Timonis."

"He's Berna's father," Gustav said. "Why do you think he's so dangerous?"

"My Trait," she said. "I've tried to tell you." She'd spent hours trying to explain to him the dozens of little things that, for her, added up to Rahm being an extremely dangerous man—the most dangerous man she'd ever met—but he couldn't see it. He kept going back to the fact that Rahm was Berna's father, as though that somehow made it impossible for him to be a threat to them. Rather than simply trusting her Trait—the way he would if she'd made an observation about the weather—Gustav kept questioning it. It was annoying. The only thing that kept her irritation in check was the understanding that he questioned her Trait because he so often questioned his own.

"Should I get more wood?" Gustav asked.

"I'll go," Pia said. She pulled her hat down and headed away from the warmth and light of the fire to the window they were using to access the building.

Wet snow clung to her as she walked along the path to the woods. She filled her arms with a bundle of fallen branches and turned to head back. And stopped. A light was moving through the woods coming from the direction of the town. She quietly dropped the wood and ducked behind a tree.

The light moved away from her, heading in the direction of Setberg. Careful to remain hidden and quiet, she followed. The light stopped and she edged closer, peering out from behind a tree.

Half a dozen figures stood huddled around someone holding

a single lamp. Pia wasn't surprised that Rahm was in the centre of the group.

She Concentrated on the others and then nodded. Pirates. She recognized some of them even in the dark.

"All we ever wanted was a way home." That was Ursa Ozlinch, who was no longer quite so bulky after months of reduced rations. "So we're beholden to you."

"You should make it to Setberg by dawn," Rahm said.

"We can take both boats?"

"I have no need of them," Rahm replied.

"And no hard feelings on our part on account of Edur," Ursa said. "He caused grief, let me tell you."

"Pirates die," Rahm said. "Now get going before I change my mind. And remember what I told you."

"You can count on us," Ursa said. "On the sea and on Strongrock."

Rahm held the lamp out to the pirate captain, and she took it. Pia watched the small group until she lost sight of the light.

"See anything interesting?"

Pia looked over her shoulder. Rahm stood a few feet away, leaning against a tree. She rose and faced him.

"I did," she replied. "You've kept your side of the bargain. The pirates are gone." She paused. "Except for the one who's dead."

Rahm shrugged. "Pirates die."

"So you said. It's time to tell Gustav that it's our turn to keep the bargain."

"Gustav," Rahm said. "He's not like you."

"No," Pia replied. She thought it was a good thing; that Gustav not being like her was a strength. But she suspected Rahm felt it was a weakness. "He's better in many ways."

"Maybe," Rahm said. "But he doesn't know himself, not like you do. Who taught you so much about yourself at such a young age?"

She didn't think he expected an answer, but she gave him one anyway. "Henrik Ottosen. And one day I'll kill him for it."

Rahm laughed out loud, a sound of real surprise. "Ottosen." He shook his head. "There's a man with more than a few enemies. Which one will get to him first?"

Pia shivered as her Trait activated. She kept her eyes on the path in front of her as she walked past Rahm towards the warehouse. And a few more pieces slipped into place.

Rahm wanted something Undone, that was what he'd told them, and that was true. But it wasn't the only reason why he was here; why he had sailed a small boat from the Sapphire Sea to the Pale Sea. She tried not to worry about the man who followed her back to the old warehouse. Tried not to worry about someone who had casually killed a man, even if he was a pirate. And tried not to smile at the thought that Rahm was here to kill Ottosen.

DAG REREAD THE list of goods. She was grateful that it was mostly beans and grains with a dozen crocks of olives, but it only filled the hold halfway. Inger and Esma hadn't been able to find more food: at least not stores that were dried, cured, or pickled and ready to ship.

"I hope to be back in two or three weeks," she said as she handed the list to Inger.

"I've been promised some pickled fern shoots by then," Inger said. "Adao Machado should be back from the south."

"That would be excellent." Rafael's uncle was heading to Tobei and Yedris and had promised to look for supplies on his travels.

"He might end up with a hold full of dried seaweed," Inger said, making a face. "It's an acquired taste."

"It's good in stews," Esma said. "If you use the proper spices."

"Starving people will be grateful," she said. "Oh, there's Charis."

"The council meeting went well enough," Charis said as he entered the office. "Floros wasn't there. I was told that she is off on important personal business. Everyone else begrudgingly accepted me onto the council, but there will be no more additions."

"It seems strange that Floros didn't attend," Dag said. True to his promise, Jurgus had delivered an official council request for Charis to join them.

"She seems to have some influence even when not present," Charis continued. "Audra is clearly in her camp and Nilus is opposed. Jurgus seems to be on the fence a little. He was not happy that Floros was absent."

"I wish I could have been there," Dag said. Her Trait would have helped discover any hidden agendas, but Fair Seas Alliance representatives only attended Arressan council meetings for very specific reasons, and then they had to be asked. There had not been a request for the head of the Merchant Adventurers.

"Other than the decision not to increase the number of councillors, not much happened," Charis said. "Just angry councillors blaming each other for backing or not backing Floros and Pinho."

"That's exactly the type of situation that reveals hidden alliances and plots," Dag said. "See if you can get Inger an invitation to the next meeting."

"I'm not sure I'll be able to help," Inger said.

"Your Trait has changed," Dag replied. "You might figure out more than you think you will. Besides, another perspective is always useful."

"I can probably convince enough of the others that Inger's presence would be a good thing," Charis said. "At least in the short term."

"Audra in particular wants to make sure the relationship with the Alliance is good," Esma said. "I can ask her to invite Inger."

"Yes," Charis said. "It would be better coming from you anyway. Some of them don't like my relationship with Inger."

"Some of them do," Inger said. "They think the favours I can do for you are more important than the favours you can do for me."

"As long as we can get food shipments," Dag said. "And it doesn't jeopardize anyone's safety, do what you need to."

"Have you seen my brother?" Esma asked.

"Not since this morning," Dag replied. "I'm worried that I won't see him before I set sail." The goods were being loaded into the *Atlaine*'s hold, and she couldn't delay leaving for a personal reason.

She and Calder had both agreed that they had to part; that they had vastly different jobs to do, but she'd assumed they'd have a chance to say goodbye. Her Trait hadn't triggered, so she wasn't worried that this was anything more than Calder's task taking longer than expected.

"I'll make him feel bad about taking so long that he missed sending you off," Esma offered with a grin.

"How very sisterly of you," Dag said. "I should be back in a few weeks."

The door to the office opened, and Rafael stuck his head in.

"Captain Demer says that the *Atlaine* is loaded and ready to set sail," he said. "And that there's a good wind that she doesn't want to miss."

"Coming," Dag replied. "Say goodbye to Calder for me." She hugged Esma.

She took Charis's hands. "Look out for my sister." Then she stepped into Inger's embrace. "This hasn't gotten easier," she said. "This time when I return, you'd better be here."

"I'll do my best," Inger said. "And you come back safe."

"I'll do my best," Dag echoed her twin. Then with a wave, she headed out the door to join Rafael.

CALDER EYED THE sky. It was getting late; there was a very real possibility that Dag and the *Atlaine* would leave before he returned to the Merchant Adventurers office.

He'd been following his Trait through the streets of Messanos, and now he stood in front of what he hoped was his final destination. But was it a place for answers or more questions?

The narrow dirt track he'd followed had passed between two houses and had ended at the single step that led up into a house. The small, white-washed structure was built right against the rocky cliff that rose up behind it. A weathered door and tiny window were set into the front of the building, facing the street.

There was nothing else here: no trees, no fences, no other doorways. Just solid rock rising up behind the small house.

He gave a mental shrug and walked up to the door and knocked.

The door opened a fraction, and a single brown eye peered out at him. When the door opened wider, Calder looked into the wary eyes of the Pilalian street vendor who had helped him find the suicide assassins.

"I'm not even that surprised," the man said. He stepped aside. "Come in."

Calder entered a dimly lit space. After staring out at the street for a moment, the man shut the door and turned to face him.

"What more do you want from me?" the vendor asked. "I already took a risk when I gave you information."

"I am sorry if I put you in danger, and I hope this visit does not add to that," Calder said. "To be truthful, I'm not sure why I'm here."

"I suppose you won't leave until I give you some sort of answer." The man sighed. "I was just making tea. Join me." He stepped past Calder and headed to a small stove that was tucked along a wall.

"Thank you." Calder looked around the small space. The room they were in looked like the main living space. Besides the stove, there was a table and three chairs as well as a small, upholstered bench. At the back a curtain hung from the rock face, hiding what he assumed was a sleeping alcove. Since it had been dug right into the rock, it would provide some relief from the heat in the summer.

The man handed him a mug.

"Thank you," Calder said again. "I am sorry to disturb you, and I don't want to make your life difficult."

"*More* difficult," the man replied. He sighed again and sat at the table placing his mug of tea on the scarred wood in front of him. "I know why you're here."

Calder sat down opposite him. "Will you tell me?"

"I don't think I have a choice," he replied. "Otherwise, that Trait of yours will keep finding me."

"How do you know I have a Trait?"

"I assumed you did, and now you've confirmed it," the man replied. "Son of Rahm."

"Do you know where my father is?"

"No. But I know where he isn't, and he isn't in Messanos. Or anywhere on the Sapphire Sea."

"How do you know that?" Calder asked.

"I heard it from more than one reliable source," the man replied. "The same way I knew where to find the one you were looking for the last time we spoke."

"*Most Pilalians find you eventually*," Calder said, repeating what the vendor had told him when they met.

"Yes."

"And the suicide assassins? Where are they?" Calder's first stop had been to their training compound, but it had been empty.

"Is that the Pilalian you seek?"

"No." He'd hoped to find a link to Pinho: maybe he had. "I'm looking for Fihaldo Pinho. Do you know where he is?" He paused. "Or where he isn't?"

The vendor laughed. "That is the better question. I know that he is not in Messanos. I also know that he is not in Pilalia."

"So, he's in the south," Calder said. Then something clicked, and his heart clenched. "Is he heading for Zelesso?"

"I know he is not there today," the man said. "But tomorrow?" He shrugged.

"Thank you," Calder said. "For the tea and the information." He stood up to leave but at the door, turned to face the vendor. "I hope I will not disturb you again."

"But you will if your Trait tells you," the man said.

Calder nodded and left. If Pinho was already on his way to Zelesso, he had to get there as soon as possible. It was already too late to warn the city, so now he had to figure out how to defeat Pinho.

He expected Dag was on her way to Tarklee, so he would have to do those things without the *Atlaine*. Without the ship's speed, without its crew, and without its guns and cannon.

NADEZ DID HER best to ignore Ottosen, who stood beside the door to the warehouse, nodding and waving to the crowd that had gathered to watch the food being delivered.

"What's he up to?" Lauma asked from her side. They were across the street, in the shadow of a building.

"I think he's trying to be the saviour of the city," Nadez said. "To what end, I have no idea."

"It won't help him get elected Grand Freeholder," Lauma replied. "Not as long as me and mine cast the vote for Byholt."

The last of the goods were unloaded from the final wagon. Sture looked their way, and Nadez raised a hand. Ottosen noticed and scowled at them before pasting a smile on his face.

The Clan Freeholder then made a big show of thanking the wagon driver as he sent him on his way.

"He's taking credit for returning food he most likely stole from us," Lauma said. "And we can't do anything about it."

"At least we have it," Nadez replied. "Sture will inspect it and let us know if he can tell if it was from the latest warehouse theft, or from the earlier robberies."

"Ottosen would do that, wouldn't he?" Lauma shook her head. "Return goods from more than one theft just to make sure we know that he was behind them all."

"And revel in it," Nadez replied. "But he doesn't know that we

have Fricis and his family. A tenuous tie to Ottosen is still a tie."
She sighed. "No matter that he's creating some good will for
himself today. Come on, Ottosen is leaving so let's go talk to
Sture."

The crowd was already thinning as they made their way across
the street to the warehouse. A few people glanced at them, but
most of the chatter Nadez overheard was praise for Clan
Freeholder Ottosen.

She shared a grimace with Lauma. It infuriated her that the
two of them had done so much hard work over the winter to keep
people fed and ration the food in an egalitarian way, and now
Ottosen, through treachery, theft, and grandstanding was
overshadowing them.

"Glad to be done with that bit of acting," Sture said when they
reached him. "Come on, the last load should be sorted by now. I'll
compare what just arrived to the list of what was stolen from each
of the warehouses." He led the way to a small office.

There was only a single chair, so Nadez and Lauma stood in
front of the table Sture sat down at. He lined up a few papers in
front of him.

"Here's the list," a woman said from the doorway. She stepped
into the small room and passed the paper she held to Sture.

"Thank you," he said absently, his eyes scanning the list. He
pushed one paper on the desk towards Nadez and Lauma. "Looks
like everything on this list."

Lauma leaned over the paper. "The most recent theft," she
said. "All returned."

"And about half of what's on here," Sture pushed another
paper forward.

"From the first warehouse that was robbed?" Lauma asked.
"You're certain?"

"Aye," Sture replied. "That was the only warehouse that had
dried fish stored in straw and that's what's been returned."

"Was that because there's not much of a market for it?" Nadez
asked. "Most meals from the feeding centres are based around
either dried or fresh fish, so perhaps no one was willing to pay for
it?"

"Food is food," Lauma said. "I think Ottosen is taunting us."

"A slight to worry about another day," Nadez replied. "Sture,
can you send copies of this list to Lauma and me? Lauma, I

41

assume you will revise the plan for meals at the feeding stations?"

"I'll do that as soon as possible," Lauma said.

"Excellent," Nadez replied. "We have to assume Ottosen is trying to show the people that he cares, but to what end? And did he steal the food in the first place to do this or has something changed?"

She said goodbye and headed out into the city. She had very few resources, but there was one person who she thought might have an idea.

CHAPTER 4

"WHAT DID YOU say to Timonis?" Gustav asked as he eyed the ice boat. It looked to be in good working order, and the sail Rahm had handed him was dry.

They'd arrived in Nurmi last night, and Rahm had made Pia and him hide while he dealt with Clan Freeholder Timonis. His favour, as Rahm had called it. Gustav didn't like owing Rahm anything, but it wasn't like he'd had a choice.

"Nothing you need to know," Rahm said. "Now get that sail up and let's get to Lavais Port and your Unmaker."

Gustav rolled his eyes and stepped into the little boat. It was still two hours before dawn, and the dock was quiet and empty.

As soon as Gustav had the sail up, Rahm, carrying the tiller, stepped into the boat. He slid the tiller in place and sat down in the stern. Pia clambered past them both and sat in the prow.

"Ready to go," Gustav said. He picked up an oar, ready to push them away from the dock when Rahm gave the signal.

"I should make you call me captain," Rahm said. "Shove off."

"A captain for this little sailboat?" Gustav set the oar against the dock and pushed. "That would make you a lot more like Timonis than I would have ever guessed." As soon as they were clear from the dock, he dug the blade of the oar into the ice and shoved the boat to port.

Rahm laughed. "He does think he's important."

The boat jerked as wind caught in the sail. Gustav put the oar down in the bottom of the boat and leaned against the mast, facing Rahm.

"And smart," he said.

The Pilalian laughed again. "Which makes him easy to manipulate," he said.

"Really? I had no success making him do anything, not even when I used my Trait." Gustav shook his head. "I've never met anyone so convinced of their own importance."

Rahm stared at him, and Gustav did his best not to squirm. He'd thought the man's laugh meant that he was letting his guard down. Now he realized that wasn't the case. He sighed but didn't avert his eyes. A man like Rahm would take that as weakness. It had taken some time, but now he agreed with Pia: Rahm was very dangerous.

"I threatened him to get him to agree to my terms," Rahm said finally. "He only complied when he realized that I was more than prepared to carry out that threat. So you are not wrong in your assessment of Timonis. I thought she was the smart one." He gestured to Pia. Gustav looked over his shoulder and met her gaze. She flashed him a hand signal to keep to their plan, and he nodded.

He turned back to Rahm with a grin and tried to force Charisma to work. "She's a lot smarter than me," he agreed. "But I always try to figure out what went wrong when my Trait doesn't work."

He and Pia had promised to take Rahm to Jarri, and they would. They would even tell Jarri to do his best to Unmake whatever Rahm wanted destroyed.

But they were not going to tell Rahm that Berna was the person in charge in Lavais Port.

He had no idea what the Pilalian would do when he found out, but he was tired of not having any advantage. Rahm had spoken about Calder, not with fondness, exactly, but he thought the man really did care about his children.

"Does your Trait fail you often?" Rahm asked.

"Not often," he replied. "But it's very inconvenient when it doesn't work."

"What happens when it doesn't work?"

"In the case of Clan Freeholder Timonis, I was forced to agree with his assessment of himself as a brilliant Freeholder. And let me tell you, he can talk about himself for hours."

"Not something he does in my presence," Rahm said.

"So, he's not too stupid to recognize a dangerous man," Gustav said.

"What else," Rahm said, "has happened when your Trait didn't work?"

"I was poisoned. By yet another Clan Freeholder."

"Which one?" Rahm asked in a way that Gustav knew wasn't just casual interest.

"Tarmo Holt."

"Timonis, Holt, you've had to deal with the worst Clan Freeholders," Rahm said.

"And the best," Gustav said. Rahm seemed to have relaxed, so he did too. "Between Pia and I, we've been assigned as Lauma Strauskas's assistants for a total of two days."

"Ah yes, my wife. When did you last see her?"

"A few months ago," Gustav replied. "Just before midwinter." He sighed. "The Interim Grand Freeholder was organizing ice fishing in the harbour."

"Feeding her people," Rahm replied. "I suppose now she considers everyone in the Three to be her people."

"She doesn't want more food riots," Gustav replied. "No one with a heart would: they're dangerous."

"I'd let them riot," Rahm said. "When the dust settles perhaps there would be fewer mouths to feed."

Gustav looked at him, his mouth hanging open.

"Don't look so shocked," Rahm said. "Besides, it's not like that will happen. I don't have that kind of power."

"Tarmo Holt did," Pia said from prow. "And he was planning on doing pretty much that. Did he get that idea from you? I know you knew him."

"Maybe we both got it from someone else," Rahm said.

"That's why your relationship with Lauma failed," Pia said. "She realized that you were the type of man who could consider such a thing."

Rahm's face darkened in anger, and Gustav worried that he was going to climb over him to get to Pia.

Then suddenly, the Pilalian shrugged.

"We parted ways years ago," he said casually, but Gustav knew his uncaring attitude was forced.

With one hand behind his back, he signalled to Pia to be quiet and that he would be too.

Rahm's sore point, his weakness, seemed to be his family. He'd said that Calder knew him, and Gustav suspected Lauma did too. But did Berna? And would threatening to tell her make Rahm do anything different?

CALDER PACED THE deck of the *Spice Runner*.

"We'll be there by dusk," Adao Machado said when his pacing brought him to the wheel.

"I know, and I thank you," Calder said. "I don't mean to imply you are at fault." As he'd feared, Dag and the *Atlaine* had already set sail by the time he arrived back at the Merchant Adventurers office. But Luck was still with him. Rafael's uncle had been there collecting coin to purchase food for when Dag returned, and he'd quickly agreed to ferry him to Zelesso.

"You're just restless," Adao finished for him.

Calder nodded. He was also nervous.

Esma joined him. "There's an excellent stew for supper," she said. "You should eat. I'll keep watch."

"Thank you, I will." He wasn't hungry, but they had no idea what they would find in Zelesso. Who knew when he would have a chance at another meal?

The stew was very good, but he expected that on a Pilalian spice ship. He was too keyed up to savour it though. When his bowl was empty, he dropped it off amongst the rest of the dirty dishes and headed back up to the deck.

"Esma suggested the two of you would prefer to go ashore on the near side of the city rather than have us sail to the main docks," Adao said. He gestured to the bow where Esma stood, a spyglass in her hand. "She said you would swim rather than have us lower a dinghy."

"That's a good idea," Calder said. Until they confirmed whether Pinho was anchored off Zelesso, they had to be careful. Esma knew the city, and he trusted her to get them to shore undetected, even if it meant getting wet. They could change the plan if Pinho's ships weren't at anchor when they reached the city. "When we're closer to Zelesso, I'll send her back with directions for where to drop us," Calder said. "We won't want to swim too far."

He left to join his sister at the bow. She glanced at him before handing him the spyglass.

"I haven't seen any sails," Esma said.

For the next few hours, they traded the spyglass back and forth. When they were close enough to see the city, Calder put the spyglass to his eye. There: the shadows of masts were dark against the reds and oranges of the sunset.

By his count, three large ships were anchored just offshore of the main dock area. It had to be Pinho. There were so few ships left that it would be an incredible coincidence for three traders to be at anchor in Zelesso right now.

"Pinho's here," Calder said. He handed the spyglass to Esma, who took a quick look.

"I'll go tell Adao," Esma said. "And guide him in."

A few minutes after she left, orders were called for the *Spice Runner*'s sails to be lowered and the ship started to slow. They turned into the narrow channel that led to the dock where the *Hakon* was kept. It was much too shallow for Pinho's larger ships, but the *Spice Runner* would be able to get in closer to land. It was dangerous to get too far into the channel: if they were seen by Pinho, a single ship could block the exit, trapping the *Spice Runner* until the tide went out and stranded them.

"We swim from here," Esma said as she joined him. "The tide is on the way out, and Adao only has an hour before it will ground him."

"All right," Calder replied. "I don't see any signs of Pinho or his men: hopefully, that means no Zelessans have told him about our arrival."

"I'd be angry if anyone helped him," Esma said. She turned and he followed her back to Adao.

"Be safe," Adao said. "I'll try to secure as much food as I can and get it back to Inger."

"Thank you," Calder replied. "For all your help."

A sailor came up to them. "A rope ladder is ready on port," he said.

Calder met Esma's eyes. "Let's go."

Esma stepped over the port gunwale and silently climbed down into the water. Calder tied his boots together and slung them around his neck before following his sister. The water was warmer than he'd expected, and he let go of the ladder and started to swim. Esma's strokes frothed the still water, the gentle splashing the only sounds Calder could hear.

When he looked over his shoulder, the *Spice Runner* had already turned around and was sailing away from the city.

Esma reached the end of the dock and hauled herself up onto it.

"All of the boats are gone," she said when he joined her on the dock. "All except the *Hakon*."

"Do you think the other boats were seized by Pinho or taken by the owners escaping him?" Calder asked. They'd been counting on the *Hakon* being here. His neighbours wouldn't know that Rahm was a Resolute, but they would have recognized that he was dangerous. Calder doubted that anyone who knew Rahm would be foolish enough to steal his boat.

"Knowing the people who use this dock, neither," Esma said. "They wouldn't have risked having their boats confiscated by Pinho so they would have left in them, but not to run. My guess is that most of them have met up somewhere to figure out what to do about Pinho."

"Do you think you can find them?" If they were going to rid the city of Pinho, they needed all the help they could get.

"I might not have to," she replied. "I need to make sure that my mother and brother are safe and if they are, they might know where everyone has taken their boats. If we're lucky they might already have a plan. At the very least they will be gathering information."

"Yes, making sure they are safe is the first thing we need to do," Calder said. His boots were as wet as his clothes, so he left them tied around his neck as they walked towards the cobbled street.

"So, WE ARE to be friends, are we?" Valda Skala's warm smile contradicted her greeting.

"I thought we already were," Nadez said. "It is lovely to see you, and I appreciate you meeting me without an appointment."

"Please, sit," Valda gestured to the chair across from the settee she rested on. "And I think I told you before that an old woman like me has very few visitors. Madara will bring us tea and then join us."

"Both would be welcome," Nadez said as she sat down. Valda

Skala didn't look any different than she had since her last visit, although she'd been thin then, too.

"Looking for signs that I'm eating too well?" Valda asked. "I fear I haven't had much of an appetite in years, so the smaller rations have had less effect on me than on many others."

"Sorry," Nadez said. "It's an automatic assessment."

"To try to determine if someone has been eating more than their fair share?"

"Yes," Nadez agreed. "And to see who *hasn't* received their share."

"Of course, to make sure we all almost starve together," Valda said. "It's a very fair approach that you and Lauma Strauskas have taken."

"The city is hungry but not angry," Nadez said. "Or desperate."

"Or rioting," Valda said. "As I said, a very fair approach. I despair when I think of what would have happened in Tarklee had Tarmo Holt still been Grand Freeholder. Oh look, there's Madara. We've no milk or sugar I'm afraid."

"I didn't expect them."

Madara poured tea for the three of them before sitting down beside Valda.

"What brings you here, Master Intelligencer?" Valda asked. "What is so important that you visit me when we are in the midst of a disaster?"

"Food," Nadez said. "What else? I know you say you rarely get visitors, but I have a feeling that not much happens that you don't hear about. I was wondering if you'd heard rumours or whispers about stolen food."

Valda sighed. "Whispers, and vague ones at that. I wish I knew more. I would much rather any food stores be in your hands than the hands of the one the whispers claim stole it."

"Ottosen," Nadez replied. "We know it was him, but we have no proof. Besides, I care much less about who stole the food than I do about how I can recover it."

"You're saying that you wouldn't try to arrest Henrik Ottosen?"

"I would not," Nadez replied. "I am not willing to do anything that might spark any unrest, not when the city is so close to the edge. That includes arresting Ottosen and whoever he hired to steal the food." She took a sip of tea and set her cup down.

"Lauma Strauskas and I both agree. All of our energy must be spent trying to keep everyone in the Three alive until spring. Then we must count on the arrival of shipments of food and the new growing season to provide enough to feed us all. Anything that distracts us from those tasks could have devastating consequences."

Valda and Madara exchanged a glance. "And that includes those who might have helped, however unwilling?" Valda asked.

"We are already sheltering the family of a person who was forced to help," Nadez replied, suppressing a frown. That glance had meant something: what did Valda and Madara know? And why weren't they sharing it with her? "I cannot guarantee this person will not be charged with a crime, but there will be no more threats against their family."

"I see," Valda said. She sighed. "I am sorry that I have no news for you. I do hope you don't feel that you've wasted your time."

"Not at all." Recognizing that she was being dismissed, Nadez drained her tea and stood up. "If you do hear anything, I would appreciate it if you could send word to me. And if you agree, I will visit again. Perhaps when we are on the other side of this misfortune?"

"I would like that very much," Valda said. "Good day."

As Nadez followed Madara through the house to the front door she wondered what Valda Skala would do: which she assumed would depend on what she wanted or who she was trying to protect. Was it Ottosen? Valda had been very interested to know that Nadez had no plans to arrest him, but why would she care? Ottosens and Skalas had never been close allies; although, being from different countries meant they were not necessarily adversaries.

She nodded to Madara and headed back to the Hall, the whole way wondering what it was that Valda Skala wanted.

IT WAS LATE afternoon by the time the little ice boat rounded the island and Lavais Port came into view. The solid ice ended a dozen boat lengths ahead of them, giving way to a stretch of water that was dotted with chunks of ice tossed by whitecaps. Past that were the docks and behind them, the town and shipyard. They were too far away for Pia to see if anyone was on the dock to watch their arrival, but a couple of small boats were out.

"Sail down," Rahm called from the stern. "Now!"

She turned and watched Gustav scramble to untie the sail, roll it up, and lash it to the mast.

"When was the last time you took an ice boat from ice to open water?" she asked.

Rahm scowled at her. "I was doing this long before you were born," he said.

"I'm sure you were," she replied. "But Gustav has done it a few times just this past winter. We would be better off with him at the tiller, don't you think?"

"No," Rahm said. "I'm in command here."

Pia shook her head and turned to face forward. She decided that she had to be ready to jump out if Rahm made a mistake. She glanced at the sky and shivered as her Trait activated. The weather was holding for now, but a storm, with high winds, was on its way. To make her point, a gust of wind caught the boat and sent it skidding sideways.

"I'd be happy to take the tiller," Gustav said. Pia recognized the worry in his voice.

"I said I'm in command," Rahm replied. "I will take this boat in. Which dock is the closest to the Unmaker?"

"The one nearest to the cradle," Gustav said. "Over towards the shipyards."

Without looking at him, Pia hand-signalled to Gustav to be ready to abandon the boat. A soft grunt was the only reply, but she took it to mean he understood the danger and was also prepared to jump clear of the boat.

The prow of the boat turned towards the farthest dock. Holding her breath, Pia grabbed the gunwale as the boat sped towards the open water. When they were closer, she saw the icy ridge of ice that had formed along the edge from waves that had been tossed up by the wind.

"Start rowing," Rahm called.

Gustav pulled on the oars, and they hit the surface of the ice with a crunch. The boat jumped forward, and a gust of wind pushed them sideways. The port runner hit a huge chunk of ice, forcing that side of the boat to lift up. Pia leaned on the port gunwale, hoping her body weight would keep that side of the boat on the ice.

The boat bucked when it hit the ridge of ice and the prow hit the water at an angle. Freezing water surged in over the gunwale. Pia took a deep breath and launched herself out of the boat, jumping towards the dock.

"Help!" she yelled and then she was in the water and the cold sucked the breath from her. Hoping that Gustav had been able to get clear of the oars, she struck out for the dock.

One stroke, two strokes, three strokes, she Concentrated on moving forward, blocking out the bone chilling cold that made her limbs so heavy that she thought they would drag her under.

Suddenly, she was hauled out of the sea and deposited into the bottom of a boat.

"Got one!" someone above her yelled. "How many of you?" she was asked. "How many overboard?"

"Three," she managed to stutter. "Two more."

"Two more overboard," her rescuer called out. "There, I see one." The boat surged forward as her rescuer manned the oars. A moment later another wet body was pulled into the boat.

"Gustav?" Pia huddled into him, hoping that despite how cold and still he was that he was still alive. "Gustav?"

He drew a deep shuddering breath, and she gulped back a sob and wrapped her freezing arms around him.

"Another boat is looking for the third one," their rescuer said. "I'll get you two where it's warm."

Shivers wracked them during the trip to shore. A good sign, Pia thought; proof that they were still alive.

Hands helped her up, and a blanket was wrapped around her. It didn't make her warm, but it blocked out the worst of the now howling winds.

"Pia?"

She looked up into Berna's worried face. "Rahm," she croaked out. "Rahm was in the boat. Your father."

And then she was bundled past Berna into a warm building. She had so little energy that she could barely stand as her clothes were stripped off. Grateful, she dropped onto a bed. A bed warmer was settled against her and heavy blankets were pulled up to her chin. It was a long time before her shivering subsided, but after that, she fell asleep.

PIA STRETCHED AND sighed. The metal bed warmer beside her was tepid now.

"How are you?"

She turned to see Berna hovering in the doorway.

"I think I'm fine," Pia said. "Gustav?"

"He's still asleep. He was in the water a little longer than you were, but the healer is hopeful that he will recover fully."

"And Rahm?" It wasn't that Pia wanted him to be safe, but if he was, she was going to let him know that she did not appreciate her life being put in jeopardy because of his stubborn need for control.

"I thought you were hallucinating when you said he was with you," Berna said. She came and sat on the side of the bed. "But there he was. He's recovering, like you and Gustav, but we've posted guards at his door."

"Guards? Why?"

Berna sighed. "I'll need to hear your story once you're up to it, but my mother has informed me that my father is a very dangerous man."

"Yes," Pia nodded. "I got that impression. Should we be worried?"

"Not unless we're his target," Berna replied. "According to my mother, Rahm is an assassin." She rose. "We'll talk later. If you want, I can heat up the bed warmer."

"Please," Pia said. She lifted the blanket, pulled out the metal warmer, and handed it to Berna who nodded and left the room.

An assassin. Of course. She already knew who Rahm's target was. She still had no idea what he needed Unmade, but she knew who he was here to kill.

She sighed. Was she happy that she wouldn't have to do it? She grinned. Yes. Especially if that target knew who and what was coming for him.

Because she had no doubt that Henrik Ottosen knew that Rahm was an assassin. Just as she had no doubt that Ottosen would not be able to stop him.

DAG STARED AT Strongrock Island. The *Atlaine* was anchored just off the beach that sat between the settlement and where the children had lived.

They were going to wait until dark and then round the point and sail past the town undetected. The assumption was that Steen and the pirates were here with the *Vassan*, but if they were wrong, and Pinho was on the island, they couldn't afford to be noticed by him and his multiple ships. All they wanted to do was head south and get through the Teeth.

"I don't see anything out of the ordinary on shore," she said to Darya, who stood beside her at the gunwale. "My Trait is quiet."

"Good," Darya replied. "Let's hope it stays that way."

"I'll keep watch," Dag replied.

"Thanks. Let me know if you see anything we need to worry about," Darya said before she turned and left.

In Dag's experience, the Strongrock pirates weren't interested in travelling by land. She thought that if anyone had investigated the rest of the island, it would have been Pinho's crew, making sure they couldn't be surprised by anyone approaching by land.

If there were no signs of anyone here, at the beach that was just a short walk from the settlement, it likely meant that Pinho was not on Strongrock.

Dag wasn't sure if she should be relieved. If Pinho was here, there was a chance he'd wait on Strongrock until the Frozen Pass opened. Dag would be able to warn Lauma and Nadez about him. With so few ships they would be challenged to figure out where and how to defend against him, but at least they would have time to prepare.

But if Pinho *wasn't* here, it meant he was still a threat on the Sapphire Sea, where Calder, without a ship, had a clear disadvantage. Would Luck be enough to defend against Pinho?

A few hours later, when dusk was settling in, Dag joined Darya at the wheel.

"The beach is still clear," she said.

"Thank you," the captain replied. "I'll want you at the bow when we pass the settlement, so you have about an hour to find yourself a meal or a rest."

"I'll be back long before then," Dag said. She headed to the mess and grabbed a bowl of stew. As she was finishing her meal, she felt the telltale signs that the ship was starting to move.

She nodded as she passed Darya at the wheel and headed to the bow.

It was a quiet night, clear and cold. A weak moon gave off very little light. Up ahead was the point, and beyond that was Strongrock Harbour.

A dozen minutes later they rounded the point, and Dag

searched the area. There was a single ship moored in the harbour: the *Vassan*. On shore there were a few lights at the tavern, but the burned hulk of the inn was dark.

As they passed the settlement, she walked along the port gunwale, keeping her eyes trained on shore, but no warnings sounded. She didn't see a single person, although a couple of times the sounds of shouting drifted across the water to her.

Then they were past the harbour and moving out into the open sea.

"The tavern was very quiet," she said when she reached Darya and Rafael. "With no signs of Pinho and his ships."

"Just the *Vassan*," Rafael agreed. "Maybe Steen has fewer pirates than we thought?"

"Or they're behaving better," Dag replied.

"We'll reach the Teeth in the morning," Darya said. "Get some rest, and that's an order."

"I'm going now," Dag replied. She said goodnight and headed down to the captain's cabin. Hers still, despite her protests that it was rightfully Darya's.

She studied the map for a few minutes. Nothing had changed: the spot on the map she'd pointed out to Darya still felt right to her, still felt like the place to enter the Teeth.

Though it was much farther south of where they'd crossed before.

She crawled into bed hoping that she was right and they would make it through to the Pale Sea.

"PINHO IS USING both taverns by the docks," Saba said. She put down her empty laundry basket and sat down at the table across from Calder. Esma and Kasim sat to either side of him.

"He has three ships," Saba continued. "All with full crews. And Floros has been seen with him."

"So, this is where she went," Calder said. "Pinho must have picked her up from Messanos."

"What use is Floros to Pinho now?" Esma asked. "She no longer has complete control over the council."

"In part because Audra can't get what she wants from her," Calder said. "Maybe Floros thinks Pinho can help her supply timber?"

"Lauma would have to agree to sell to one of them," Esma said.

"Not if Pinho pirates the timber," Calder replied. "Three ships—four if he can recruit the pirates and the *Vassan*—would be more than enough to target Byholt. The Three still only have two ships and a couple of log haulers." That didn't even take into account that one or more ships might have sustained damage— or been destroyed—over the winter. "Ships are being built in Lavais, but we have no idea when the first one will be ready to sail."

"The only good news," Saba said. "Is that Pinho's crew is getting more unruly every night." She grinned. "They insisted on being served *the best of everything,* so they've been served beer that has been brewed at double strength."

"How many sailors are left on the ships?" Calder asked.

"We've been watching the crew changes, so based on that, we believe that no more than five sailors remain on board each ship," Saba said. "And that the *Fair Winds* probably only has two."

"Do they know why?" Calder asked. Five crew members were the minimum required to sail a ship that size. To have less than that on one of the ships seemed strange.

"Our best guess," Saba replied. "Is that Pinho doesn't have enough crew. If he kept a bare bones crew on each ship, he might not have enough to secure the city. Too few in the taverns and Zelessans might try to capture them."

"That's probably it," Calder replied. "Even drunk sailors are a deterrent. Your network has done an incredible job of gathering information."

He and Esma had arrived last night, and this morning, Saba had gone in search of information. Her network consisted mostly of women going about their daily household tasks: shopping, visiting elderly or ill relatives and neighbours, and what Saba had just done, hanging laundry out to dry.

She would head back out in a few hours to gather the clothes and would no doubt hear more news.

Once they had enough information, they could come up with a plan. He was counting on Esma finding those who'd left in their small boats. If they wanted to defeat three ships, they needed to be on the water, and the *Hakon* was not enough.

"I can go watch the *Hakon*," Kasim said. "In case anyone shows up there. Including Father."

"I don't think he's in the city," Esma said. "He'd be here if he was."

"It might be too dangerous for him to come home," Kasim said. Esma snorted, and Kasim glared at her. "For us, not for Father," he added.

"He would have sent word if he couldn't come himself," Saba said. "He knows I would never forgive him." She sighed. "Although, I'm not sure I will anyway. All those lies for all those years."

Calder met Esma's eyes, and he raised his brows. He hadn't said anything to Saba about Rahm, so who had, and what did she know?

"I told her," Kasim said. "At least I told her what Esma told me, even though I'm not sure that's the whole truth."

"I know that Rahm is an assassin," Saba replied. "Which explains why he is always so secretive about everything." She shook her head. "I feel so foolish for having trusted him."

"We all trusted him," Esma said. "But that's his fault, not ours."

"I think the important point is that given who and what Rahm is," Calder said. "And that both Pinho and Floros know, he would have the freedom and ability to make that known to his family."

"You don't think he's here," Kasim said. "That there's no point watching the *Hakon*."

"I actually think watching the *Hakon* is a good idea," Calder said. "As long as it can be done safely. We'll need the boat, so we have to make sure it's not *borrowed* by anyone. And if someone else who docks there returns, it would be a chance to find out where the rest of them are. Once we have a plan, Esma will need to be able to find them *and* convince them to help."

"I'll watch the *Hakon*," Kasim repeated.

"No," Esma said. "I'll go."

Calder blew out a breath. "I won't insist if the two of you," he looked first at Esma and then at Saba, "decide against it, but I think Kasim should go. Esma shouldn't even be in the city; if she's seen by the wrong people, it might raise alarms."

"Then *I'll* go," Saba said.

"You're part of the network," Calder said. "No one else can do that. Besides, when was the last time you visited the *Hakon*? We can't do anything out of the ordinary."

"It's been a year," Saba said. "You're right; Kasim is the only one who can go."

"I know a back way," Kasim said. "I don't even need to be on the street."

"I'll tell him what he needs to do," Calder said. If anything happened to Kasim it would be his fault. He would have gone with his brother, but like Esma, he was not supposed to be in the city. And as a stranger, his presence might be seen as suspicious even by those he wanted to help.

"I'll talk to him too," Esma said finally. "I know who to trust."

"Good." Calder sighed. Kasim was the age he was when he'd become an Intelligencer, but he did not have the ten years of lessons he'd had. Nor did he have his Trait. They had just a few hours to try to give him enough information to keep him safe. How he hated sending those he cared for into danger.

CHAPTER 5

GUSTAV GROANED AND opened his eyes. He was warm and dry, but he couldn't suppress a shiver.

That had been an awfully close call. He'd been afraid when Rahm had refused to let him pilot the boat and then, when Pia signalled that he should be ready to jump, his heart had raced. Her warning had been enough to make him sit a little differently, so he'd been able to jump free of the oars when the boat started taking on water.

If Pia hadn't signalled him, or if he hadn't seen it, he could have been tangled up in the oars and dragged under. With water that cold, seconds mattered.

As it was, he was grateful that someone had already been out in a boat and they had seen them. It almost made him wonder if Calder's Luck came from Rahm.

His stomach growled, and he shoved the blankets to one side and rose reluctantly. They'd managed to get him into his own bed, so at least dry clothes were at hand. Once dressed, he grabbed the bed warmer and headed to the kitchen area.

Pia was already sitting at one of the tables along with Berna and Kaja.

Berna poured him some tea, and he sat down heavily. "Pia," he said. "Thanks. I owe you."

"We'd have all been fine if Rahm hadn't insisted on being at the tiller," Pia said. "His stupidity almost killed us."

"Not stupidity," he said. "All right, some stupidity. I just don't think he trusts anyone and hasn't for a very long time." He paused. "I also think that there's something else driving him."

"The Unmaking?" Berna asked. "Pia told us about the bargain you made with him. He would get rid of the pirates, and you would ask Jarri to try to Unmake something."

"We need to honour that," Pia said. "Especially now that we know he's an assassin."

"He's a what?" Gustav asked. He paused. "Rahm is the Resolute. Of course. Nadez told Ottosen that she knew who the Resolute was and that he would be surprised if he ever found out." He turned to Kaja. "It's true, isn't it?"

Kaja looked from him to Berna and then nodded. "Neither Lauma nor Nadez wanted anyone to know. Not even you."

"*Skit*," Berna said. "I don't blame you, Kaja, but I will be having words with my mother. This means we need to be even more careful with Rahm. I'll be the one to deal with him," she said. "In the hopes that he won't harm his own child."

"Pia and I should be with you when you talk to him," Gustav said. "Since we're the ones who made the bargain with him."

"I'm still going to shout at him for risking our lives," Pia said.

"Do you think that's wise?" Berna asked. "Given what we know about him?"

"He'll expect it from Pia," Gustav said. "He might actually think something's changed if she doesn't."

"He won't kill me," Pia said. "Not over this. And we don't want to make him nervous and give away any small advantage we might have."

"I'm not sure we have an advantage over a Resolute," Berna replied. "Even if he is my father."

"But we do," Gustav said. "And it's exactly because he *is* your father. Pia and I told him that we knew you, but we didn't tell him that you were here in Lavais Port."

"He has no idea that you know he's an assassin," Pia said. "I don't think he wants you to know."

"I need to eat," Gustav said. "And Kaja needs to tell us everything she knows about Rahm. Then we need to figure out how to use the little advantage we have—the surprise of Berna being here and in charge when he needs something Unmade—to make sure Rahm goes away without causing any harm."

"Is that the goal?" Kaja asked. "To simply let him get what he wants and then leave?"

"I doubt he wants to harm my mother," Berna said. "Or the Three. I'll have a conversation with him about what else he's doing. Pia, we'll need you and your Trait to try to figure what he's lying about. Because knowing my father, he'll be lying about something."

NADEZ STEPPED OUT of the shadow and into the centre of the street.

She'd been watching the warehouse for half an hour, and now it was just after midnight. She had two more warehouses to check before she could head for bed.

Ever since the last theft, she'd visited all the warehouses that still stored food every night. Her sleep was poor anyway; hunger and worry kept her awake, so she decided that she might as well put her time to good use.

She did her best to make her visits random; although, the warehouses were all well-known, so it would be simple for someone to find and follow her.

So she wasn't surprised that someone was. She strolled towards a cross street, but as soon as she turned the corner, she ran to a nearby alley.

She flattened herself against a building and waited for a few minutes before poking her head around the corner.

Someone was standing in the middle of the street. Oddly, they were just standing there, a dark cloak and hood covering them from head to toe. As if they were waiting.

"I'm here," she said, stepping out of the alley. "If you're looking for me."

"Master Intelligencer," the cloaked person said. The voice was too muffled for Nadez to even identify it as a man or a woman, let alone someone she recognized. "A mutual friend asked me to tell you that there is a gift for you at the New Bridge warehouse." Then the figure turned and went back the way they'd come.

Nadez stared after them. That warehouse was the place where Joosep had been held captive. Was that deliberate? Or was it simply convenient? At this time of night, it should be quiet, even if it were housing people.

Puzzled, she took a roundabout path to the warehouse.

The street outside was empty when she arrived, and just a single lamp hung beside the door. She opened the door and stepped into the dimly lit interior.

A hand cart sat a few feet from her. A tarp covered it, and when she lifted the tarp, she saw sacks of grain and a few crocks. She didn't have to look into the crocks to recognize that they contained preserved cabbage.

A mutual friend indeed.

Someone coughed near the back wall, and she paused. The shapes of sleeping people lined the floor along the back. The cart had been put here recently—and quietly—enough that no one had noticed it or been disturbed when it was left.

Careful not to make too much noise, Nadez pulled the cart through the door. She'd take this to Sture and have him check it for spoilage before adding it to the tally of food available to feed the city. She'd also ask him if he could tell which warehouse it had come from.

She had no idea how she'd done it, but she was certain that Valda Skala had arranged for the return of some of the stolen food. Who else would it have been? What she didn't know was how or why.

KASIM HURRIED IN from the kitchen and stopped in front of Calder and Esma.

"I just saw Ismini down at the dock," he said. "She and the rest are out at the marsh. I didn't tell her anything except where to get some supplies, but you can probably catch her before she leaves."

"I'll try to talk to her," Esma said. "We need to know exactly how many boats and people we have."

"Tell them we are coming up with a plan," Calder said. "But we need their help."

"I will. Let's go," Esma said to Kasim. The two left through the kitchen to head out into the back alleys.

Calder focused on the map of the town in front of him. The two taverns Pinho had commandeered for his men were marked, as were his three ships. But in case the map was discovered by someone loyal to Pinho or Floros, everything else they knew was kept in their heads.

And what they knew for certain wasn't much.

Pinho seemed to have somewhere around fifty men total,

including the twelve or so who were on watch on board the ships at any given time. Calder hoped that watch changes would provide them with an opportunity to catch Pinho's men off guard, so Saba was gathering more information. But winning against three ships from land, even with help from their small boats, would be difficult.

According to Saba's network, Pinho had been treading lightly in Zelesso so far. He had control of the harbour and monitored any goods leaving or arriving, but he had made no requests for anything other than food and drink for his men.

However, Pinho had called a meeting with local leaders and the most prominent merchants. Calder expected that Pinho was finally ready to make some demands.

The front door opened and closed, and Saba entered the room.

"He's done it," Saba said. "Pinho is demanding a protection fee from every household and merchant. Anyone who can't pay will have to work for him until he deems the debt paid off." She sat down across from him.

"Good." Because Pinho hadn't made life difficult for anyone, the network had heard whispers that many people were prepared to live with his rule. This should change all of that. "Who was the most surprised?"

"The local leaders, of course," Saba said. "Floros has been assuring them that nothing would change. The merchants had expected something. They know they always have to pay someone. But the amounts are crippling."

"Does anyone know what Pinho will do with the people who end up working for him?"

"Other than make sure that everyone is in debt to him?" Saba asked. She shook her head. "There are rumours that he's creating an army, but with only three ships what threat does he pose? I doubt he'd be able to take Messanos by force."

Calder shook his head. "I don't think that's his goal. I still think he's planning on targeting Byholt," he said. "Three ships could carry enough men to take a northern logging camp hostage, especially in early spring when only a dozen or so loggers are on site. If Pinho can promise to supply Audra with timber, he might be able to control the Arressan council again. The Frozen Pass won't be open for at least three or four weeks, giving him plenty of time to train his recruits. Some Zelessans might even like this."

There were always angry and entitled people with few skills and fewer prospects ready to ally with a tyrant.

"Then we'll need to make sure it doesn't happen," Saba said. She grinned.

"You learned more?" Calder asked.

"Pinho might be making some strategic plans, but his men live by a schedule," Saba said. "Watch changes are every twelve hours, midnight and noon."

"All at the same time?"

"So far every watch change has been the same," Saba said. "A single dinghy rows out and swaps a new crew for the old. Which means that twice a day half of Pinho's men are on the water: some in the dinghy and the rest on the ships."

"There's a good chance the ones on board the ships are watching their replacements the whole time," Calder said. "What about Pinho? Where is he likely to be?"

"He spends his nights on board the *Defensor*," Saba said. "He usually eats in the tavern and then goes to the ship, along with a couple of his men, long before the watch change."

"So the *Defensor* would have more than the bare minimum crew, along with a seasoned captain," Calder said. "And either the First or Second Mate. That's what I'd do and leave the other officer on shore to make sure the crew doesn't cause too much trouble in the taverns." He looked at the map and pointed to the ship that was farthest from shore. "Is the *Fair Winds* the last ship to have its crew replaced?"

"Every single time," Saba replied.

Calder grinned. "Good. In the morning you can start spreading the word to the owners of the small boats. Tomorrow at midnight we'll make our move."

DAG STARED OUT across the water. The Teeth rose in the distance, a field of white spires. Even this far south, the breeze was cold, and she hoped the sea between the spires wasn't frozen.

Ansdottir's old crew had said the pirate captain sailed through the Teeth farther north, in a fairly straight line between Strongrock and Tarklee, and only in summer. She and Calder had gone through the Teeth farther south, but that had been in a small sailboat. But just because no one had done it here, didn't mean it couldn't be done.

She had to assume that she would find a path. There was no other option.

"Anything?" Rafael asked. He stood beside her at the starboard gunwale, also peering out to the east.

"Not yet," Dag replied. She'd been looking for an hour already. She feared that if they were forced to enter the Teeth farther north, there was a much greater chance that they would encounter ice.

The potential to be frozen in place and incur damage that could disable or even destroy the ship, thereby endangering the crew, was something she didn't want to think about.

So there *had* to be a path.

She stared at two spires off in the distance, and the itch started between her shoulder blades.

"I think I see something," she said. She pointed. "Between those two large spires."

"It looks pretty tight," Rafael replied. "I'll ask the captain to take us closer so we can get a better look."

Alone at the gunwale, Dag studied the spires. The space between them was narrow, but she thought the ship would fit.

As they drew alongside, she stared past the spires. A clear path opened up just beyond them. The itch subsided, and she nodded to herself.

"This is it," she said to Darya when she joined her on the bridge.

"We have a steady but gentle wind," Darya said. "And four hours of daylight. Is that enough time?"

"I think so." Dag wished she could be more confident. "It's pretty open once we get past the first two spires."

"Getting past them will be the challenge," Darya said. "But if that's the way, then that's where the *Atlaine* will go. I have to bring her around. I'll need you and Rafael at the bow until we're safely out, so I suggest you take a rest now."

Rafael was in the mess, and she joined him with a mug of tea.

"Captain said we're going in." She paused. "You need to tell me if the ship is too wide."

"You're not sure?" Rafael asked.

"I'm certain there is a path through the Teeth here," Dag replied. "But I'm not an expert on ships or Traits. It's possible that my faulty knowledge of the *Atlaine* is informing my Trait."

"Ah, you think that a mistaken understanding about the width of the ship is allowing your Trait to see a path even if the ship won't fit through it." Rafael nodded at her tea. "Drink up. I'll give you a tour."

Dag drained her tea and followed Rafael.

She'd been to the hold before, but she'd never really noticed how the hull bulged at the water line and then narrowed to the keel. After an explanation of the draft—the vertical distance, on the outside of the ship, from the waterline to the keel—Rafael had her pace the entire width. She paced the same spot up on deck.

With a better feel for the ship, Dag stood at the bow and stared at the Teeth now. She closed her eyes, and when she opened them, her Trait activated. Her new knowledge hadn't changed her belief that the *Atlaine* would fit between the two large spires.

She glanced at Rafael. "We can make it."

"Good," he replied. "Because we're heading in."

It was a tight fit—too tight. Dag ran from starboard to port. "We're too close," she called to Rafael. "We need another two inches."

Rafael's order was relayed back to Darya.

Slowly the space between the hull and the spire increased. Dag leaned over the starboard gunwale as they neared the spire. There was a soft scraping sound, and then the ship was past it.

Back at the bow, Dag saw clear sea for a handful of boat lengths. She pointed out a patch of ice to Rafael. "We need to turn right at that ice."

For two hours, Dag took them on a winding path through spires and ice. She held her breath as they passed over a stretch of submerged spires, testing her new understanding of the depth the ship required.

Finally, they reached open water. A cheer went up when they left the last spire behind them.

"Well done," Rafael said. "There were a couple of places where I was worried that we wouldn't make it."

"Including where we entered," Dag agreed. "Did it damage the ship?"

"A little," he said. "Captain will want to have someone take a look at it when we have a chance."

"There will be an opportunity in our next port," she said. "We're far enough south that we'll pass Lavais on our way to

Tarklee. I would very much like to stop and see how the shipyards are progressing. I'll see if Darya agrees."

"I'm sure she'll want to take advantage of having someone look at the hull," Rafael said. "Lavais Port has more experienced shipbuilders than Tarklee."

PIA OPENED THE door and entered the room. Rahm stared at her as she crossed the floor to sit down at the table.

"When do I get to meet the Unmaker?" he asked. "We struck a deal."

"Which did not include you almost killing us all," Pia said. "Because you were too stubborn to let Gustav have the tiller."

Rahm's mouth twitched in a small smile. "But here we are, alive. At least, I assume Gustav made it."

"No thanks to you," Pia said. She glared at him. "Gustav and I were pulled into the same boat. I should have said that there were only the two of us."

"Why didn't you?"

Pia sighed. "A question I keep asking myself."

"You did the right thing," Rahm said darkly. "I am extremely hard to kill, and if I had lived and found out that you'd done that, things would not go well for you." He leaned back in his chair. "Now, we had a bargain. When do I meet this Unmaker?"

The door opened, and Gustav entered.

"Ah, so you are alive," Rahm said. "Good. Between the two of you, I expect our bargain to be kept. Or else I will hurt Pia."

"I know we made the deal," Gustav said. "But the representative of the Interim Grand Freeholder did not. They have final authority here."

Pia kept her eyes on Rahm. He seemed to believe Gustav. It was the truth, after all.

"Let me speak to this person who represents my wife," Rahm said.

"So you can threaten them as well?" Pia asked. "I thought Lauma Strauskas was your former wife? Are you sure she would want this bargain to be kept?"

"Don't try to go back on our deal, little girl," Rahm said. "I will take this whole settlement apart to get what was promised me."

The door swung open.

"Make sure you don't kill the Unmaker while you're doing

that." Berna strode into the room and sat beside Pia. Kaja followed her and stopped and stood beside Gustav. "Isn't that what you do, Father? Kill people?"

Pia Concentrated and was able to suppress a shudder when Rahm's eyes bore into hers. Then he pasted a smile on his face and turned his attention to Berna.

"Well, isn't this a happy reunion?" he said.

"After foolishly almost killing the three of you, and putting good people at risk by requiring rescue?" Berna asked. "I think not. Besides, it's been what, five years? If you'd wanted a reunion with me, you had plenty of time."

"Your mother told me to stay away," Rahm said.

"And you always do what Mother tells you? She'll find that amusing." Berna shrugged. "Or maybe not. I think she's had a lifetime of your lies, and I know that's another one."

"What do you know?" Rahm asked.

"That you are a Resolute. Oh yes, your secret is out. Calder told us. He also said that you knew about the threat to Mother's life: that a suicide assassin had been commissioned."

"I had no idea *she* was in danger," Rahm said. "That she was Interim Grand Freeholder and therefore the target. That was not my doing or my fault."

Berna frowned. "There he is, the father I remember. Nothing was ever your fault, was it?"

Rahm looked calm, but Pia could tell that he was furious. She hoped Berna knew what she was doing. Rahm probably wouldn't kill his daughter, but everyone else in Lavais Port might be at risk.

"There were circumstances that you could never understand," Rahm said.

"Like the fact that you were killing people for coin?" Berna asked. "I suppose assassination must be very lucrative; you did give quite a lot of coin to Mother over the years. Was that to ease your conscience?"

"That was to take care of my family," Rahm said. "I will *always* take care of my family."

"That would include both families, I guess," Berna said. "The one here and the one in Zelesso."

Rahm's eyes narrowed. "How do you know about them?"

Berna laughed. "Calder *is* my brother. You might not talk to any of us, but we certainly talk to each other. Mother, me, Calder, and Yakop. I especially want to meet Esma. I've always wanted a sister, and I hear she's just a few years older than me." She paused. "And Kasim is younger, yes?"

Below the table, Pia clenched her hands into fists. If she'd known that Berna was going to goad Rahm like this, she would have cautioned her. Maybe Berna hadn't known it herself.

Berna's anger certainly seemed real.

Pia believed Rahm when he said he wanted to take care of his family. She thought that was a driving force in his life. But what would he do if his family, if *both* his families, rejected him?

She unclenched her hands. She didn't know if Berna understood signalling or not, but she tried anyway. Berna sighed and nodded.

"But all of these family squabbles can be dealt with another time," Berna said. "Although, Father, you should be prepared to make amends with all of us."

"I will do whatever I can," Rahm said.

Pia relaxed because *Rahm* relaxed.

"Good. I'll let Mother know," Berna said. "Right now, we are dealing with near-starvation and untrustworthy Clan Freeholders."

"I've already warned Timonis," Rahm said. "I expect you will hear about his sudden and heartwarming decision to share his food. I trust that Pia and Gustav told you I solved your pirate problem?"

"They did, and I thank you," Berna replied. "For your help with Clan Freeholder Timonis, as well." She paused. "But you did neither of these things for free."

"My conversation with Timonis was a courtesy," Rahm said. "But the pirates? That was the bargain."

"Yes. The bargain. We will keep it," Berna said. "So, whatever you want Unmade, you can hand it to me, and I will make sure there is a sincere attempt to Unmake it." Berna looked at Pia. "And an attempt is all I will promise. I understand that no other guarantees were given to you." She held her hand out over the table, palm up.

Rahm shifted in his seat. "There were no other guarantees," he agreed. "But I must put what I have into the hands of the Unmaker myself. It's not that I don't trust you," he said. "There are other reasons."

Berna withdrew her hand. "Very well. But I will let the Unmaker decide when they are ready. Until then, please remain inside." She pushed her chair back. "Father." Berna nodded and left, followed by Kaja.

Pia watched Rahm watch his daughter leave. Then he turned his glare onto her.

"You didn't tell me she was here," Rahm said.

Pia shrugged. "We told you we knew her. You never asked how." She stood up. "There's just us three in this building right now," she said. "Gustav and I will fetch some tea. I imagine the Unmaker won't take very long to decide when to try to Unmake your item."

"We'll be back soon," Gustav said. He left the room, and Pia was right behind him. She closed the door and took a deep breath.

She hoped Jarri was able to do it. Despite Rahm agreeing that an attempt was all he expected, she worried how he'd react if his item couldn't be Unmade. Better to get his item Unmade and let him leave Lavais Port as soon as possible.

"YEP," STURE SAID. "From the first warehouse theft, same as the other cart."

"You're certain?" This was the second cart of food that Nadez had been directed to. Like the first one, she'd been followed by a cloaked figure who told her that a mutual friend had a gift for her.

"See these crocks?" Sture pointed to a stamp on the side of one crock. "We had fifty of them taken that first night. I checked around after the theft and they were the only ones like them in the city."

"So, they are returned goods," Nadez replied. "But why?"

"And returned by whom?" Sture asked.

Nadez had a very good idea of the whom: Valda Skala. But why was she returning food, and how was she doing it? That Valda had access to the food implied that Clan Freeholder Skala was behind the thefts, and Nadez was certain that it had been Ottosen.

"This makes half of the crocks recovered?" Nadez asked.

"Aye. And about a quarter of the grain," Sture said. "I'll send that out to be ground and get the cabbages distributed by end of day tomorrow."

"Thank you," Nadez said. "I'll give the tally to Lauma." She took the paper Sture handed her and stuffed it into a pocket.

Outside the warehouse, a warm wind blew up from the south. The sun was shining, and she had hope that they would all make it to spring.

At this time of day, Lauma would most likely be down at the harbour supervising the ice fishing.

Nadez was almost there when she heard a sudden boom, followed by a second, louder, crack. Cries and shouts from the harbour drifted to her.

Running now, Nadez squeezed past two people who had stopped just at the edge of the dock.

Booms and cracks echoed across the harbour. Shading her eyes against the glare off the ice, Nadez looked out towards the mouth of the harbour.

Half a dozen figures were on the ice running towards the city.

"Get these ice boats out there now!"

Nadez turned to find Lauma at the very end of the dock, pointing at two small ice boats that were beside her. Before Nadez could reach her, Lauma stepped into a boat, untied it, and grabbed the oars.

A second person jumped into the other boat, and soon the two of them were rowing towards the running people.

Three people from the ice were able to climb into Lauma's boat, and in a few minutes the sail was up. Lauma sat at the stern, and the boat skimmed across the ice, heading farther out.

It wasn't until Nadez looked to see where Lauma was heading that she saw the hole in the ice; a stretch of black water with chunks of white ice bobbing in it. Someone lay flat on a floating piece of ice and there—someone else was in the water.

She turned and ran to the people who lined the dock, watching.

"Blankets!" she called. "We need blankets. Who has a space nearby? We need a warm room with a fire."

"My shack is right there," a man said, pointing to a small wooden structure at the edge of the dock. "You can bring them to me. I'll get the fire going, and I have some old tarps you can use."

Nadez followed him into a single room. It was a fishing shack; old nets and traps lined the wall. The fisherman pulled two cloth tarps from a bench and handed them to her.

"I'll get the fire hot," he said.

"Thanks." Nadez hurried back outside and down to the edge of the dock.

Lauma's boat was in the open water at the centre of the ice, now. Nadez held her breath as Lauma's passengers leaned over, making that side of the boat dip low. The little boat bobbed upright when someone was dragged into it.

She'd have words with Lauma later: they could not afford to lose her. The Three could not afford to lose her.

Lauma's boat continued towards the person who was stranded on ice. Someone in the bow reached out and pulled them over the gunwale.

As soon as that person was in the boat, it headed back to the edge of solid ice.

The second boat had turned around on the ice, its stern facing the black water and Lauma's boat. A few minutes later the second boat, its sail up and straining against the wind, started to move towards the city, towing the other boat. Lauma's boat hit the edge of the ice head on, and the boat hovered for a moment before it was pulled up onto the ice.

The crowd on shore cheered as both ice boats headed in.

As soon as the boats reached the dock, Nadez handed off the tarps.

"There's a warm room up this way," she said. She led the way to the fisherman's hut.

The two who had been saved were taken into the hut. Nadez stood just inside the door, and was joined by Lauma, who shut the door, keeping the warmth in.

"We lost a man," Lauma said. "He'd already gone under by the time I got out there."

"You saved two," Nadez replied. "I don't think anyone else could have done that."

"It's my fault they were out there," Lauma said. "I'm the one with ice fishing experience. I'm the one who said it was safe to go out today."

"We're all doing the best we can," Nadez replied. She knew she couldn't convince Lauma that this wasn't her fault. She knew it because if the positions had been reversed, she wouldn't listen to anyone. She'd blame herself for not knowing everything, for not managing everything.

Responsibility for what happened: good and bad, was the price of being a leader.

CHAPTER 6

CALDER STARED OUT at the dark Zelesso Harbour. He'd been watching for hours: none of the three ships had moved all day, and other than when the watch had changed, he'd seen very little activity on board.

The watch change at noon had happened exactly as it had been described. All twelve replacements rowed out in a single dinghy, and starting with Pinho's flagship *Defensor*, visited each ship. Once the final change was made at the *Fair Winds*, the dinghy headed back to the dock.

The trip back was loud, with sailors laughing and shouting as they rowed. Once at the dock, they jumped out and headed for the nearest tavern. Careless and carefree: Calder was counting on the midnight crew being much the same.

A pebble landed near him, and he crept back through the scrubby bushes to the hole in the fence.

"Esma signalled," Kasim whispered. "They're ready."

"How many boats?" Calder asked. "And people?"

"Fourteen. And twenty on board. Twenty-one if you include me."

"No," Calder said. "You're the communication link, and that's a vital task." He couldn't see his brother in the dark, but he heard him sigh. "Please see if Saba has any news. Watch change starts in fifteen minutes, so be back here by then."

A soft scrape in the dirt was the only sound when Kasim left.

Rather than disturb the bushes, Calder stayed where he was. Any little thing could disrupt the plan, including a stray cat noticing him and waking people up.

He took a deep breath. The plan would work; it had to work.

"Calder?" Kasim was back.

"Here."

"Nothing new," Kasim said. "The next watch has been in the tavern, as usual, but they all stopped drinking an hour ago."

"Thanks." Pinho's crew was showing some discipline. He wished he knew if it was out of loyalty or out of fear for their captain. "It's time. Let Esma know I'm going."

"I will," Kasim replied. "Good luck and stay safe."

"You too." Calder eased away from the fence. Good Luck. He was counting on it. He only hoped Luck wanted what he wanted.

The water was cool when he slipped into it. He figured it would take ten minutes to swim to the *Fair Winds*. Ten minutes when the two men on board would be at the bow, watching as the dinghy with their replacements headed first to the *Defensor* and then to the *Pathfinder* before turning towards their ship.

By that time, Calder needed to be on board.

Sound travelled far over water on a still night like this, but the rowers were making more than enough noise to cover the small splashes he made as he swam.

He heard them reach the first ship; sailors laughed and shouted in greeting; the boisterous conversation continuing as the dinghy left the *Defensor*.

Calder had reached the stern of the *Fair Winds* when he heard a second chorus of greetings. He had only a few minutes now.

Luck was with him. Ropes dangled over the gunwale, and it only took him a moment to climb up onto the deck. He cut a length of rope and wrapped it around his waist.

Bare feet padding silently on the wood of the deck, he carefully made his way to the prow. Two men stood there watching their replacements being rowed their way.

"Did you hear something?" one asked. He turned and his mouth widened in surprise when Calder stepped out of a shadow.

"Sound the alarm!" the sailor said as he rushed towards a bell.

Calder surged forward and tackled the man before he could grab the bell rope. His momentum carried them both towards the gunwale. Calder shoved the man to the left, sending them both crashing into the second man. The two sailors sprawled onto the deck while Calder regained his balance.

One sailor got to his knees, yelling for help, and Calder pushed him back down. He fell on his companion, who grunted in pain.

They were both shouting now, but Calder ignored them and grabbed the top sailor, uncoiled the rope around his waist, and quickly tied the sailor's hands and feet together. The second sailor was trying to get to his feet, so Calder pushed the tied sailor on top of him, sending them both tumbling onto the deck. Using the end of the rope, he secured the second man's hands and feet, hobbling them together.

With his knife, Calder cut the sleeves off one sailor's shirt and stuffed a sleeve in each man's mouth, silencing them.

He heard shouts from the water below the bow, and after making sure his captives were secure, Calder leaned out over the gunwale. Five Zelessan boats surrounded the dinghy. Even in the dark, he recognized the *Hakon*.

He grabbed a lamp and waved it back and forth twice, paused to count to eight, then waved it to port once.

A lamp on one of the boats was lit. Ismini sat in the stern, pointing a pistol at the dinghy. Then the little band of boats, with the dinghy in tow, headed towards the *Fair Winds*.

By now, lights dotted the shore, and angry shouts and a low whistle drifted across to him. Two dinghies set out from the dock, one heading towards the *Defensor* and the second heading in his direction.

It was too dark for Calder to see how many men Pinho had sent this way, or whether they had guns. The group of Zelessan boats was on his starboard side, and he left the bow to toss down a rope ladder before he returned to the bow to watch the dinghy.

"We captured all twelve."

Calder turned to find Esma beside him, staring out over the gunwale.

"We should have all the prisoners on board and locked below decks in five minutes." She gestured to the two bound sailors. "I'll add these two."

A shot rang out and Calder pulled Esma down to the deck.

"That answers that question," he said. "At least one gun on that dinghy."

"And now everyone knows," Esma replied. She grinned. "We

have a gun too, if we need to use it."

That had been their biggest worry, after Calder being able to take the *Fair Winds* by himself.

Having the little flotilla unknowingly head directly into guns. Now that they knew, they would move to the second part of the plan.

Three people joined them, and with Esma's help, they dragged the two sailors away.

The dinghy was slowing as it approached the ship.

Esma re-joined him in the prow, both of them staying below the gunwale: out of sight and hopefully out of range.

"Will they try to board us?" she asked.

"I don't think so," he replied. "The other dinghy is almost at the *Defensor*. I think this one wanted to keep us busy until they made it to Pinho. Look, they're trying to turn away." The dinghy below them was now arcing away from the *Fair Winds*.

"Maybe Pinho will leave," Esma said. "Now that he knows we'll resist him."

"Or he might use his cannon." Pinho had run from Rahm, but would he run from this? If he was looking to build an army and steal timber, this could be his very last chance. "He's spent years trying to gain control in the Sapphire Sea. I doubt he's ready to give up."

By now, almost a dozen small boats from their flotilla surrounded the *Fair Winds*. A shot echoed across the water, and the man holding the tiller in the dinghy slumped over.

The rowers tried desperately to keep the dinghy heading away from danger, but in moments, the flotilla was on them.

It took just a few seconds before Pinho's sailors were captured.

"That's another seven," Esma said. "Added to the fourteen locked up, we have almost half of Pinho's men."

"He still has enough to crew both those ships," Calder replied. "And we're still outnumbered."

The dinghy finally reached the *Defensor*. Orders echoed across the water, and the sailors scrambled on board.

Calder strained to see what the *Defensor* was doing. More lamps were lit on board Pinho's flagship, and sails were being unfurled. "I don't think he's leaving," he said. "No, look. They're using the anchor to turn the ship and point the stern, and the cannon, at us."

"We'll need a few minutes to get these new prisoners on board," Esma said. "Then we can haul anchor."

"Don't rush," Calder replied. "The *Pathfinder* is between us and the *Defensor*. I doubt Pinho will risk losing both ships to his cannon."

Esma left to secure the prisoners, and he watched Pinho turn his ship and point his stern-mounted cannon.

"*Skit!*" His heart sank when he realized what Pinho was doing; what his target was.

Pinho wasn't aiming at the *Fair Winds*: he wasn't risking destroying the other two ships. He was aiming directly at the main docks of Zelesso.

Pinho was going to attack the city.

"YOU'RE SURE ABOUT this?" Gustav asked again. "You can wait, or even not do it. Rahm *is* a Resolute."

Jarri shrugged. "A Resolute who wants something from me. I'll be fine. There's not much left for me to Unmake in the shipyards, so it would be good to do something useful."

"All right," Gustav said. They were in the smallest shipyard workshop. A few broken and burned bits were scattered across a large table that took up half of the floor space. "Pia, Kaja, Berna, and I will all be there. He won't tell us what he wants Unmade, and remember, we did not give him any guarantees. So, if you can't Unmake it, don't worry."

"I'll do my best," Jarri said. "We might as well do this now."

"Do you want Janni to come?"

"No. She's really busy," Jarri said. "She thinks they'll get the mast made today."

"That's great," Gustav said. He led the way outside. The mast was one of the last things completed before the ship was assembled.

"Yeah," Jarri replied. "The ship might be ready to launch next week. They've already started dressing timber for the second one."

"Who's naming her?" Gustav asked. Usually whoever commissioned—and paid for—a ship named it. But this ship had no owner unless you counted the Fair Seas Treaty Alliance. Everyone involved had worked for very little pay, so they all should have stake in it.

"Some of them, including your da, wants Janni and I to name her," Jarri said. "I guess we have to start thinking of something."

"Ask for help picking a good name." Gustav didn't envy them. The wrong name could be bad luck for the ship and crew.

He opened the door to the office. "We're here," he called out. "Jarri's ready."

"I'll get my father," Berna said. "Hi, Jarri. Are you sure you're up to this?"

Jarri nodded as he closed the door. "I'm looking forward to a challenge," he said. "I assume this is a tricky thing to Unmake since he's brought it all the way from the Sapphire Sea."

"I didn't think of it like that," Gustav said. He really looked at Jarri: he'd filled out over the past season despite the poor rations. His face had more colour, and his eyes were brighter. He just looked more . . . solid.

"All right," Berna said. "I'll meet you at my desk." She headed to the room they'd assigned to Rahm. They hadn't locked him up, but he'd behaved and kept to himself anyway.

Jarri led the way to the office and sat down at the desk facing the door. Gustav stood behind him, watching the entrance.

There were only three chairs, and they'd agreed beforehand that they wanted Rahm sitting beside his daughter with the desk between him and Jarri.

"Hi, Jarri," Pia greeted him when she and Kaja arrived.

Berna led Rahm into the room, indicated a chair, and sat beside him. Pia leaned against the wall, where she could see everyone's face, and Kaja closed the door and stood in front of it.

"This is your Unmaker?" Rahm asked. "I was expecting someone a little older." He shook his head. "The Three seems very short on experience."

"Calder is experienced," Berna replied. "Despite being a few years younger than Jarri."

"Calder has done more field work than me," Jarri said. "Our Traits dictate the type of work we do."

"Jarri, this is my father, Rahm," Berna said. "I'm sure you've been told that he is a Resolute assassin?" Jarri nodded. "Good. Father, this is Jarri. Hand him whatever you want Unmade so we can get this business over with."

"I will not expose what I want Unmade with all of you looking on," Rahm replied. "The rest of you can leave the room."

"If we leave, Jarri leaves," Berna said. "Without attempting to Unmake anything."

"We had an agreement," Rahm said, staring over Jarri's head at Gustav. "Are you going back on your word?"

"Our agreement did not define the conditions," Gustav replied. "In Lavais Port, Berna Strauskas defines those conditions on behalf of the Interim Grand Freeholder."

"You can always petition Mother," Berna said calmly. "But we are not leaving you alone with Jarri. For all we know you have nothing to Unmake and want to make sure that someone else can't get their item Unmade. You are an assassin, after all."

Rahm's face darkened, and he glared at his daughter. "You are accusing me of making a bad faith agreement. Daughter or no, that is a dangerous thing to do."

"You expect me to believe anything you say after all the years you spent lying to your family?" Berna asked. "Would you trust *you* if the situations were reversed?"

"I lied to protect you," Rahm said. He frowned and then sighed. "And I *would not* trust me if the situations were reversed. But that is because I have learned not to trust anyone. If you have learned that too, I bear some blame." He looked around the room and sighed again. "I suppose the Unmaker would just tell you what it is anyway." He pulled something from a pocket, placed his hand flat on the desk, and slid it across to Jarri before lifting his hand.

Gustav leaned over Jarri's shoulder. It was a coin of some kind, with an image etched onto it.

Jarri picked it up and turned it over. "Kaja?" He held it out, and Kaja took a step closer so she could see it clearly. She studied the coin for a few minutes before nodding and returning to her place in front of the door.

"What was that all about?" Rahm asked.

"Kaja was curious," Berna said. "Jarri, can you do anything with it?"

"How do you want it Unmade?" Jarri asked. "I can destroy the coin."

"It's a token," Rahm said.

"All right," Jarri said. "I can destroy the token, meaning that I can make it into smaller pieces." He brought the token closer to his face and squinted at it. "But I'm not sure that will change its . . ." He paused. "*Function.*"

"The function is the only thing I need Unmade," Rahm said. "Especially if the smaller pieces would all retain that function."

Rahm actually looked worried at that possibility.

"It's possible they would," Jarri said, his voice low and quiet. He set the token back on the desk and stared at it. "I need to be very careful, so this might take a while."

"But you can do it?" Rahm asked.

Jarri looked up at him and grinned. "Oh, I can do something, but you want me to do the *right* thing." He looked over at Berna. "We have time for tea."

"I'll get it," Pia said.

"I'll help," Kaja said.

"That's better," Jarri said once they'd left and closed the door. "I thought Unmaking things at the shipyard got me used to people watching me work, but they were making you—and therefore me—nervous. So, this function, what does it do?"

Jarri was still bent over the token and instead of answering, Rahm stared at his head.

Jarri looked up at him. "I can't Unmake what it does if I don't *know* what it does. And I will not agree to be alone in this room with you. So, you have a choice. You can tell all of us so I know what I'm trying to do; I can attempt to Unmake this without understanding its purpose and run the risk of making things worse for you; or I can refuse to try something that may be dangerous to me."

"Father," Berna said. "If Jarri decides not to attempt this because you have not given him the information that he needs, I will decide that the bargain has been fulfilled. I will not let him put himself at risk because of your stubbornness and need for secrecy."

Rahm closed his eyes for a moment. "You're right. It is a dangerous object. I don't know how it does what it does, but it compels me. The token is held by whoever hires me."

"To kill someone," Berna said.

"Yes," Rahm agreed. "They pay me to kill someone and hold the token until the task is done. And every day, every hour that I am away from the token it . . ." He paused. "At first, it's like an itch that I can never scratch. Later, if I take longer to fulfil the task, it gets worse."

"Pinho hid your token for months," Kaja said, surprising Gustav. "Until Dagrun Lund found it and returned it to you."

"What did that do to you?" Berna asked.

"It made me willing to do almost anything in order to make it stop," Rahm said. "And before you ask, I was willing to die to end my misery, but I can't kill myself and so far," he grunted, "no one else has been able to either."

"How did this token get tied to you like that?" Jarri asked.

"There was a ceremony," Rahm said, "when I was a child. My father sold me to a man I will *never* call by name. He conducted a ceremony that I don't really remember, and then he trained me."

"That's why you never speak of your family," Berna said.

"*You* are my family," Rahm said.

Gustav looked down at his feet. Rahm's admission that he'd been sold startled him: he knew it happened, but he'd never really thought about the consequences. That the one sold would never trust anyone ever again. That had to be when the assassin had first learned not to trust, and Gustav couldn't blame him. If your own father betrayed you, you had to assume that anyone would.

"I understand so much now," Berna said, her voice sad.

"I do not want your pity!" Rahm said. "Uhn." He grunted, and his head dropped to the desk with a thud.

"Father?" Berna shook his shoulder. "Father!"

"It's done," Jarri said.

The token was still on the table but . . . Gustav leaned over for a closer look. It was no longer shiny. What looked like years of grime darkened the surface, obscuring the symbols.

"Father!" Berna shook him and he groaned.

Suddenly, the door flew open.

"A ship!" Pia called. "A ship is just outside the harbour! There's too much ice so an iceboat has gone out."

"The *Tazeyar* is here already?" Berna asked.

"No," Pia said, grinning. "It's the *Atlaine*. Calder and Dagrun back with more food! Hurry!" She ran out of the room.

Gustav itched to follow. The first ship of the season was always exciting, but for the *Atlaine* to be here, with news and probably food from the Sapphire Sea, that was cause for celebration.

He turned back to Rahm. "Is he alive?" he asked Berna, who still sat beside her father.

"He's breathing," she said. She shook him again but there was no response.

"You go," Gustav said. "I'll send Jarri if Rahm wakes up."

"Thank you." Berna rose, looked down at her father, and sighed. "Thank you, Jarri. You did something. We won't know what until he wakes up, but I'll be back as soon as I greet the ship."

Gustav sat down in the chair Berna had vacated.

"I'll go see if they had a chance to make tea," Jarri said, and before Gustav could stop him, he left.

Gustav turned back from looking at the open doorway to find Rahm staring at him.

"Don't say a word," Rahm said. He scooped up the token and stared at it. Then he laughed. "Our bargain is complete." He pocketed the token and rose to unsteady feet. "Don't try to stop me," he said. "I have something I need to do."

"You still have a commission," Gustav said. "But with your token Unmade, isn't the compulsion gone?"

"I hold my token," Rahm said. "There has been no compulsion for this final task. It is fitting that my last assignment is for someone I would not want to, nor dare to, turn my back on." Then he was gone.

Gustav wondered if he should try to follow him but then decided not to. Their plan had been to do their best to fulfil Rahm's bargain and then have him leave.

Now he was gone.

Gustav stood up just as Jarri returned with two mugs of tea.

"Rahm woke up," he said to the older Intelligencer. "He said that your Unmaking worked, that the bargain was complete, and then he left. Come on. Unless you really want tea, we're free to go greet the *Atlaine*."

CALDER STARED OUT at the *Defensor*. It was almost in position now. One of the small boats had been sent ashore, and he could hear calls and shouts along the waterfront warning people to get out.

"The last of the prisoners has been put into the hold," Esma said as she joined him. "They're locked up but not bound, like you asked."

"Thanks." He assumed the sailors would be able to break out

of a locked hold eventually: he had no wish to condemn them to drown, and there was no way to guarantee he would have time to free them. He looked up: the mainsail had been raised, and the canvas shone in the moonlight. A gust of wind caught the sail and it billowed out causing the ship to strain against the anchor.

"It's time to raise the anchor," Calder said. "Then everyone else needs to get off this ship."

"You too," Esma said. "We can just point it at the *Defensor*. I don't think Pinho has enough room to get out of the way."

"I would," Calder said. "I have to assume Pinho is at least as good a captain as I am. If he is, then we risk being worse off than before our actions of tonight. Pinho will have all of his ships and crew, and he will know that there is organized opposition to him. We can't let that happen."

"Even if it means destroying two ships?" Esma asked.

"Even if it means destroying all *three* ships," Calder replied. "At least if none of us had a ship, that would put us on the same footing. Although, the city would have the advantage because of the resolve of its people." He turned to his sister. "That's what Pinho is trying to destroy. He's trying to kill the defiant spirit of Zelessans and make them either cower in fear or try to gain an advantage by working for him. Any loss is worth not allowing that."

"Including you?" Esma asked softly.

Calder sighed. "Yes."

"I don't like it," Esma said. "You're not even from here. It should be one of us making this sacrifice."

"You're from here," Calder said. "That makes me one of you. Besides, I'm the only one who has captained a ship like this." He grinned. "And I *have* done this before and lived."

"Your Luck better be working," Esma said.

"It hasn't failed me yet," Calder said. "Come on. I'll see you to the *Hakon,* and then I'm raising the anchor."

"You really think the *Pathfinder* crew will just let us board?" Esma asked.

She followed him to the stern.

"There are no officers on board," he said. "Without discipline, I expect all eyes will be on the *Fair Winds* and the *Defensor*." He grinned. "It should be quite a distraction. But everyone needs to be careful."

"Ismini is in charge," Esma said. "She already used her pistol and won't hesitate again, if needed."

"Good. Time to go," Calder said. "For both of us."

He hugged Esma before she climbed over the gunwale. Two small boats were tied up to the stern of the ship. One was the *Hakon* and the second was for him, assuming he had time to escape.

As soon as the *Hakon* was safely away, Calder pulled the peg from the winch and started winding the wheel to raise the anchor.

He was sweating by the time the anchor was up and tied it off. The *Fair Winds* was already surging forward, so Calder ran to the bridge and grabbed the wheel. He set course directly for the starboard side of the *Defensor*.

A loud boom echoed across the water when the cannon was fired, followed by the sound of wood splintering in the city.

Calder didn't hear any cries or screams, so he had hope that the warnings had been enough to keep people safe even if property was damaged or destroyed.

A cloud skidded across the moon, and the night got darker. Calder smiled: Luck was giving him an advantage.

The *Fair Winds* slipped past the *Pathfinder*. All five crew members were at the city side gunwale, watching the *Defensor* fire on Zelesso. They cried out when they saw him, but by then he was already out of range of any guns they might have.

The *Defensor* had had enough time to reload the cannon when the sky suddenly cleared. A shout came from Pinho's ship: the *Fair Winds* had been spotted.

A flurry of orders were called out, and the topsail was unfurled as the *Defensor* headed away from the city, out towards the open sea. Calder changed course, and there were multiple shouts from the deck of his quarry.

He grinned. No doubt Pinho had expected Esma's plan: that the *Fair Winds* was empty and would sail right past.

The *Defensor* tacked to starboard, and Calder turned the wheel to follow, keeping the bow of the *Fair Winds* pointed directly at the starboard side of the *Defensor*.

Pinho changed course twice more, and Calder changed with him. The *Defensor* was picking up speed now, but the *Fair Winds* had been sailing with full sails far longer than the *Defensor* and was gaining on the other ship.

In another few minutes, he would catch Pinho. A door up ahead banged open; the prisoners had escaped the hold and were now on deck

There were grunts and shouts of pain as they stumbled into his trap: loose pins and pegs strewn across the dark deck.

Calder eyed the *Defensor*; he made a final adjustment in anticipation of Pinho's next move before he tied off the wheel. In the predawn light, he could see sailors scrambling on the deck and in the sails of the *Defensor*.

It was time to go. He stepped past the trap he'd set to make sure the course he'd set couldn't be changed and ran to the stern. The small dinghy was still trailing the ship. He pulled out his knife and cut the rope before slipping over the gunwale into the sea.

A moment later, Calder pulled himself into the dinghy. He heard shouts and screams from on deck: barefoot sailors had stepped into the shards of glass he'd spread out around the wheel.

He grabbed the oars and started rowing, his eyes on the stern of the *Fair Winds*.

He heard the crash, wood cracking and tearing, and then the *Fair Winds* shuddered to a stop.

Pinho had made the move he'd anticipated, and the *Fair Winds* was firmly embedded in the starboard side of the *Defensor*. He looked over his shoulder. The small flotilla was already on its way.

Esma passed him in the *Hakon*. "We've secured the *Pathfinder*," she called. "It's in need of a captain."

He grinned. "I've just lost my ship," he called. "So I'm available."

A few minutes later, he set foot on a second ship that used to belong to Fihaldo Pinho.

CHAPTER 7

"RAHM IS HERE? Right now?" Dag stared at Berna, almost not understanding what she'd just said. She and Darya had just stepped out of an ice boat onto the main dock at Lavais Port.

"I was as surprised as you are," Berna replied.

"I need to see him," Dag said. "Is he in the office? Is someone keeping an eye on him? Has he hurt anyone?"

Berna nodded. "Gustav and Jarri are with him."

"Unmaking his token," Dag said and hurried past her towards the main office building. Up ahead, the door opened.

"Gustav?" Dag called out as the younger Intelligencer exited the building. Her steps faltered when she saw Jarri.

Dag started to run. "Are you both all right? Where is he?" she called out. "Rahm, where is he?"

"He's gone," Gustav said when she reached him. "He left a few minutes ago. I don't know where he went. And we're both fine."

"His token?" Dag asked. "Jarri, did you Unmake it?"

"I think so," Jarri replied.

"Yes," Gustav said. "Rahm said it was done."

Dag ran past them and scanned the ground near the door. But the snow was old, and she couldn't tell if any of the footprints were new. She walked around to the back of the building and stared out past the small town, hoping her Trait would show her where he was.

But her Trait was silent.

"I'm sorry," Gustav said when he joined her. "Pia and I made a deal with him. Rahm's help with the pirates for Jarri's help Unmaking his token. We didn't really want him around after that was done. Was there something you wanted from him?"

"Just to make sure he hasn't hurt anyone," she said. "And because Rahm always has secrets, I think it's better to know where he is."

"You mean safer," Gustav said.

"Yes," she agreed. "I mean safer. He's gone now, so that is also safer. For Lavais Port, anyway." She turned to retrace her steps to the front of the building. "Come on. I don't have much time. I need to get some goods unloaded and get to Tarklee as soon as possible."

"You know who his target is," Gustav said.

"I do," Dag replied. "I *had* planned on being weeks ahead of him." She hadn't expected to stop him from killing Ottosen. Token or not, Rahm was still a Resolute. Who knew if Rahm had another target?

It took just over an hour, using the ice boats, to unload some beans and barley to supplement the food of Lavais Port and the surrounding settlements.

One of the shipbuilders was brought out to look at the hull. The damage was minor and only required a small amount of resin to make sure the ship remained watertight.

Pia offered to take some supplies to Solvig's warehouse, since she wanted to visit her sister, and Berna was going send a group to Nurmi. Now that Ursa Ozlinch and her pirates were gone and Rahm had spoken to Timonis, it would be safe to deliver some food. It would also be added proof to the townspeople that the Interim Grand Freeholder continued to look out for them.

Gustav asked to go to Tarklee with her.

"Can you spare him?" Dag asked Berna. They were in Berna's office. Dag had wanted her account of her father's visit, as well as an update on the new ship. At least she could give Lauma good news about that: the ship was almost ready to launch. "Kaja might be the better choice to send."

Berna sighed. "If I send Kaja, my mother will enlist her as her personal assistant, and I might never get her back."

"Won't she do that with Gustav?"

"She might try." Berna grinned. "But Gustav will get

sidetracked. Besides, Nadez probably needs his talents more than my mother needs an assistant."

"All right," Dag said. "Gustav comes with me. Is there anything else you need? I can stop here on my way back to the Sapphire Sea."

"We need an experienced captain and some crew for the new ship," Berna said. "We have plenty of sailors and even a captain or two, but none who have navigated through the Frozen Pass and have trade contacts in the Sapphire Sea."

"I'll make sure we send people with experience," Dag replied. "Inger will help with getting goods in Messanos, but we can't afford for anything to happen to this ship." She was already worried about the *Tazeyar* and the two log haulers, the *Oakhaven* and *Tove's Folly*. Berna said it had been a bad winter even this far south: it would have been worse in Tarklee and Byholt.

"Who is it?" Berna asked. "I know you know. Who is it my father is going to kill?"

"Henrik Ottosen," Dag said.

"Really?" Berna said. "Why? Father told Gustav *this task is for someone I would not want to, nor dare to, turn my back on.*"

"That's true," Dag replied. "Calder made a bargain with an assassin, just as Pia and Gustav did. The head of the suicide assassins was holding Rahm's token. Calder asked for the token in exchange for her choice of Rahm's final target. She chose Ottosen." She met Berna's eyes.

"The attempt on my mother's life," Berna said. "This is evidence that Ottosen was behind it."

"I think so. And for whatever reason, the suicide assassins were not happy with Ottosen."

"I am not in favour of my father killing people," Berna said. "But I see what he meant when he told Gustav that he wouldn't dare turn his back on them. You'll tell my mother, of course."

"Yes." Dag sighed. "I hate giving bad news, but there seems to be so much of it." She sighed. "I must be on my way. If you see Gustav, tell him we're sailing in an hour. If he's not on board, we will leave without him."

"My guess is that Gustav has already said his goodbyes and is waiting for you on deck," Berna replied. "Expecting you to try to throw him overboard if he can't talk you into letting him come."

"You're probably right," Dag said. "Maybe I'll let him squirm." She rose. "I may not come ashore next time I'm here, but I'll send news with the captain we bring you." She left and made her way to a waiting iceboat.

"WE HAVE TO send the fishermen back out," Nadez said. "It's been three days." She was standing in front of Lauma's desk. The Interim Grand Freeholder was staring out the window. In fact, ever since the ice in the harbour cracked and one man was lost, she'd spent much of her time staring out the window.

"Not until it's safe," Lauma said. "I won't risk any more lives."

"Lives are at risk if we can't feed everyone," Nadez said. "We need the fish or we won't last until spring. And the people know it. They line up at the warehouses now because they're afraid we're going to run out of food."

"Calder and Dagrun will be here soon," Lauma replied. "We can hold off until then."

"And when they do show up with the harbour still partially frozen," Nadez said, "we'll need the boats to ferry goods in from the ship. We might as well get them out now."

"When the *Atlaine* arrives, we can use the reinforced boats to break the ice," Lauma said. "The *Tazeyar* should be safe enough by then."

Keeping the ice clear from the *Tazeyar* all winter had been a formidable task, but they'd accomplished it so far.

"We still can't afford to lose that ship," Nadez said. "But I will check in with Captain Eklund. Perhaps he can spare an ice breaker for a few hours each day to clear enough ice to fish on open water. Would that make you confident enough to tell the fishermen to go back out?"

"If there is clear sea, then yes," Lauma said. "But I will not force anyone back out onto the ice."

"That is fair," Nadez replied. No one but Lauma blamed her for the death. Every single person knew that there were risks but also knew that they had to take them. "Thank you." She paused. "We should also discuss the returned food."

Lauma turned to look at her. "What's to discuss? You spoke to Valda Skala, and she apparently arranged to have a good deal of the food returned."

"But Ottosen stole it," Nadez said. "How can Valda have had

it returned?"

Lauma sighed. "We agreed we would not arrest Ottosen for this," she said. "You said that she was very interested when you told her that."

"I did," Nadez replied. "What does that have to do with this?"

"Valda has lived a very long time as a key member of Clan Skala," Lauma said. "First as the wife and now as the mother, of the Clan Freeholder. I don't ever remember a Clan Freeholder being arrested, and I'm fairly certain neither does she."

"Some of them should have been," Nadez said. Far too many seemed to be murderers.

"But none have been," Lauma said. "To someone like Valda, that would be a terrible outcome." She paused. "Perhaps—to her—even worse than food riots."

"You're saying she was perfectly willing to let people starve rather than allow Ottosen to be arrested?" Nadez was shocked. "Valda seems so nice."

"She's survived, even thrived, in a Clan Freehold that passed from her husband to her son," Lauma said. "Something that did not happen because she was *nice*."

"But why return the food when I said I wouldn't arrest Ottosen?"

"Because food riots would also be a terrible outcome," Lauma said. "People would die, maybe even members of her own Clan Freehold."

"But for Valda, not the worst outcome," Nadez said.

"No," Lauma agreed.

Nadez sighed. She hated Clan Freeholder politics: was that why she'd ignored them for so long? Better to concentrate on what she could control.

"I'll let you know what Eklund says," she said. "About the ice in the harbour."

She left Lauma's office and made her way outside.

Wind whipped around a corner as she headed to the temporary offices for the Merchant Adventurers. The previous office had burned the night Calder had rammed and sunk Margit Ansdottir's ship. An old fisherman's hut had been co-opted, and even though everyone kept calling it temporary, Nadez had a feeling this would be the permanent office.

It was right on the water and there was a window that allowed someone inside to keep watch on the *Tazeyar*.

"Captain Eklund," she said when she entered. He was sitting at the desk that was in the centre of the small space.

"Master Intelligencer," he greeted her. "Please, sit. You have news?"

Eklund kept a list of all seaworthy craft along with the skills of the people who owned and worked them. Once Lauma gave the all clear, he was the one who would actually tell the fishermen they could now fish in open water.

"She wants to make sure it's safe," Nadez said, dropping into a chair.

"It was my call as much as hers," Eklund said. "And I'd make the same decision today. We needed the fish: we still need the fish."

"I know. The fishermen are well aware of the risks, both of fishing and not fishing." Nadez looked out the window. The *Tazeyar* sat in a circle of ice-free water. "If you can spare an ice breaker for a few hours each day, we could break up some of the ice. It's not safe to be on, but it's too thick for anything other than an icebreaker to cut through." She turned back to him. "Lauma will agree to send the fishermen back out when the sea is clear of ice."

"I can do that," he said. "Now that the nights are no longer quite so cold, trapping the *Tazeyar* in ice thick enough to damage the hull is less likely every day. I'll send a crew out today."

"Thank you. I'll have Lauma take a look at what your crew does this afternoon. I'm sure she'll let you know if she thinks it's enough."

Nadez stood up, and Eklund rose as well.

"I'll tell the crew now," he said as he led the way to the door.

"Thank you," Nadez said. She followed him outside, but when he turned to go down to the dock, she headed back towards the town.

Instead of going directly to Lauma to tell her the plan was in motion, she made her way to the closest warehouse.

More than a dozen people were lined up in front of it. She watched as they waited their turn to go inside to receive rations. Four guards managed the process of checking each name against the list before allowing them to pass.

Nadez sighed. At the moment, people were being patient, but

she knew that a single rumour that the food was gone could turn the crowd into a desperate and dangerous mob.

Getting fishermen back out into the harbour would help quell any rumours of food shortages. She hoped.

PIA TUGGED HARD on the rope and finally dragged the sled over the clump of grass.

For the most part, it had been easy. The sled, put together by the shipbuilders, had smaller versions of ice boat runners. Even partially loaded down with barley and beans, it had been easy to pull it across the deep snow all morning.

But now she was at the highest part of the trail, and the wind had scoured the path clear of snow. Every few yards she had to struggle to free the runners from a tangle of dried grass or a bush.

She didn't have far to go though. She'd been over this trail a few times this winter, visiting Frida and sharing news with Solvig.

The last time she'd visited had been three weeks ago. There had still been five people at the warehouse, but three had returned to Lavais Port with her, leaving Frida and Solvig alone. Solvig wouldn't leave her warehouse, and Frida had wanted to stay with her. She felt useful, her sister had told her; she had a place where she felt like she belonged.

In Lavais Port she would just be Pia's little sister and not expected to do anything or help in any way.

As much as Pia would have liked to have Frida with her, she was proud that her little sister was becoming so independent. That had been her goal for the two of them; to get them somewhere safe and to become self-sufficient. If you didn't have to rely on anyone else, you would be less likely to lose your power to them. Even with Solvig, the sisters made sure they were always doing their share of the work.

Frida had grown up so much in just a few months. She was so different from the girl who had been rescued from Ottosen's household. Pia had no wish to jeopardize Frida's new confidence in herself, so she agreed to let her sister live where she felt useful, here with Solvig.

She finally reached deeper snow. Her boots sank into it, making it harder for her to walk, but the easy way the sled skimmed across the surface made up for it.

The warehouse came into view an hour later.

Snow had been cleared away from the main door, and a trail of smoke rose from the chimney.

Frida stood on the dock, looking out across the water.

"Frida!" Pia shouted. "Frida!"

Her sister turned and then waved. "Pia!" She started to run towards her.

Pia walked faster, pulling the sled behind her. By the time Frida reached her, she was almost out of the snow and into the cleared area.

"I didn't expect you for another week," Frida said, launching her into her arms. "But I'm glad you're here. Come on. Solvig is out in an ice boat. I have to throw her the rope when she returns. What's that?"

"That," Pia said, "is supplies from the Sapphire Sea. The *Atlaine* came through the Teeth, from the Sapphire Sea."

"That's very good news." Frida grabbed the rope and started to pull. "It sure will be nice to have something other than dried fish. Unless that's what you brought. Then it will be nice to have more dried fish."

"No dried fish," Pia said. "Beans and barley."

"Oh, wonderful," Frida said. "Although we have a new person who made the dried fish taste better. He's Pilalian, and Solvig said his way with spices reminds her of Calder."

Pia slowed. "When did this Pilalian arrive?"

"Last night," Frida said. "He'd been in Nurmi but left when the pirates started taking over. Did you see him in Lavais Port? He said he stopped there for a night but that he needs to get to Tarklee. Solvig told him he should have taken the road out of Nurmi instead of crossing to Lavais Port."

"How long is he staying?" Pia asked. Frida pulled at the rope, and Pia was forced to walk at her pace.

"I think just one more night," Frida said. "He tried to bargain with Solvig for her ice boat, but she said no."

"She might want to hide the sail," Pia said. Rahm wouldn't hesitate to steal a boat, but would he kill for one? She knew he was going to Tarklee to murder Ottosen, but that was a commission he had from before. Now that his token was Unmade, was he still an assassin?

"Look, there he is," Frida said. "Oh, Solvig is coming in from fishing. I have to go throw her the line." Frida took off toward the dock at a run.

Pia stopped, her eyes going to the warehouse. Rahm stood in the doorway, a mug of something in his hands.

She knew the moment he recognized her. Rahm tensed, and Pia lifted a hand to wave.

A moment later, Rahm raised his mug in her direction. She could see his grin from where she stood, and it did not make her smile in response.

Her heart beating faster, Pia started walking towards him as quickly as she could. She needed to talk to Rahm alone. She *had* to make sure he understood that she wasn't going to do anything to get in his way, that she wouldn't even tell her sister and Solvig who he was.

Just in case he was willing to kill to keep his secrets.

CALDER STOOD BEHIND and slightly to one side of Ismini: Esma was on her other side. It was just after dawn, and a crowd had gathered in the square near the dock.

"Zelesso is secure," Ismini said to the crowd. "Thanks to Zelessans!"

A cheer went up, and Calder scanned the crowd, looking for people who weren't celebrating. There would be some who would not be happy, especially anyone who stood to profit off Pinho. But if any were here, they were cheering with the rest of the crowd.

"That'll teach anyone to use force against us!" someone shouted from the crowd.

"Where's Pinho?" someone else called. "Make him pay the way he wanted us to pay."

"Make him pay!" the crowd started chanting. "Make him pay!"

Ismini held her hand up, and eventually the crowd quieted. "We are still searching the bay," she said. "So far, we have not found Pinho either alive or dead."

Along with the five crew members from the *Pathfinder,* they'd recaptured ten of the fourteen they'd imprisoned on the *Fair Winds.* Nineteen bodies had been retrieved from the wreckage along with eight of Pinho's sailors pulled alive from the sea.

Only the *Defensor* was completely destroyed. Calder hadn't been out to see the damage, but word was that the *Fair Winds* could be saved. It made him feel a little less guilty about his part in the destruction of much-needed ships.

The most troubling development was that they had not been able to find Pinho or seven or eight of his crew.

"If you want to help," another man said, stepping forward. "And if you have a boat, we need more people to help search. At least three per boat, mind you. For your own safety."

"Will fishing boats help?" someone asked.

"Every boat will help," Ismini replied. "Sign up over there with Takis." She pointed to the man who had just spoken, and soon half a dozen people had surrounded him.

"We have Floros."

Calder turned to find Kasim at his side.

"She was waiting for us," he continued. "She didn't even try to flee."

"Where would she go?" Calder replied. "Even if she could find a boat, I doubt she knows how to sail or row. Besides, people like her always believe that they can find an angle to play to survive and turn the tables." He shrugged. "And often it's true. She was losing control of the council in Messanos, but once here, alongside Pinho, she had authority. Let's do our best to make sure this time she doesn't have a chance to recover her political power."

He took one last look at the people offering to search for casualties: sailors he was responsible for killing or maiming. He had hoped that more would be found alive; although, finding Fihaldo Pinho safe and sound would create a different problem.

He followed Kasim and Esma to a small building not far from the dock.

"It used to be the office of our Overseer," Esma said when she held the door open for him. "When we had one of our own managing our affairs: before the Overseer position was eliminated and all of the decision-making power was consolidated with the Arressan Council in Messanos."

The building consisted of a single room. Floros was seated in the centre, her arms bound to the arms of her chair. A couple of men ringed her, and an older man stood directly in front.

"You!" Floros spit when she saw Calder. "This is all your fault."

"I'm quite certain that this young man did not make you betray your own people," the older man said, turning. "My name is Omer. You must be Esma and Kasim's older brother."

"Calder Rahmson," Calder replied. "An Intelligencer for the

Fair Seas Treaty Alliance."

"I understand that you are also the son of both Rahm and the current Grand Freeholder," Omer said.

"I am," Calder agreed.

"Omer used to be the overseer of Zelesso," Esma said. "We think he should have that title and responsibility again."

"He's not fit," Floros said. "By holding me hostage, he is a traitor to Arressa."

"You're the traitor," Esma said. "You were working with Pinho who was trying to place an unsanctioned levy on this city for his own purposes."

"He was doing what?" Floros asked with exaggerated surprise. "I had no idea." She smiled. "You have no proof I had any part of such a vile scheme. Untie me now, and I will not tell the council that you held me hostage."

"I can claim you as my prisoner," Calder said. "I am an agent of the Three. I have the right to charge you with interfering with the Treaty Alliance's agreements with Arressa, which would give me the authority to hold you and transport you to Tarklee where you would stand trial."

Floros's smile slipped off her face, and Calder nodded. "I think you understand. Even if you are found not guilty, this entire process could take months, maybe even years. All of which you would spend as a prisoner of the Fair Seas Treaty Alliance." He shrugged. "I doubt you will like my mother, or that she would like you."

"What do you want?" Floros asked.

"You were already told what the Three wanted," Calder replied. "For you to no longer be on the council."

"You do not have the power to insist on that," Floros said.

"No," Calder agreed. "But as I said to you before, as the son of the largest timber supplier in Byholt, I can say that Clan Freeholder Strauskas will not sell to anyone she doesn't trust. And that includes Arressa if you are a council member."

"I think arresting Floros and taking her to Tarklee would mean that she's off the council," Esma said. She took a step closer to Floros. "If I were you, I'd think about your options." She turned to Calder. "Come on, we have more work to do. Omer, is this a safe enough place to hold Floros?"

"This will do for today," Omer said. "Come back later, and

depending on what she decides, we can take her somewhere for the night. Our current lock-up is filled with Pinho's men, and we don't want her in with them."

"What will you do with them?" Calder asked.

"We'll keep them locked up until we know where Fihaldo Pinho is," Omer replied. "If he's dead and no longer a threat, we'll ask the Arressan council to banish them from Arressa and let them find their own way home."

"I'm sure the *Pathfinder* has someplace secure where we can hold Floros," Calder said. "We can put her there for the night. She's coming with me anyway. The only decision is whether I leave her in Messanos once she's renounced a seat on the council for the rest of her life, or I take her to the Pale Sea when the Frozen Pass opens."

"Both good options," Esma said and grinned at him. "We'll come and collect her later, Omer."

Esma led the way out of the building and back down to the dock.

"I'm going out to look for Pinho," Esma said. "Kasim, you should go check on Mother. Calder, do you want to come with me?"

"Yes," Calder said and followed Esma to the *Hakon*.

Finding Pinho was the priority.

RAHM GLARED AT Pia as she approached the warehouse.

"What name did you tell them?" she asked when she reached him. She looked over her shoulder: Frida was still trying to throw a rope to Solvig, who waited patiently in an iceboat.

"Hakon," Rahm said. He visibly relaxed. "I take that to mean you aren't going to give me away?"

"We want the same thing," Pia replied. "I can help you."

"Maybe we do want the same thing," Rahm said. "But that doesn't mean I want or need your help."

"Dagrun Lund just left Lavais Port heading to Tarklee. She will get there before you. If you steal that," Pia gestured to the boat Solvig was now tying off at the dock, "you may be sailing into a harbour on high alert. Looking for you. I can help you get to Tarklee without sailing into the harbour."

"Was my son on the ship?" Rahm asked.

"No. Just Dagrun."

"What help can you give me?"

"I can have Solvig take us across to the mainland as far north as possible and set us ashore near the road," Pia said. "Because I'm an Intelligencer, there's a man with a cart and horse who will take us into the city, no questions asked. And I can make sure we don't get caught in a late spring storm." She eyed him up and down. "You are not dressed for that kind of weather, and it can kill."

"I'm hard to kill," Rahm said.

"You *used* to be hard to kill," Pia replied. "Before your token was Unmade. You might not want to casually risk your life in case that has changed. Since I very much want you to complete your task, I don't want you to risk your life either."

Rahm studied her for a moment, and then he laughed. "All right. I will let you help me. We leave in the morning."

"We leave in the morning," Pia agreed. "I hear you are a passable cook. I look forward to your evening meal." The last was said more loudly as Frida and Solvig reached them.

"He has a way with spices," Solvig said. "Not unlike our mutual friend Calder."

"Another Pilalian?" Rahm asked. Solvig nodded. "It's in our blood." He winked at Pia as he turned to head back inside the warehouse. "A few more minutes and the fish stew will be ready," he called over his shoulder.

"He said he's going to Tarklee," Pia said to Solvig. "If you can ferry us across and land us north near the road, I'll go with him."

"Aye, I know a place where I can set you ashore," Solvig replied. "Are you sure you'll be safe with him?"

"Probably," she said. "I'll feel safer knowing he's not here."

Solvig sighed. "Me too. Come on, he really is a good cook."

"A BOAT CAME in, Master Intelligencer."

Nadez looked up from the list of food supplies she was studying to find Sture in her office door.

"Is it the *Atlaine*?" she asked. The arrival of the ship would mean more food, something they desperately needed. Sture shook his head, and her heart dropped. "Bad news then?"

"I don't know," Sture said. "An ice boat just entered the harbour. They should arrive at the dock soon."

"Thank you, Sture." Nadez handed the list back to him.

"Please have someone let Lauma know."

"Already done," Sture replied.

Nadez nodded to him and then strode out of the warehouse, past the four guards, and into the street.

She was standing on the dock, watching the ice boat sail across the harbour, when Lauma joined her.

"Is it Gustav again?" Lauma asked.

"No," Nadez replied. She shaded her eyes against the glare of the sun on the ice. "I don't recognize them." Two people were in the boat, that much she could see, but their faces were covered, and their heads were down as they struggled through the shifting chunks of ice near the docks.

"It's from Byholt," Lauma said, surprise in her voice. "I recognize that boat. It belongs to Thorben, a friend of my son's. I think that's him in the bow."

The man in the bow was leaning out of the boat, pushing the larger pieces of ice out of the way with an oar.

"And Noak has the tiller," Lauma continued. "Come on. These two won't have any trouble reaching the dock." She stepped onto the dock and waved. The man in the back of the boat lifted a hand in response.

"Lauma Strauskas," Noak called when they were closer. "Grand Freeholder, I'm glad you're not too proud to come meet us."

He was near enough that Nadez saw the grin that accompanied his words. Beside her, Lauma chuckled.

"I needed to see for myself," Lauma said. "The kind of fool who would travel so far in an ice boat. Turns out it's an old fool."

"Not so foolish that I didn't get old," Noak replied.

The boat was almost at the dock now. The man in the bow tossed a rope, and Lauma stepped forward to catch it. She pulled the boat in, and the younger man stepped out.

"Good to see you, Thorben," Lauma said. "I hope you have good news about my son?"

"Yakop is fine," Thorben replied. He took the rope from Lauma and tied it to a ring before grabbing the gunwale and pulling the boat up against the dock. Noak handed him a second rope, and Thorben secured that one as well.

Noak climbed onto the dock and faced Lauma.

"Everyone in Langin is fine," he said. "Byholt villages south of

Langin are also doing well. We have enough food to get us through to spring. Tight rations, of course, but we'll all survive."

Lauma introduced the two to Nadez before she turned back to Noak.

"Byholt villages south of Langin," Lauma said. "What of the Nordmerian villages?"

Noak sighed. "That's why we've come, but I'd appreciate it if we could talk somewhere warmer."

"Of course. We'll meet in my office. Nadez, could you bring us some tea before you join us?"

"I'll be there in a few minutes." Nadez headed back to the Hall. Not having assistants meant that she and Lauma took turns getting tea for their meetings. Fifteen minutes later, she was carrying a tray through the door to Lauma's office.

Noak and Thorben, their faces red and chapped from the cold, had taken their coats off and were sitting across from Lauma, who was behind her desk.

When she saw Nadez, Lauma cleared some papers from the desktop to make room for the tray.

Lauma poured tea while Nadez retrieved a chair from the outer office.

"First warm thing in almost a day," Noak said, cradling the mug in his hands. "The ice was solid for most of the trip south. It broke up around Falkis, and after that, we mostly had clear sea." He took a sip of tea. "But the harbour here was a little tricky."

"The ice is clear outside the harbour?" Nadez asked. "Clear enough for a ship?"

"Aye, it's clear," Noak said. "Though you can't sail very far north."

"South looked fine," Thorben said. "At least as far as we could see."

"So a ship could reach the harbour?" Nadez asked. "We are hoping the *Atlaine* is on its way from the Sapphire Sea."

"That's a bit of welcome news," Lauma said. "Noak, I assume that what brings you here is more of the unwelcome type. It's not a fun trip even this close to spring."

"Food, what else?" Noak said. "As I said, Byholt is fine. We know how to put food up for winter, and Yakop and I, with help from Thorben and others, have been making sure all the small villages have enough rations. Then one day Thorben sailed farther south into Nordmere. Where things are not fine."

"People are starving, almost," Thorben said. "Every village I landed in was in the same predicament."

"We shipped them food," Nadez said. "Nordmere and Byholt received their shipments first, in the fall. Did we not send enough?"

"Perhaps they didn't ration properly?" Lauma asked.

"Can't say what they did early on," Thorben said. "Maybe their rations weren't strict enough. Or maybe they didn't get all the food you sent." He looked over at Noak, who nodded grimly.

"Keep going," Noak said.

"None of the people I talked to said anything about shipments from Tarklee," Thorben said. "They said they put up as much food as they could and were fishing, but the weather had been bad and none of that was enough. They also told me that they could buy food from Clan Freeholder Ottosen's people, but that only a few were willing to pay his price."

"What was he asking for?" Lauma's expression was dark. "These people don't have much, so what was he asking for?"

"Allegiance to him," Thorben said. "He made that offer only to the people living on Holt and Seppa lands. He's offered no help to his Freeholders."

"That *skit karl*," Lauma swore. "He's either punishing Saulia Holt and Karl Seppa for thwarting him or he's trying to coerce them into supporting him in the future. Meanwhile he lets his own people starve."

"He won't have any more success," Noak said. "As soon as Thorben told us, Yakop and I gathered as much extra food as we could and sent it to those who needed it."

"You had extra?" Nadez asked. She knew that Byholters prided themselves on being self-sufficient, but to have extra food when shipping had been disrupted seemed unlikely.

"Not so much as extra," Noak said. "Byholters know what hunger is, and missing a few meals is not that. No, we went on smaller rations and sent what we could. But we can't ask anyone to reduce their rations more."

Lauma sighed. "I'll need to check with Sture," she said. "I'm not sure we have much to spare."

"Anything will be better than nothing," Noak said.

"And it will let the people know you care," Nadez replied. "I'm going to have to talk to Saulia Holt and her uncle Karl Seppo and see what they knew about this."

"Will they have food to send?" Noak asked.

"They shouldn't," Nadez replied. "Every Clan Freeholder was supposed to give us their food stores so we can distribute it evenly to everyone, no matter what country or clan they belong to."

"That doesn't mean they did," Noak said.

"No, it doesn't," Nadez replied. She had to wonder if the stolen food—the food Valda Skala had been returning to her—had been meant for this purpose. If Ottosen had planned on doing this same thing in Tarklee: trading food for support.

CHAPTER 8

THE *HAKON* SAILED directly into a wave, and seawater splashed Calder's face. He turned to Esma, who grinned at him from her perch at the tiller.

"Sorry!" she called, but she didn't look sorry.

He shook his head, wiped the water from his eyes, and returned to scanning the sea in front of them.

The *Fair Winds* was off to their starboard side, with what was left of the *Defensor* in front of it: the interiors of cabins and the hold open to the air.

Wreckage of wood, ropes, and sails littered the water. A small boat ahead of them dragged something from the sea, a body, tangled up in rope.

The entire stern of the *Defensor* had broken off and was missing, and the wheel, where Pinho most likely had been commanding his crew, had disappeared with it. The cannon had been mounted on the stern; a heavy enough chunk of iron to drag that part of the ship down into the sea.

"Starboard," he said, pointing towards a larger piece of debris just past the damaged prow of the *Fair Winds*.

Esma shifted, and the little boat skimmed past the ship. Calder took a look as they went by. The ship wasn't taking on water that he could see, although the hull had been pierced in a few places above the water line and the keel was no longer true. It looked sound. And repairable.

"I'll bring the *Pathfinder* out later," he said to Esma. "And tow the *Fair Winds* closer to the dock. Where's the nearest shipyard?"

"Messanos," his sister replied. "But the Master Shipbuilder is here in Zelesso. She refused to work for Pinho and has family here."

"That's good for us." With someone who knew what they were doing, the *Fair Winds* might not even need to go anywhere else for repairs. "Careful," he called out. They were almost alongside the wreckage.

Calder grabbed an oar and set it against the wood. It turned when he pushed at it. "It's the wheel deck," he called out. He stared at the water that surrounded them, but he didn't see any signs of life.

"Do you see any crew?" Esma asked. "Dead or alive?"

"Not so far." Calder pushed another floating piece of debris out of their path. Where was Pinho? Had he died? Had he sunk with the stern of the *Defensor*? Or was he out here somewhere, hiding in the ruins of his ship, waiting until the searchers left?

"Nothing here," he called out. "Try up ahead." He pointed to what looked like a cabin door floating in the water.

An hour later, they pulled a body out. The woman had a gash on her head that went down to the bone, and her right hand was crushed in a mangle of rope.

"We should head back," Calder said, looking at the sky. "I need to find a crew for the *Pathfinder* so the *Fair Winds* can be towed to port. It will also get the ship out of the way and allow the searchers a better view of the wreckage."

"All right," Esma said. She pushed the tiller hard to the right, and the *Hakon* arced towards the city.

Once at the dock, the dead sailor was lifted from the boat and placed in a line with other bodies. Calder slowly walked down the line.

"Are we sure Pinho isn't here?" he asked when he reached the end of the row. He'd counted fifteen dead, about half of them men he guessed would be Pinho's age, but they were all dressed like simple sailors.

"He's not here," Ismini said. "With the one you just recovered, we think we're missing six, maybe seven sailors. And Pinho."

"We might still find him," Calder said, though he didn't think they would. "I need to find a crew for the *Pathfinder*. Do you know who can help? The *Fair Winds* looks fairly seaworthy, so I'm going to tow her in."

"We'll ask Nomiki to take a look at her once we get the ship close enough," Esma added. She turned to Calder. "I'll find Kasim. He and I know enough to crew for a few hours."

"I can bring three sailors with experience," Ismini said. "Will that be enough? Most of the others are still out searching."

"I can make do with that," Calder agreed. He stared out to sea as he waited, but the *Fair Winds* and what was left of the *Defensor* were too far away for him to see what was happening.

Esma returned with Kasim and Saba in tow.

"I'm not much of a sailor," Saba said. "But I'll help if I can."

"Can you sail the *Hakon*?" Calder asked. "We'll need someone to bring it back here once we're all on board. I'd prefer not to tow it, as well as the *Fair Winds*."

"I can manage that," Saba said. "I'll follow you and pick you up once you anchor the ships."

Ismini arrived with three people Calder didn't know. She did a quick introduction, and then all eight of them settled into the little sailboat.

It rode low in the water, and if the weather had been worse, it would have been dangerous, but they made it out to the ship safely.

Ismini remained in the *Hakon*. When the *Pathfinder* was in place, the *Hakon* would take the tow ropes over to the *Fair Winds*. Ismini would secure the tow ropes, stay on the *Fair Winds*, and make sure nothing went wrong during the trip to port.

Once on board the *Pathfinder*, they all pitched in to get the mainsail up. Calder headed to the wheel and pointed them at the *Fair Winds*.

Esma knew only basics of sailing a ship this size, and Kasim even less, but Ismini's recruits were experienced. In less than an hour, the *Pathfinder's* stern was positioned in front of the *Fair Winds'* prow. The main tow rope was handed down to Ismini in the *Hakon*, and a few minutes later she boarded the *Fair Winds*, dragging the rope up with her. Once the two ships were tied together, one of Ismini's sailors scrambled across with more ropes.

When half a dozen lines connected the two ships, Ismini

signalled that she was ready. Calder set course for the main docks of Zelesso.

A crowd had gathered at the dock to watch, and Calder heard them cheer once he was close enough to release the anchor. Ismini waved from the prow of the *Fair Winds*.

"I've dropped anchor," she called. "Some of the sailors and I need a few minutes to untie the tow ropes and check the hold for damage."

"All right," Calder replied. "I'll have Saba fetch you as soon as you're ready. Kasim, haul the tow ropes over and stow them." His half-brother nodded and headed up to the stern gunwale.

Calder helped the rest of the crew take down and store the sails. Once that was done, he did a quick inspection of the ship. The *Pathfinder* had already been searched for any of Pinho's men and to make sure no lamps were still lit, but he wanted to confirm nothing dangerous was on board.

When he was done, he went back up on deck.

"Calder," Esma called. "We're ready to go ashore."

He jogged over to her and held the rope ladder as she stepped down into the *Hakon*.

"I already took Ismini over," Saba said to him when he sat down in the prow. "I was told that the *Fair Winds* is not taking on water."

"That is good news," Calder said. He stared at the dock as the little boat sailed towards it.

Takis met them on the dock. "Still no sign of Pinho," he said. "But one of the small sailboats is missing." He gestured to the bodies lined up. "And one of the two Zelessans who were in it was found dead."

"We have to assume that Pinho is alive," Calder said.

"And that he had help from someone we thought we could trust," Takis said.

"Who was it?" Esma asked.

Takis said a name Calder didn't recognize, but Esma swore.

"I grew up with him," Esma said.

"Place a watch on board the *Fair Winds*," Calder said. "It can still be sailed, and if Pinho has seven sailors, he has enough to crew it. I need to get Floros on board the *Pathfinder* and head to Messanos. The council needs to be told that Pinho has not been found."

"I DON'T SEE a path," Dag said. She'd been staring at the mouth of Tarklee Harbour for an hour, hoping her Trait would find a way for them to get close enough to be seen by the city. Up ahead, chunks of ice stretched across open water, ending at an expanse of solid ice that she couldn't see the end of. Somewhere past that was the actual harbour and the city.

"We'll need to anchor here," Darya said. "I'm pretty sure Gustav is ready to get in a dinghy."

"I'm sure he is," Dag said. "And I'm inclined to let him."

Jaak and the younger Intelligencer had shared competing tales of sailing small boats: Jaak along the coasts of Pilalia and Arressa, and Gustav travelling from Lavais Port to Tarklee in the dead of winter.

"He's probably the only one who can do this safely," Darya replied. "None of my crew has much experience with ice."

"I'll tell him to get ready," Dag said.

"I'll send Rafael with him," Darya said. "Let me know if you need any more rowers."

"Thanks. I think just Rafael, Jaak, me, and Gustav. More than that might make the dinghy too unwieldy. I'll send someone back when we have a plan for offloading the goods." They had to get the food off the ship somehow. She hoped Lauma and Nadez could figure out how to do that.

Gustav and Jaak were standing beside the dinghy with a group of sailors, ready to lift it over the gunwale and launch it.

"You're steering," she said to Gustav. "I'll watch from the bow." She turned to Jaak. "You and Rafael will row. Let's get this boat in the water."

Rafael joined them, and once the dinghy was launched, the four of them climbed into it. Dag settled in the prow, staring ahead, searching for a safe way into the harbour.

There was a stretch of clear sea, but ice crept out from the shore and huge chunks of ice floated in the water, the biting wind sending them spinning and turning.

"You sailed in a wind this cold for how long?" Jaak asked Gustav.

"Most of a day," Gustav called out. "And it was worse than this. Colder, anyway."

"Port," Dag called out, pointing to her left.

The prow of the little boat turned toward the clear path. After calling out a few more directions, they were closing in on solid ice.

"It looks fairly solid almost half way to the docks," Dag said, turning to face Gustav. "We'll need to get on the ice."

"No other option," Gustav replied. "We need some speed, and Dagrun, I need you to come back and sit by me to weigh down the stern so the bow can slide up onto the ice."

"Sure." She squeezed past Rafael and Jaak and crouched down in front of Gustav.

"Go hard now," Gustav called out, and the two rowers grunted as they put more effort into their strokes.

The bow hit the ice with a crunch, and then it angled up onto it. The keel of the little boat scraped across ice. Without runners, the boat tilted to one side. Rafael and Jaak took one last stroke in water and then the oars dug into ice.

"Go up to the bow," Gustav said to Dag, and she scrambled up the slight incline and wedged herself as far forward as she could.

They were completely on the ice now, and the angle made it hard for Rafael and Jaak to move them forward. They both pulled their oars from the oarlocks and stood up, pushing against ice, trying to make the boat slide across it.

"We made it," Dag said. "We're on the ice. But it will take us hours to get to the dock." More rowers in the dinghy would have made their shift onto the ice even more dangerous.

"You sound surprised," Gustav said.

"A lot could have gone wrong," Dag replied. "And still could." She peered out across the frozen harbour. A half a dozen small boats were on the sea between the ice and the docks. Closer to the city, a ship sat in an expanse of open water: a good sign, she thought, that it had survived the winter. A small boat with a sail turned towards them. It slowed as it reached the ice, and then a moment later, it surged up onto it.

"An ice boat is on its way," she said, turning to Jaak and Rafael. "You can stop pushing us."

"Good," Jaak said, sitting down. "This would have taken forever."

The ice boat was closer now, and a figure stood up and waved. Dag waved back.

"We're with the *Atlaine*," she called out. "We have supplies for

Tarklee!"

"That's good news," came the reply.

The little boat was even closer now, and Dag could see that the person she'd been talking to was an older man.

"I'm Dagrun Lund," Dag said. "Intelligencer. We've come from the Sapphire Sea with food. We need to see Lauma Strauskas and Nadez Norup as soon as possible. Can you take us?"

"Aye, and very glad to meet you," the man said. "I'm Mads. I'll take you directly." He peered at Gustav. "You're the lad who sailed an ice boat from Lavais Port, aren't you? Come on aboard. I came out fishing by myself today, so I have room for all four of you."

Mads brought his boat alongside the dinghy, and the four of them stepped across to it.

"Take a long time to get to the dock that way," Mads said as they all settled in his boat.

"We had hoped that the harbour would be clear of ice by now," Dag replied. Wind caught in the sail, and the little boat turned and pointed towards the city.

"We all did," Mads said. "But we've managed so far in spite of the ice, though we're clearing it from closer in."

By the time they were halfway to the dock, another four boats had joined them, and a crowd was gathering on land.

Dag didn't see Nadez, but she spotted Lauma and waved.

SAULIA HOLT DIDN'T offer her tea.

Nadez sat down in the chair the Clan Freeholder indicated. This wasn't a social visit anyway.

"We've had word from Byholt," Nadez said. "That includes some serious allegations regarding Nordmerian Clan Freeholders. What do you know?"

"Word about what?" Saulia asked. "You must be more specific."

"I am here in my official capacity as the Master Intelligencer and a representative of the Fair Seas Treaty Alliance," Nadez said. "I am talking about food distributed to northern Swyford that was seized by one or more Clan Freeholders who then offered it to starving people in exchange for support. Is that specific enough?"

"Yes," Saulia said. "I have no information for you."

"But you know about this," Nadez said. Saulia hadn't lied, but Nadez didn't think she'd told her the truth either.

"Was that a question?" Saulia asked. "Or a statement?"

Nadez sighed. Saulia had known; perhaps she'd even been threatened by Ottosen.

"I already spoke to Melker Skala," Nadez replied. "At least he's been doing his best for his people. A few times this winter he's sent any food he could spare north."

Saulia's eyes widened.

"You didn't know that," Nadez said. "Yes, Clan Freeholder Skala has tried to feed his people and ensure that they cannot be taken advantage of. Unfortunately, that means Ottosen has been able to target your and your uncle's freeholders." The lower-level freeholders didn't own land, so losing their support wouldn't affect anything officially, but the people who managed the land for the clans could do subversive things that affected the productivity, and therefore the profitability, of the entire Clan Freehold.

"I have no information for you," Saulia repeated. "If that's all, I have work I need to get back to."

Nadez got to her feet. "I wish you trusted Lauma and me," she said. "It would make your life easier."

"You're wrong about that," Saulia said. "Trusting the wrong person can make me vulnerable. I can't afford to let anyone take advantage of me."

"You need to figure out who you can trust," Nadez agreed. "If you change your mind, you know where to find either me or Lauma." She left the room and made her way to the front door.

The snow on the ground was over a week old and no longer white due to smoke and ash from fires that had settled on the surface.

She headed past an empty fountain and through streets lined with tidy houses. Then she turned down a lane and stopped at the gate that led to Henrik Ottosen's estate.

Saulia Holt was right about one thing, trusting the wrong people would make you vulnerable. She didn't trust Ottosen, and she wasn't planning on questioning him today: she needed guards with her when she set foot inside his estate.

A plume of smoke rose from the main chimney, proof that

someone was home, although it was quiet, and she didn't see any guards. Which surprised her: ever since they'd taken Frida Engen from his apartment in the Hall, Ottosen had stayed here, behind his constantly guarded walls. She nudged the gate. Oddly, it wasn't locked and swung open a few inches.

Nadez grabbed the gate to close it and was about to turn to walk away, when something in the thick brush just beyond the gate, caught her eye.

She pushed the gate open and took a couple of steps closer. It took a moment for her to realize she was looking at the sleeve of a jacket.

She swept aside an evergreen limb. A man lay face down in the snow: the missing guard, she guessed. She checked for a pulse, but judging from the peculiar angle of his head, his neck had been broken. The body was still warm though.

She backed away from the body and peered towards the house. Now the sense of quiet seemed dangerous, rather than peaceful.

The gate rattled, and she turned to see Ottosen's Provisions Manager, Rein Chebek, step through it.

"Rein," she called out. "It's Nadez. Over here."

He gave her a puzzled look and walked over to her. His eyes widened when he saw the dead guard behind her.

"What's happened?" he asked.

"I don't know," she said. "I was wondering if this was a good time to speak to Clan Freeholder Ottosen and found the gate unlocked and the guard dead."

"We need to get to the house," Rein said. "The whole family is there."

"We have to go slow," Nadez said. "Whoever did this might still be here. Come on. You know the property; there must be a way we can sneak into the house without being seen."

Rein nodded and stepped past her, leading the way through the trees. There was a narrow path that followed the fence around to the back of the house. The back door was open.

"Is that usual?" she asked Rein, gesturing to the open door.

"No," he said. "The doors are kept locked, and guards patrol constantly: one during the day and two at night. I can't imagine anyone leaving the door open. If one was found open, it would be closed, locked, and reported immediately."

"So either whoever killed the guard is still here," Nadez said. "Or they left it open on their way out. Is there another way into the house?"

Rein nodded and led her to a small side door. When he unlocked it, they entered a storage shed half full of cut wood. A second door opened into a small hallway that Rein said was near the kitchen.

The kitchen was empty, but it looked like the cook had been preparing a meal. Nadez gestured to a door at the far end.

"Cellar?" she asked. Rein nodded, and she took a couple of quiet steps to it. The door was locked, and she stepped aside as Rein unlocked it.

They found them in the cold room. Alive, thankfully. Ottosen's wife, Tessan, and the three Ottosen children, along with a cook and a housekeeper, had been tied up with gags stuffed into their mouths.

"Is he gone?" Tessan Ottosen asked once her gag was removed. "Rein, where's Henrik?"

"We don't know," Rein said. "We came in through the woodshed and came down here first." He untied her hands.

"The guard at the gate is dead," Nadez said. The housekeeper was untied and turned to the smallest child, a girl who looked about eight. Nadez started working on the ropes that bound the cook.

"How many were there?" Nadez asked. "How many people broke in and tied you up?"

"I only saw one," Tessan said. "He was dark, I think he was Pilalian. We were all in the kitchen."

"How did he get into the kitchen?" Nadez asked. "Which way did he come from?" What she wanted to know was had he encountered them on his way in the house or on his way out.

"I didn't see," Tessan said. She got to her feet, and the youngest girl clung to her.

"He came from the main hall," the only boy said. "And he was fast. I saw the door open a crack, and then he was there. I believed him when he said he'd kill us."

Every single head nodded.

"Did he kill Father?" the older girl asked. Her voice quavered, and Tessan pulled her into a hug.

Nadez blew out a breath. "I don't know," she said softly. "But since it might not be safe, you all have to stay here while I check."

She headed up the stairs alone. She didn't think Ottosen was alive. Just as she didn't think whoever had killed him was still in the house.

Ottosen was in his study.

He'd been strangled. It looked like he'd been facing the killer when he died. She suspected that the Clan Freeholder was already dead when the intruder encountered his family and servants and locked them in the cellar.

Rein joined her. "He's gone, right? The man who did this is gone?"

"He's gone," Nadez said.

With no idea of how Rahm had gotten to Tarklee, she couldn't be certain, but what other Pilalian had reason to kill Henrik Ottosen?

She'd have to let Lauma know, of course. There was a very good chance that her former husband, Rahm the Resolute, had assassinated Henrik Ottosen.

And there was justice to it, she thought, more than the Three could have delivered: that a man who had claimed his power through assassination was felled by it.

GUSTAV TOOK ONE last guilty look over his shoulder. Dagrun was talking with Lauma Strauskas, probably trying to figure out how to get the food from the *Atlaine* across the icy harbour to the city.

He should probably stay and help, but he wanted to take a look around Tarklee first and get a feel for how the city was coping. Besides, he'd spent all winter in Lavais Port, where he knew everyone, and everyone knew him. The anonymity of the streets of Tarklee was liberating.

The city was calm; although, from what Mads had told them, food was being tightly rationed. The people out on the streets looked drawn and tired, but he didn't sense any anger or resentment. So whatever Lauma and Nadez had done over the winter had at least got them to this point: a calm city and new food shipments from the Sapphire Sea.

According to Mads, every boat that could be fitted with blades had been, and anyone who was willing was ferried out to the ice to fish as much as possible. Lauma managed distributing the fresh fish to the feeding centres, which were responsible for doling out rationed meals to registered citizens.

Everyone could register, even if they were only in the city for a day, and you could only register at one centre. Lists were checked each night to stop people from getting double rations.

How Lauma Strauskas had dealt with people getting extra rations went a long way to explaining why the streets were calm. Instead of simply punishing people, she'd investigated and discovered that most were trying to help sick neighbours. After that, Lauma had made sure that those who couldn't make it to the feeding centres were supplied with either rations or meals.

He hated to think what would have happened if the election had gone ahead and Tavet Timonis had been Grand Freeholder during this famine.

He crossed the bridge and headed to the old warehouse where Joosep had been held. It was in a part of the city that had always struggled; he figured that if the process wasn't working, it would be apparent in this type of neighbourhood first.

The lineup started at the door, turned the corner, and continued just past the old stable. A woman came out of the stable door: three young children trailed her.

"What's on the menu today?" a man asked her as she and her family squeezed through the crowd.

"Fish!" half a dozen people called out, and a few in the crowd chuckled.

"Aye, it's fish," the woman said. "It's fresh, not dried, and I'm happy to have it."

"Me as well," the man said. "Although I'll still be hungry."

"The Grand Freeholder is doing the best she can," a second man said. "And it's a sight more'n any of the others ever did for us. Asides, we all get the same, rich or poor."

"Sometimes we get better," the first man said. "Last week we got fresh fish and my cousin over near the Hall got dried."

The line shuffled forward, and someone else left through the stable door.

Gustav walked towards the front door of the warehouse.

"You need to register," someone said. "You can't get a meal unless you register."

He couldn't see who the speaker was talking to, so Gustav edged closer. A woman stood at the door, barring someone from entering, but whoever she was talking to was shorter than the people that surrounded them.

Gustav didn't think anyone from the ship had come here for food, so whoever it was, if they were newly arrived in the city, they must have taken the road. Then he had a terrible thought. What if the pirates hadn't all left for Strongrock?

He craned his head and stepped around a few people trying to get a better view, but he still couldn't distinguish an identity.

The man in front of him moved his arm and—

"Pia!" he called.

She froze, and he could tell she was getting ready to run. He pushed his way to her, grabbed her arm, and pulled her out of the lineup.

"I thought you were visiting Frida?" he said, releasing her arm. "Why are you here?"

Pia glared at him. "I did visit Frida," she said. "And then I decided to take the road and come to Tarklee."

"But why are you *here*?" he asked again, gesturing to the warehouse. "You know you can eat at the Hall; that you *should* eat at the Hall." He paused and stared at her. "Rahm," he said, and she flinched. "You came here with Rahm. Did he threaten you?" He looked around, but he didn't see any sign of the Pilalian.

"He's not with me," Pia said.

"Then why aren't you at the Hall?" he closed his eyes. "He didn't force you to do anything, did he? You helped him because you want . . ." He leaned in closer. "Ottosen dead."

"Yes, now leave me alone."

"Come on," he said. "Let's leave the food here for these people."

He walked away not really sure if she would follow him. He was almost at the bridge before she caught up to him.

"You're not mad at me?" Pia asked. "For helping Rahm?"

"He was at Solvig's, wasn't he?" Gustav asked.

"Yes, and I desperately wanted him away from there," she said. "Away from Frida. But I also wanted what he wanted."

"No one is going to blame you," Gustav replied. "You got a Resolute away from innocent people, and you lived through it."

"But he's going to complete his task," Pia said. "And I'm glad he will."

"Could you have stopped him?" Gustav asked. "Or should we have tried to kill him before we even got to Lavais?"

"We wouldn't have been able to," Pia said. "But you could have gotten away and warned everyone."

"Just like you could have gotten away when Timonis sent his guard after me," Gustav said. "After I told you to leave. Instead, you stayed and helped us both escape."

"That's not the same," Pia said.

"Why?" Gustav asked. "You didn't leave me, and then I didn't leave you."

"Tripping that guard was easy, killing Rahm would be impossible."

"See?" Gustav said. "Even your argument assumes we weren't going to talk him out of anything. To stop him, we would have had to kill him. Which you just said was impossible. So, it's not your fault that he's going after Ottosen."

"I still helped him."

Gustav shrugged. "Did he give you a choice? He didn't give us one when we made our bargain. Besides, don't forget that his target was given to him by Calder Rahmson. Rahm's own son, and an Intelligencer. Do you think Calder wants Ottosen dead too, or do you think he had no other choice about giving his own father an assassination target."

"He probably had no choice," Pia said.

"Exactly. I think that most people don't have a choice when it comes to Rahm. For all we know, that's part of what his token does. I'm quite sure Dagrun Lund has no plans to get in Rahm's way."

"You really think that?"

"Yes, but you can ask her yourself, once we've found ourselves a meal."

CHAPTER 9

CALDER CALLED OUT an order and the mainsail was shortened. Messanos was still a distant speck, but he planned on a slow approach.

He was still getting a feel for how the *Pathfinder* handled, as well as how best to work with its new crew. He'd done this before: captained a new ship and a new crew, and it always took a few days to get everything and everyone working together.

"Do you think Pinho is here?" Esma asked. Even though she had little experience sailing a ship this size, she was acting as First Mate: because he trusted her.

"He's had enough time to come this far," Calder said. "I suppose it depends on whether the city still holds allies he can count on."

"You don't think so."

"I wouldn't come here if I were him," he replied. "Not without a ship."

"He could try to steal this one back," Esma said. "It's obvious even to me that we would not be able to hold off an experienced crew."

"An experienced crew in a ship, yes," Calder said. "But Pinho is in a small sailboat. One that is carrying as many men as it can hold. He'll either try to capture a trader like the *Spice Runner* or he'll make for Strongrock."

"That's a long way to travel in such a small boat," Esma said.

"Especially if it's loaded down with so many men."

"I've travelled farther," Calder said. "You do what you have to if you're desperate enough." If Pinho *was* headed to Strongrock, Calder had to wonder what terrible decisions he might make. That many men in that size of boat would make even a weak storm potentially deadly.

"I'm going to speak to Floros," Calder said. "You take the wheel. Keep it pointed at the city, and if the wind picks up, send someone to find me."

"I don't think she'll give in," Esma said.

"Then she's coming with me to the Pale Sea," Calder replied. He wasn't sure all of his current crew would be willing to sail that far, but Messanos would have sailors looking for work. It would mean another few days getting used to them, but the Frozen Pass wouldn't be clear of ice yet anyway.

Floros had been put into the cabin closest to the captain's quarters. A bored looking Kasim stood in the hallway outside it.

"Did she say anything?" Calder asked his brother.

"Not about resigning," Kasim said. "But she's had plenty to say about her poor treatment. Are we in Messanos?"

"Almost," Calder replied. Kasim had begged to come on this trip. Calder knew he'd assumed he'd be up on deck learning to sail the ship instead of being trapped down here guarding Floros. But he was here because Calder trusted him. He shook off the feeling that he was becoming like Rahm—that there was no one other than family that he could trust. Not that Rahm seemed to actually trust *his* family.

He unlocked the door and handed the key to Kasim before entering the cabin.

Thekla Floros glared at him from the chair she sat in. Her hands were tied together behind her back, but other than that, she could move around the cabin freely.

"I will never renounce my country," she said.

Calder sighed. He stopped just inside the door, out of range in case she decided to try get up and try to attack him.

"That's not what's being asked of you," Calder said. "And you know it. Besides, you've been accused of treason by the Overseer of Zelesso. I'm here to tell you that we will arrive in Messanos soon."

"There is no Overseer," Floros said. "So any charges of treason are false. I will make my case in front of the entire council. Then we'll see who has the power."

"You're not setting foot on land until a decision is made," Calder said. "I will notify the council of your circumstances, but unless all members are willing to make the trip out here, you will not be making your case in front of them."

"You can't do that!" Floros said, panic creeping into her voice. "You are in Arressan waters, so Arressan laws apply."

"I am the captain of this ship," Calder said. "Arressan laws do not apply. Consulting the Arressan Council is a courtesy, as is giving them the opportunity to investigate Omer's charges against you. Either way I expect you will no longer be a member of the council."

"You have no authority to remove me from the council," she said, lifting her chin.

"The current council does." Calder knocked on the door. "Someone will let you know what the council's response is."

"Will you really take her all the way to Tarklee?" Kasim asked once he was back out in the hall and the door had been relocked.

"If I have to," Calder said. He didn't want to. Having a viper like Floros on board a ship with a new crew was a risk he really didn't want to take. "I'm hoping Charis has a better option."

An hour later, the ship was close enough to drop its anchor.

Assuming that the *Pathfinder* would be recognized as a ship belonging to Fihaldo Pinho, Calder ran four flags up the mast, signalling that the ship was under control of the Three.

A dinghy was lowered, and he got ready to set out for Messanos alone.

"Remember," he said to Esma, who would be in charge in his absence. "On board a ship, you are the law. I should be back in a few hours. If I'm not," he paused. "If I'm not, it means that the Arressan Council can't be trusted. You are to put Floros in a dinghy and head back to Zelesso."

"I'm not leaving you here," she said.

"You have to. I don't expect it to come to that and besides," he said. "I have Luck. It often works in unpredictable ways, but it does work, and I will be safe. I need you to be safe as well."

"I don't like it," Esma replied.

"Neither do I," Calder said. "That's the worst-case scenario, and I don't expect it to happen, but you need to know what to do if it does. You are not to come after me. And honestly, I expect to be back in a couple of hours."

He climbed over the gunwale, and in a few minutes, he had the oars in place and was heading towards the city.

"Calder!"

He looked over his shoulder. Inger Lund was on the dock, waving at him. He closed his eyes in relief. If Inger was safe, it meant Charis was still on the council and that it was unlikely Pinho had arrived before him to cause chaos and division.

When he reached the dock, he threw a line to Inger, who tied the dinghy up.

"You have a ship," she said. "There must be an interesting story behind that."

"There is," Calder said. He stepped onto the dock and hugged her. "But the more pressing issue is that I have Councilwoman Floros on board. Omer, the former Overseer of Zelesso, has charged her with treason. The council needs to discuss that and if they feel there is not enough evidence for them to convict her, then I will accuse her of interfering with the Fair Seas Treaty Alliance's agreements with Arressa."

Inger's eyebrows lifted. "You have been busy. Come on. I'm expected at the council meeting, and you are the solution to their major problem."

"Acquiring timber to build ships?" he guessed.

"Yes," Inger replied. "Though now they'll need to deal with Floros."

"STURE WILL TALLY everything up and determine what goes where," Lauma said.

"You're very efficient," Dag said. In less time than she'd expected, Lauma had organized the offloading effort.

Lauma didn't want to risk putting too much weight on the ice, so they were ferrying smaller amounts of goods from the *Atlaine* using the few ice boats they had. At that point, the risk was moving from ice to water. A barge had been pulled up as close to the ice as possible. Goods would be transferred onto even smaller boats that would be pulled the final few yards to the barge. Everyone would be safe and there should be minimal chance of losing any of the food.

"Mads said you're the one who organized the ice fishing," Dag continued.

"I have plenty of experience," Lauma said. "All I did was teach a few people what I do every winter. Sture is the one who's been managing the food stores in the warehouses. He's the reason we're all still alive."

"We're all fortunate that he's here then," Dag replied. And the Three was fortunate that Lauma was in a position where she could make the biggest difference.

"There's Nadez," Lauma said, pointing back towards the city.

Nadez was hurrying towards them, and Dag waved.

"You're here!" Nadez called. "With supplies?"

"With supplies," Dag replied. "Dried beans and barley along with some olives. Nothing too exotic."

"We've all been surviving on fresh and dried fish," Nadez said. "Beans, barley, and olives sound plenty exotic." Her smile fell, and she leaned in close. "Did Rahm arrive with you?"

"Rahm?" Lauma asked. "What makes you ask about him?"

"He's here already?" Dag asked. "Ottosen?"

Nadez nodded. "I just came from his city estate. Henrik Ottosen is dead. His wife, children, and servants had been locked up but are otherwise unharmed."

"Rahm killed Ottosen?" Lauma asked. "How did he even get here?"

"I really thought there was time to get the food unloaded," Dag said. She ran a hand through her hair. "I had no idea he could even beat me to Tarklee. He had just left Lavais Port when I arrived. He'd made a bargain: he would manage the pirates in Nurmi in exchange for help from an Intelligencer."

"A bargain," Nadez asked. "With Berna?"

"With Gustav and Pia," Dag said. "Although Berna upheld it. Rahm spoke to the pirates, and they left Nurmi. Apparently, he also warned Timonis to behave, and extra food was *found*."

"My former husband did not do that for free," Lauma said.

"He wanted his token to be Unmade," Dag said. "And Jarri did that. Rahm was gone by the time I reached Lavais Port. The bargain had been completed, he didn't hurt anyone there, and he left on foot."

"Do you think someone helped him get to the mainland and the road?" Nadez asked.

"Maybe. He could have stolen what he needed or used force,"

she said. "My mission was to get this shipment of food delivered to Tarklee. Not to search for Rahm or get in the way of a Resolute."

"I might have been able to stop him," Lauma said. "If I'd known, I could have waited at Ottosen's estate until he showed up and talked him out of it."

Dag shook her head. "This was his final commission, and a target chosen by the suicide assassins. A choice Calder gave them. You might have stopped Rahm from killing Ottosen today, but I'm sure there's a reason why they're called Resolutes. Rahm would have completed this task eventually."

"Would you have told Ottosen about your former husband?" Nadez asked, looking at Lauma. "He would have used that information to harm you, and that could threaten the people of Tarklee and maybe even everyone in the Three."

"So, we do nothing?" Lauma asked.

Dag met Nadez's eyes, and they both nodded.

"Over the years Ottosen and his mother used assassins to get what they wanted," Nadez said. "I may have some sympathy for his wife and children, but not for him. He did seize food that was shipped north and used it to force people to support him."

"What?" Dag asked. "How did you find out?"

"A couple of Byholters arrived recently with that information," Lauma said. "Nadez, did you find proof?"

"No," Nadez said. "But now that Ottosen is dead, Saulia Holt might be willing to provide some."

Lauma sighed. "I doubt it matters now. Do you think the transition to a new Clan Freeholder will be smooth? I really don't want to deal with any more trouble."

"I have some hope," Nadez replied.

"Look," Dag called out. "I can see the barge. It's on its way back to shore." Whatever problems the news of Ottosen's death brought, at least the food was arriving.

GRATEFUL, PIA TOOK the bowl of fish soup. It had been a long time since she'd eaten in the Hall. Rather than lead her to the usual dining room, she'd followed Gustav into a small room where they joined a couple of other people in a lineup outside of what turned out to be a kitchen door.

She and Rahm had eaten at Pavil's house, but that had been

last night at supper. When asked, Pavil had harnessed his horse to a sled and driven through the night to drop them at the outskirts of Tarklee.

Rahm had disappeared then, and after declining Pavil's offer of a ride back to his house, Pia had gone in search of a meal.

"I've had worse," Gustav said after eating a spoonful of soup. "And I've had better."

"Same here." Pia spooned up some soup and swallowed. The hollow feeling in her stomach was subsiding. She ate another spoonful.

"Pavil makes a good fish soup," Gustav said. "He learned what spices to add to it from Calder *Rahmson*."

"Yes, we stopped at Pavil's," Pia said. "Rahm is a good cook, too. He made a stew at Solvig's warehouse." She spooned the last of her soup into her mouth and savoured it for a moment, before swallowing. She would still be hungry, but at least she could think about something other than her next meal.

"What was it like travelling alone with him?" Gustav asked.

"It was quiet," Pia said. "He doesn't really talk much." She looked over at Gustav. "Which is good because when he does talk, it's usually because he doesn't like something that you're doing."

"And he's really not a," Gustav leaned in closer, "Resolute anymore?"

"He didn't tell me, and I wasn't about to ask." She pushed her bowl away and glared at Gustav. "Whatever Jarri did to his token, it didn't make him less dangerous."

A pair of men walked by talking in low whispers. She tensed until she heard what they were talking about: the ship that had arrived.

"Come on," Pia said. "I need to find Nadez." If she could warn the Master Intelligencer before Rahm killed Ottosen, she might be able to restore some of the mistrust bringing him to Tarklee would cause. Nadez didn't need another reason to doubt Pia's commitment to the Intelligencers, and she'd just given her a big one.

Pia wasn't sure how to fix it, wasn't sure how to regain Nadez's trust so that she could continue to be an Intelligencer.

"WE'RE HERE FOR the council meeting," Inger said to the woman who had answered the door. "On behalf of the Fair Seas Treaty

Alliance."

"You're late," the woman said. "They were expecting you half an hour ago." She opened the door and stepped aside. Raised voices drifted out through the open door.

Inger shrugged. "I bring excellent news."

Calder followed Inger into the room. It took a few moments, but the room eventually quieted, and the four councillors looked up from the table they were sitting around. Charis's back was to them, and he had to turn around. He grinned and nodded at Calder.

"Council members," Inger said. "Calder Rahmson has returned from Zelesso. I believe he has at least some of the answers you are looking for."

"Welcome," Nilus said. "What news of Zelesso?"

Jurgus leaned back in his chair, and Audra, the woman who was desperate for timber, plastered a smile on her face.

"Fihaldo Pinho was there," Calder said. "Along with Thekla Floros. They were attempting to extort Arressan citizens."

"Extort how?" Jurgus asked.

"There was a demand for coin from every business and household," Calder said. "The amount was set high enough that most would not be able to provide it."

"What was the penalty if they did not comply?" Charis asked.

"One person from each household or business to work off the debt," Calder said. "An effort we suspected was to raise an army."

"That's quite a deduction," Jurgus said.

"Who is this *we*?" Audra asked.

"Me, my sister Esma, and Omer, the former Overseer of Zelesso," Calder paused. "As well as Ismini and Takis, who along with the rest of the city, helped defend Zelesso from Pinho's attack."

"He attacked Zelesso?" Nilus asked.

"You must be mistaken," Audra interjected. "I doubt Pinho would do that, and Thekla would never harm Arressans."

"It's pretty hard to mistake a cannon being fired from a ship directly into the city," Calder said. "And as for what Thekla Floros would do, you may ask her yourself. She's on board the *Pathfinder*. I'd be happy to escort all of you out to the ship so you can question her."

"I'll go," Charis said. "Nilus?" The older man nodded.

"You need to bring her here," Jurgus said. "This is an Arressan Council matter."

"She's not leaving the ship until this council has made a decision," Calder said. "Omer would like her charged with treason against Arressa. If you find that you do not have enough evidence, I will charge her with crimes against the Three and take her to Tarklee."

"What was the name of your ship?" Audra asked.

"The *Pathfinder*," Calder replied.

"That's one of Fihaldo Pinho's ships," Audra said. "That belongs to Arressa."

"It's a spoil of war," Calder replied. "And I would think that Pilalia would have a better claim on Pinho's property than Arressa." He paused. "Although a second ship, the *Fair Winds*, is being repaired in Zelesso. It needs a captain and crew, as well as an owner. Pinho's flagship, the *Defensor*, was destroyed during the fight."

"You are saying that one of the two surviving ships will be handed over to Arressa?" Jurgus asked. "That is welcome news. I find the request to question Councillor Floros on board the *Pathfinder* quite reasonable under the circumstances, so I will go as well."

"I won't," Audra replied. "I will not witness her humiliation at being held prisoner."

"My dear," Jurgus said to her. "If she's found guilty of treason then she's no longer on the council. Which means Calder Rahmson will tell his mother to sell us timber."

Audra looked at him, and Calder thought her frown was a little less deep.

"Is Pinho dead?" Charis asked. "You destroyed his ship, so is he dead?"

"We don't think so," Calder replied. "We did not find his body, and one of the small sailboats that had been searching for survivors did not return."

"Where do you think he went?" Charis asked.

"Strongrock," Calder said. "Maybe south to Yedris, or here, to Messanos."

"Can we all agree that the guard should be alerted to watch for Pinho?" Charis asked. Nilus and Jurgus both nodded. Audra crossed her arms over her chest and stared straight ahead.

"I'll let them know," Charis said. "Let's go see what Thekla Floros has to say."

Calder looked over at Inger, who rolled her eyes before turning to open the door.

Calder followed her out of the room. Now he wasn't sure he wanted to leave Floros here even if the council charged her with treason. Audra clearly didn't consider Floros or even Pinho as threats. With Charis and Nilus on one side, the deciding vote seemed to be Jurgus.

WHEN NADEZ FINALLY made her way to her office, she was surprised to find the door open.

She peered into the outer office. Gustav sat in the chair at the assistant's desk, his feet on the desktop.

"Does this mean you're offering to be my assistant?" she said, entering the office. "I heard you came in on the *Atlaine* and was wondering when you'd show up."

"I took a look around town," Gustav said. He moved his feet from the desktop to the floor. "Then I ran into someone who was hungry, and we came here for a meal."

Nadez's eyes followed his across the room.

"Pia! I didn't know you came on the *Atlaine* too," Nadez said. Pia looked at the floor instead of meeting her eyes. "Except you didn't, did you?"

Nadez closed the door and headed to the inner office. "Come in here, both of you."

She sat at her desk and watched the two young Intelligencers as they slowly entered her office. Once the door was closed and they were all seated, she tapped her fingers on the desk.

"Where is Rahm now?" Nadez asked.

"I don't know," Pia replied.

"But you helped him get here."

"Yes." Pia looked up and met her eyes. "Partly to get him away from Solvig's warehouse."

"And Frida," Nadez said. "He doesn't know Swyford very well. Could you have led him back to Lavais Port?"

"You've never met Rahm," Gustav said. "He knows when he's being lied to."

"Does he?" Nadez turned her gaze on Gustav.

"Pia and I met him in Nurmi," Gustav said. "I thought he was going to kill us, but then he found out we were Intelligencers, and we made a deal. Not that we had a choice. He already knew what he wanted; he needed Jarri to Unmake something. But he didn't trust us." He paused, and Gustav's usually sunny expression darkened. "I still thought he'd kill us before we got to Lavais Port."

"He almost did," Pia said. "By capsizing the ice boat we were in. For all we know, he had planned to dump us in the water in the hopes that we would drown, and he could arrive at Lavais Port without anyone knowing who he was."

"I think he just wasn't willing to give up control of the boat," Gustav said. "And then didn't have the experience to take it from ice to open water. But he wouldn't have worried about us dying. Not when killing people is just a job to him."

"Did he do it?" Pia asked. "He did. That's how you know he's in Tarklee. He's already assassinated Ottosen."

"He has," Nadez said. She stared at Pia. "I needed to ask *why* you helped him get here. You took the road, I assume?"

"Yes. Are you going to punish me?"

"No." Nadez paused. How much should she tell them? Pia could use her Trait to figure it out. She might as well ease her mind. "Both Dagrun and I feel that there would have been no way to stop a Resolute. Ottosen's fate was sealed the moment Calder let the suicide assassin pick him as their target." She stopped there. She wasn't about to tell them that as far as she was concerned, Ottosen deserved what he got.

"Oh." Pia seemed surprised. "So am I still an Intelligencer?"

"If you want to be," Nadez said. "I do have something to discuss with you that might change your mind. Gustav, will you leave us?"

The youth nodded, and Nadez watched him leave the room. No doubt Pia would repeat this conversation to him later, but that would be her choice.

She turned to Pia. Where to start?

PIA SQUIRMED. NADEZ'S intense stare was making her nervous. But the Master Intelligencer had already told her she could still be an Intelligencer. She glanced at the door wishing she'd left with Gustav.

"I discovered something about you and your sister," Nadez

said. "About your family."

"What?" This was not what Pia had expected. "I know who my family is. My mother and father farmed land owned by Clan Freeholder Ottosen. My family has done that for generations. But my parents were both only children, so there's just Frida and me left."

"Your mother's father was not a farmer," Nadez said. "And there has been a grave injustice that we can correct."

"Injustice? About what?"

"Your mother's father should have inherited the Clan Freehold," Nadez said. "Instead, Henrik Ottosen did."

"What?" Pia was confused. If her grandfather on her mother's side could have inherited, that meant . . . "I'm related to Ottosen? Did he know?"

"I don't believe he knew," Nadez said. "If he did, he would very likely have had your grandmother and mother murdered, just as he had your grandfather assassinated."

Pia sat back, stunned. She hoped Ottosen had seen Rahm coming, she hoped he had been terrified at the end. "Why are you telling me this?" She wished she didn't know that she was related to that *skit karl.*

"With Ottosen's death, there is a chance to restore your line as Clan Freeholder," Nadez said. "It won't be easy—"

"*No!*" Pia shouted the word. "No. Why would I want that?"

"There is a great deal of land and coin attached to that inheritance," Nadez said. "Why wouldn't you want that?"

"Because I hate everyone in that household," Pia said. "And I love being an Intelligencer."

"What about Frida? I thought you wanted stability for her?" Nadez seemed genuinely puzzled.

"I do," Pia said. "And there would be no stability for Frida amongst that Clan. They locked her up and starved her." Pia couldn't believe Nadez had suggested this. "There is no one I could trust to keep Frida safe." She paused. "You just said Ottosen murdered a man you claim is my grandfather. What if he had my parents killed too? How is Frida going to be safe with any of those people?"

"I don't think Ottosen's wife had anything to do with any murders," Nadez said. "She wasn't even married to Henrik at the time."

Pia took a deep breath. "Tessan Ottosen could very well have known about any and all murders. And she was the one who locked up Frida and gave the orders not to feed her. I will *not* let that woman near my sister. I don't want any of it. Not the land, not the coin, and certainly not those terrible people as my *clan*."

"All right." Nadez leaned back in her chair. "I'll stop making enquiries."

"Enquiries?" Pia repeated. Fear clutched her heart. "Who else knows about this?"

"No one in the Ottosen clan," Nadez said. "I spoke to Lauma about this, and then there's the person I received this information from."

"Good." Pia wasn't relieved though. This was dangerous knowledge; dangerous for her and Frida if the wrong people found out. "Can I go now?"

Nadez nodded, and Pia left the office. She had to stop herself from running through the Hall. But she couldn't outrun this. Couldn't outrun the fact that she was related to the man who had done so much harm to her and her sister.

She didn't slow down until she was in the hallway that led to her old student room.

Ottosen was dead. As long as the new Clan Freeholder didn't know about her and Frida, they should be safe. She hoped.

CHAPTER 10

"JURGUS, FINALLY," THEKLA Floros said. "Someone with the authority to free me. Untie me right now."

Calder followed Nilus, Jurgus, Charis, and Inger into the small cabin. Floros was standing, an angry look on her face. There wasn't enough room in the small space, so Esma hovered in the doorway.

"Captain Rahmson has final authority here," Charis said. "You run a shipyard, surely you know enough about the laws on ships to know that."

"I wasn't speaking to you," Floros hissed. "I was speaking to Councilman Jurgus. Please release me."

"Charis is right," Jurgus said. "I don't have the authority. Besides, you've been accused of treason."

"By whom?" Floros said. "This so-called captain isn't even an Arressan."

"I am," Esma said. "You've been formally accused by the Overseer of Zelesso. And I bear witness to your crimes."

"Since there is no Overseer," Floros said, "there can be no formal accusation from one. And you are the daughter of a known assassin, so anything you say is suspect."

"There's no Overseer because you convinced the council the position wasn't needed," Nilus said. "I trust Omer's word, as well as that of Esma."

"As do I," Charis said.

All eyes turned to Jurgus. "I believe that Omer has accused Thekla Floros with treason, and that is enough for me to vote to detain Thekla for questioning," Jurgus said.

"You can't," Floros said. "Jurgus, why are you doing this? You have always been my ally."

"No, I have not," Jurgus said. "I have always done what I thought best for Arressa." He turned to Calder. "We will need to interview more witnesses. Can you help us do that?"

"What do you propose?" Calder asked.

"Well, I would like to see the damage Pinho caused to Zelesso myself," Jurgus said. "My preference would be for the entire council to travel there on the *Pathfinder* and have the trial there. It saves making witnesses come here. But you are the captain of this ship, so I can only ask."

"I agree to take the council to Zelesso," Calder said. "Charis, do you know any seasoned sailors? We need a captain and crew for the *Fair Winds*. We might as well bring them too."

"I can recruit everyone you need," Charis said. "I also agree with going to Zelesso."

"As do I," Nilus said.

"Good," Calder said. "We'll leave Floros on board, and I'll do my best to be ready to sail in a day." He was relieved with the decision. It meant that Floros was still his prisoner and that multiple witnesses would be able to speak out against her.

"That accomplished quite a lot," Esma said as he locked the cabin once everyone had exited.

"Yes, it did. Come on, I'm going to need your help assessing Charis's recruits."

"THIS IS THE last of it," Darya said.

"Good. How long until the *Atlaine* is ready to sail?" Dag asked. They were standing on the dock, watching the barge being unloaded. Sture was a few feet away from her, calling out orders.

"Three hours," Darya said. She grinned. "The crew could probably get ready in two, they're so eager to get back to the Sapphire Sea and out of this cold."

"It should be warmer the next time we're here," Dag said. She was already starting to worry about what goods they would be able to buy in Messanos. The pirate coin they'd found on

Strongrock was nearly depleted. Lauma had given her more, but Captain Eklund needed coin too. As soon as the harbour and the Frozen Gap were clear of ice, the *Tazeyar* would set sail for the Sapphire Sea.

Dag was still amazed at how much work had gone into saving the *Tazeyar* over the winter, but constant ice breaking for months had done the job. The ship was seaworthy. All it needed was some warm weather for the rest of the ice to clear from the harbour and the Frozen Pass to open.

"I'll let Captain Sorenson know we're almost ready to leave," Dag said. "And that he can get his crew ready to board." Sorenson was excited to captain the new ship and wanted both he and his crew in Lavais Port, ready as soon as the new ship was launched. Dag was relieved to have someone experienced and trusted at the helm.

The Three had managed to survive this winter, but every single ship and every single trading mission would be needed to make sure they were prepared for next winter.

Lauma thought it could be two or three years before trade was back to normal, so they had to make as many trips as possible.

"There's Gustav," Darya said. "He's helping us ferry everyone out to the *Atlaine*." She looked at Dag. "He's also asked permission to come with us to the Sapphire Sea."

"That will be up to Nadez," Dag said. "Although he is pleasant to have around." Even though his Trait didn't work on her, Gustav was eager to help and friendly. And he had some useful ice boat skills that the crew of the *Atlaine* lacked.

"He is at that," Darya said. "Time for me to see Sture and make sure our tallies match up."

"I need a final chat with Lauma and Nadez," Dag said. "I'll see you on board in less than three hours." She left Darya with Sture and stopped beside the ice boat.

"Gustav, did Captain Sorenson talk to you?" she asked.

"He said his crew will be arriving soon," Gustav said. "Fifteen in all, so I need to make four trips. Thorben offered to come on the last trip and sail the boat back."

"You're coming with us to Lavais Port?"

"I'd like to go all the way to the Sapphire Sea," Gustav said. "Can I?"

"That's up to Nadez," Dag replied. "Did you ask her?"

"Can you ask her for me? She'd probably want me to check with you anyway."

"I'll ask," Dag said. "But I won't make your case for you. That you need to do yourself. Is Pia coming with us?"

"She said she was," Gustav replied. "She wants to spend some time with her sister."

"We sail in three hours," Dag said.

She didn't have far to go since both Lauma and Nadez were at the warehouse, watching as the goods were stored.

"Is it enough?" Dag asked when she joined them. "We bought what we could get our hands on."

"It's exactly what we needed," Lauma said. "Thank you. The city will still be on rations, but we can increase the daily amount of food for everyone. And we can all breathe a sigh of relief now that we know there will be more. We'll send some of it north by ice boat."

"The Frozen Pass should open soon," Nadez added. "And there will be two more ships that can be sent for food."

"Captain Sorenson is delighted to have a ship," Lauma said. "And to get back to sailing to the Sapphire Sea. He good-naturedly blamed me for the loss of his old ship after Calder rammed the *Mischief* into Margit Ansdottir and the *Bright Breeze*."

"Any word from Clan Ottosen?" Dag asked. Any instability was a threat to Tarklee.

"No," Lauma said and frowned. "I wish I knew where Rahm was. No doubt he'll turn up somewhere at the most inconvenient time."

"He probably took the road south," Nadez said. "According to Pia and Gustav, Rahm sailed to Nurmi from Strongrock. He will likely return there the same way."

"I hope so," Dag said. "Calder and I did that trip, and even in warmer weather, it is not a journey I would want to repeat." She thought Rahm was hiding out in Tarklee, but neither Nadez nor Lauma agreed with her. Lauma was certain that Rahm would have tried to see her if he was still here. Dag wasn't so sure. Lauma knew what he was: or what he had been. There was also the matter of him murdering Ottosen. Rahm couldn't be certain that Lauma wouldn't try to arrest him if he visited her.

"One last thing," Dag said. "Both Gustav and Pia have asked to board the *Atlaine*. Pia will visit her sister. She didn't really get a chance because Rahm was there. Gustav wants to come with us to the Sapphire Sea. I told him I'd ask."

"I'd prefer if one of them stayed here," Nadez said. "But I know Gustav's ice sailing skills are needed and Pia . . ." Nadez paused. "Pia should see her sister. But I'd like one of them to return to Tarklee as soon as possible. So no, Gustav does not have my permission to go to the Sapphire Sea."

"I'll tell him," Dag said. "If that's everything, I'll head out to the ship. And yes, I will tell Calder that you are well."

"Thank you," Lauma said. "All those years when he was simply *away*, I never knew what he was doing, so I didn't worry. Now?" She shrugged. "I know what he's doing, and I worry."

"So do I," Dag said. She hugged them both before heading to the dock to take an ice boat trip to the *Atlaine*.

NADEZ WATCHED THE last group leave in the ice boat. Gustav sailed halfway to the mouth of the harbour on open water then took the little boat up onto the ice. A few minutes later, the boat disappeared around the point. The fisherman Thorben would bring the boat back when everyone was on board the *Atlaine*.

She sighed. Now that the flurry of activity was over, she felt deflated.

Guards were at the entrance of the dockside warehouse when she arrived. Sture had gone home for a few hours but would be back later for the evening shift change.

With nothing else needing her attention, Nadez returned to her office.

Lauma was waiting for her.

"I'm worried about Clan Ottosen," Lauma said as they settled in Nadez's office. "You said you had some hope of a smooth transition. Is there anything you think I can do to help?"

"No," Nadez replied. She paused. "I had thought to convince Pia to claim the Clan Freeholdership, but she wasn't interested."

"Pia? Why would you even think to consider her?" Lauma asked. "She has no support in the clan. In fact, she probably has enemies. That is a very bad idea. When you told me about her family history, I didn't realize you meant for her to try to act on it."

"It would set to rights the terrible deeds of the past," Nadez said. "I think that Pia and Frida Engen deserve the chance to gain their legacy. Besides, it would have meant a solid ally for us."

"And a short life for both of them," Lauma said. "What makes you think Henrik Ottosen was the only one behind the assassination attempts on my life?"

"You think his wife was part of that?"

"Why do you think she wasn't?" Lauma asked. "Clan Freeholder succession is very much a family endeavour. You can't do it alone, and since you have to trust someone, who better than your spouse and children? Especially since inheriting can pit you against your siblings. You're the one who said you thought Henrik and his mother were behind the death of Henrik's older half-brother."

"Yes," Nadez said. "But the mother was herself an assassin. I thought that made her an exception."

"In my experience, the women in the family are just as ambitious," Lauma said. "And heartless. Asla Holt was perfectly happy to enjoy the benefits of her husband's horrible actions. I'm sure Timonis's wife feels the same. At least Pia had the good sense to turn down your offer. Is she here?"

"No, she left on the *Atlaine*," Nadez said. "She's going to spend some time with her sister."

"Let's hope you didn't scare her so much that she takes her sister and goes into hiding," Lauma said. "Who else knows about their relationship to Ottosen?"

"Just us," Nadez said. "And Valda Skala and her companion Madera."

"Good," Lauma said. "Valda and Madera know how to keep a secret. As long as we also do that, Pia should be safe."

"*Safe*," Nadez repeated. "I never thought this would put her in danger." But that was a lie. Valda had told her that Pia and Frida would never have been born if the existence of their mother had been known to Ottosen. Somehow, she'd convinced herself that the two girls deserved a better life and that this was the way for them to get it. Lauma was right: if the wrong people learned of this, Pia and her little sister would not be safe.

There was a knock at the door to the outer office. Nadez rose to find a guard outside her office door.

"Master Intelligencer," he said. "You have to come. There's been another murder."

"Another murder?" Nadez asked.

"Yes. Another murder at Clan Freeholder Ottosen's estate."

CALDER WATCHED THE sailors as they worked aloft. Arressan was the language they all had in common, but snatches of Pilalian and Yedrissian floated down to him.

The crew Charis had found for the *Fair Winds*—a diverse crew of people of all ages and from every country that ringed the Sapphire Sea—were staying below, out of the way.

The Arressan Council, including Audra, who had decided to join the rest of them, were in the captain's cabin. The trip to Zelesso would be over in another hour which meant they would still have enough daylight for the council to inspect the damage caused by Pinho's cannon.

"They're going to let you keep this ship," Inger said. "At least that was the sentiment I overheard when I delivered tea."

"It's not really their decision to make," Calder said. "Charis knows that."

"Yes, but it would be good if they felt like they had a choice," Esma said. "Charis knows that too."

"You two talked about it," Calder said. Inger nodded. "I don't really want the ship."

"We know. But you're the most experienced captain that we trust," Inger said. "I say that on behalf of Charis and I, not the Merchant Adventurers."

"Pinho is still out there," Calder said. Until they had the man imprisoned, he would continue to be a threat. Even if he was caught, he might be able to convince someone like Audra to help him. "Do you think he has a Trait?"

"Like Ansdottir?" Inger asked. "It's possible. He does seem to inspire fierce loyalty. Traits aren't really recognized here, at least not in Messanos, so I haven't heard any speculation about one that Pinho might have."

"I suppose that's why Tarmo Holt was able to buy and steal twins and triplets," Calder said. "Although widespread knowledge about Traits might have meant some of the children would have been taken from their homes earlier." He still worried about Adjoa, the girl with the Healing Trait. Separating her from her brothers would be dangerous for the boys, but her Trait was so very strong. Adjoa had literally saved Esma's life. What would a man like Pinho do to have her Healing all for himself? Or

Henrik Ottosen, who already dealt with death? He wouldn't care about anyone left behind; the only thing he would care about was Adjoa's potential to save him from injury or illness.

"I see Zelesso," Inger said. "I'll go tell the Council that we'll be arriving soon."

"Thanks," Calder replied. "Please keep them below until we've dropped the anchor. The crew and I aren't used to each other yet, and I don't want anyone with strong, differing opinions underfoot."

"I'll do my best," Inger said as she turned to leave. "But some of them aren't very good at following orders."

"Yes," Calder replied. "Exactly."

As they approached the city, there were a couple of misunderstood orders, mostly because he had little experience captaining a ship completely in Arressan, but eventually they were in the harbour and the anchor had been dropped.

"Who goes ashore first?" Esma asked him. Despite her lack of sailing experience, she was still his First Mate.

"Me, Inger, and the council," he said. "Everyone else needs to stay on board. And again, you're in charge. No one gets on or off except us."

"Calder," Inger called. She was standing with Charis while the rest of the council ranged behind them. "Where do you want us?"

"Follow me." Calder led them to a dinghy. He called out a few orders, and a dozen sailors lowered the boat over the side.

"I'll row if you want to steer," Calder said to Charis.

"I'll steer, and the two of you can row," Inger said. She grinned as she slipped over the gunwale.

Omer was waiting for them on the dock.

"Overseer," Nilus said when he stepped out of the dinghy. "I am glad to see you."

"I am happy to see you as well, Councilman Nilus," Omer said. "Although I no longer hold the title of Overseer."

"Something we should change," Nilus said. "The entire council is here, and we can see that the position is needed in situations like this."

"He might not be interested," Charis said. "Considering the council stripped him of his title and duties just a few months ago." He stepped onto the dock. "Charis Diakos. I am a recent addition to the council. I appreciate everything you've done for

Zelesso both as an official representative and during this recent trouble."

"I'm Inger Lund," Inger said once she'd stepped onto the dock. "I represent the Merchant Adventurers for the Fair Seas Treaty Alliance."

Calder kept the boat steady as everyone disembarked, and then he joined them.

"Calder Rahmson," Omer said. "Thank you for returning so quickly. I did not expect you to bring the entire Arressan Council, but it is good that you have."

"The council wants to see the damage from the cannon," Calder said.

"Yes," Jurgus said. "Show us that Fihaldo Pinho fired on Arressans. After that we will need accommodations for the night. Then we will decide what to do with Thekla Floros. Her fate depends on what we see in the city."

"Right this way," Omer said. "People have been doing their best to make repairs, but you can still see the destruction."

The council followed Omer, and Inger fell in beside Calder, who was last.

"Do you have a place to stay for the night?" Inger asked. "Charis said that the council is going to commandeer the best tavern and inn. The other one seems a bit dodgy, so I'm not sure I want to stay there. Should we return to the ship?"

"I need to let Esma's mother know that she's safe," Calder said. "Come along and I'll introduce you to her. Saba might even have room for us."

"I'd like to meet Esma's mother," Inger said. "Lead the way."

Calder nodded and turned down a street.

DESPITE THE BITTER wind, Gustav leaned out over the prow of the ship. The *Atlaine* dipped into a trough, and when it rose it hit a wave and icy spray hit him in the face.

"It's too cold out here," Pia said. "I'm going below. Don't fall overboard."

"I'll come with you," Gustav replied. He would have liked to stay out, but he was worried about Pia. She'd been acting odd ever since they came on board, and he hoped she wasn't still concerned about her role in getting Rahm to Tarklee. Even Nadez had agreed that there had been no way to stop Rahm from assassinating Ottosen. "As long as you say you'll go exploring with me." He'd been on ships before, but this felt different, partly because an Intelligencer was in charge.

Dagrun Lund wasn't the captain; that was Darya Demer. But everyone on board knew that Dagrun was giving the directions. She was even using the captain's cabin. Gustav felt that meant he and Pia—fellow Intelligencers—would have access to every inch of this ship. He planned on taking advantage of that.

"All right," Pia said. "There's not much else to do anyway."

"Good. Let's start in the mess. I want to know how much food we need on board." He led the way below deck and along a short passage to the mess. A few sailors were huddled at a couple of tables, but at this time of the morning, only tea was available.

Gustav poked his head into the kitchen. "Cook," he said. "Have you time to answer some questions?"

"If you give me a hand sorting through these beans," the man said. "Sure."

Gustav looked at Pia, who nodded.

"I'd just as soon work for my passage anyway," she said.

"Come and sit at the worktable," the cook said. He dragged a barrel over. "Take them from here, pick out any stones and bad beans, and fill that pot halfway. While you're doing that, I'll answer any questions you can think of."

Gustav sat down at the table. He had no idea what to do.

"I'll show you," Pia said. She sat across from him, scooped up some beans, and poured them out onto the tabletop. "Pick out the stones first," she said. "Put the split ones, the really dark ones, and the shrivelled ones in a separate pile."

"Why?" Gustav could understand the stones, no one wanted to eat that in their meal, but what was wrong with the other ones?

"Because they're not good to eat," the cook said. "But they're still food. These days we shouldn't toss anything we might be desperate enough to eat later. I'm planning on seeing what I can do with them after they've been boiled for a few days."

Gustav peered at the beans and picked out a couple of stones. "How much food do you have to have on board?"

"For this trip? Captain said about ten days' worth," the cook replied. "I add three extra days in case we run into harsh weather."

Half an hour later the beans were all sorted, and Gustav knew more about provisioning a ship than he'd thought possible. Everything from water to tea to what type of diet was optimal.

"It sounds like your job is very important," Gustav said to the cook. "I had no idea."

"Most people don't," was the reply. "But try keeping a crew working during bad weather without tea and hot food and you'll see why smart captains understand that crews sail on their stomachs."

"And you have your own stores right here," Gustav said. "So they can't get mixed up with whatever's in the hold. Does anyone ever steal from the mess?"

The cook frowned. "Not if they know what's good for them," he said. "But some food and water went missing between the time it was loaded and when I double-checked just before we set sail. Not enough to make meals a hardship, but it makes me angry. The kitchen is always locked, so I'm not sure who could have done it."

"They just took food and water?" Pia asked.

"Aye."

"What food did they take? Dried beans?" Pia asked. "Or tea?"

"No." The cook looked at her. "The missing food was already cooked. Some leftover cooked beans and some olives."

"Thank you for your time," Pia said. "I appreciate all the hard work you do, and I was happy to help. Gustav, we need to check in with Dagrun."

"We do?" Pia gave a hand signal, and he stood up. "Right, I forgot. Thanks for answering so many questions."

"Glad for the help and the company," the cook said.

"What is it?" Gustav asked Pia as soon as they were out of the kitchen. "Dagrun never asked us to see her, so what happened? It's the missing food and water, isn't it?"

"Yes," Pia replied. "We need to talk to Dagrun right away. Because we have a stowaway on board, and I'm pretty sure I know who it is."

"Who?" Gustav asked, even as the answer came to him.

"Rahm," Pia said. "Who else would it be?"

"IT'S REIN," NADEZ said. "Rein Chebek, Ottosen's Provisions Manager. He is nowhere near the line of succession, so why would anyone want him dead?"

"You knew him?" Lauma asked.

They were in the office Nadez had used when she'd been investigating what Ottosen was shipping into Tarklee last summer. Rein was slumped across the desk, his eyes staring blankly at the wall. A knife protruded from his back.

"He was kind to me," Nadez said. "He even hinted at the method Ottosen and his mother used to secure the Clan Freehold."

"Then that's why he's dead," Lauma said. "He knew too much. As Provisions Manager, he might have even known about the stolen food."

"You think he had something to do with that?" Nadez didn't want to think about Rein agreeing to withhold food from starving people, but she hadn't really known him.

"Or he found out afterwards and was angry," Lauma said. She turned to the guardsmen. "Once you've interviewed everyone in the household, I'd like to see the immediate family. Nadez, do you want to speak to them with me or do you want to interview them on your own?" Lauma leaned in close. "Keep in mind that while I want to find this man's murderer, I do not want to interfere with the succession."

Nadez sighed. Lauma was right; the last thing they wanted was more instability. "I'll sit in with you." In normal circumstances catching a murderer would have been her focus, but now? She knew who had committed the first one, but she also knew that bringing Rahm to justice would be all but impossible. "Do you think Rahm did this?" she asked Lauma.

"No." Lauma shook her head. "Dagrun said his token was destroyed and that Ottosen was his last commission. I can't see him involving himself further into Clan Freeholder politics. And this seems very political."

Nadez sighed again. She hated that she was going to say this, but stability was more important. "I think we should publicly link the two murders."

"And blame them both on an assassin?" Lauma asked. "Are you sure?"

"No," she replied. "But it might keep things stable. Once we are past the threat of starvation and food shortages, we can always revisit Rein's murder."

"Thank you," Lauma said. "I know that this is a difficult choice for you. It is for me as well, but Rein Chebek is dead, and nothing we do will change that. But we might be able to prevent anymore murders."

"By letting a murderer become Clan Freeholder," Nadez said.

"Just like Ottosen," Lauma said. "Although this time it was a key member of the household who was killed instead of a rival. That tells me someone is probably going to declare themselves Clan Freeholder very soon."

"Let's hope no one else dies before that happens," Nadez said. She hated the idea of a murderer becoming the Clan Freeholder, but she couldn't be sure that a former Master Intelligencer hadn't known about Henrik Ottosen's path to power and kept quiet about it. What she did know was that Pia had been right to not want this; she had been right to be afraid.

DAGRUN STOOD IN the hold and let her eyes wander past the multiple hammocks hanging overhead. At this time of day a few of them were in use, but none of them triggered her Trait. She turned to Pia and Gustav.

"I didn't expect to find him here," she said. "Let's keep searching."

She led the way deeper into the hold. It was an empty space now with nowhere to hide.

"Maybe he's not here," Gustav said. "I mean, Cook said a *little* food was missing so really, it could be anyone. None of us is getting enough to eat these days."

"This crew is," Dag replied. "Besides, Pia's Trait says it's Rahm. Come on. He's here somewhere, and I will find him."

Remembering how she had stowed away on Ansdottir's ship, up on deck, she looked under every single dinghy.

Dag sighed and looked up at the sky. And the familiar itch started between her shoulder blades. "He's up there," she said, pointing at a figure high up in the sails.

"He must be pretty cold," Pia said. "If he's been staying up there for long periods of time."

"Rahm doesn't like the cold?" Dag asked.

"No. When we found him in Setberg, the cabin he was using was really hot," Pia said. "And when I travelled with him, he complained about the cold."

"Then he's been expecting me to find him," Dag said. She

grinned. "Let's pretend we didn't. I'll let Darya know."

"You're just going to let him stay up there?" Gustav asked.

Dag shrugged. "It's Darya's decision, but I'd rather have him up there, where we can keep an eye on him, than try to lock him up. We'll be in Lavais Port soon anyway."

Pia nodded. "He did steal food," she said. "The captain could toss him overboard, couldn't she?"

"She could," Dag said. "But all he wants is to go home, so if he doesn't cause trouble, I would be against such a harsh punishment."

"But he's an assassin," Gustav said.

"Whose final target was given to him by Calder," Dag replied. "Intelligencers used him: would it be fair to punish him for doing a task we assigned him?"

"I guess not," Pia said. "But I don't trust him."

Dag laughed. "Oh, I don't trust him, but I'm not the one who has to decide what happens to him."

"You're going to leave it up to Captain Demer," Pia said.

"I thought you were in charge?" Gustav asked.

"I'm responsible for deciding what our mission is," Dag replied. "And for navigating us through the Teeth. But Captain Demer is responsible for the safety and security of everyone on board. I have to go and let her know about Rahm so she can make a decision. You two can take turns keeping an eye on him for me." Dag left the two younger Intelligencers and headed for the wheel.

"We have a stowaway," she said when she reached Darya. "Rahm came aboard somehow and is pretending to be part of the crew."

"He's an accomplished sailor, isn't he?" Darya asked. "So he's not a danger in that respect."

"Yes," Dag said. "You don't seem surprised that we have a stowaway."

"Cook told me that food and water was missing," Darya said. "And at the last watch change a crew member told me the sailor up top didn't come down. I was going to tell you, but you were off with Pia and Gustav."

"They're watching him," Dag said. "What do you want to do?"

"Do you think he's dangerous?"

"In general, yes," Dag said. "To the ship? No. I think he just wants to get back home."

"I think that too," Darya said. "I don't like stowaways or stealing, but he is doing one of the worst tasks a crew member can do during cold or rough weather."

"Pia says he hates the cold," Dag said. "I think he assumed I would find him. It would be a kindness to bring him inside and lock him up." She met Darya's eyes, and they both laughed.

"Then we'll leave him up there," Darya said. "Until we get to Lavais Port. But we can't let him go ashore there."

"Absolutely not," Dag said. "The only place we can leave him is Strongrock Island."

CHAPTER 11

"YOU LOOK LIKE her, but you're not *like* her."

"My little brother is acting as though he's never seen a twin before," Calder said. He, Inger, and Kasim were in Saba's main sitting room while she made them tea.

"Of course, I have," Kasim said. "I have friends who are twins. But as they got older, they started to look more different."

"Dag and I do too," Inger said. "If you know what to look for."

Calder snorted. "You think you look a lot different, but the rest of us have some trouble."

"Even you?" Inger asked. "Charis says it's easy for him to tell us apart."

"He has spent more time with the two of you together," Calder said. "So maybe for him it is." Charis had shared a small sailboat with the Lund twins when they rescued Saulia Holt.

"Tea is ready," Saba said, coming into the room. "Kasim, why don't you go find out how the council inspection is going?"

"Please do," Inger said. "Charis doesn't know where to find me, so if you could tell Omer where I am, I would appreciate it."

"Sure," Kasim said and left.

"Any word of Rahm?" Saba asked as she poured tea into three cups.

"Not so far," Calder said. "It's possible he is with Pinho." Much as he didn't want his father to murder anyone else, he wasn't sure Pinho would survive an encounter with Rahm.

"If he is, then Pinho is with Rahm," Saba replied. "Following Rahm's orders."

"He might try to get to the Pale Sea to destroy his token first," Calder said. "That's what I would do, if I were him." Not only would it free Rahm from his compulsion, but no one would also be able to use the token to control him ever again, especially not Pinho.

"Would he still kill his final target?" Saba asked. "With the token gone, he won't be compelled to." She almost sounded hopeful.

"Rahm won't back out of a promise to the suicide assassins," Inger said. "Not if he wants to ever feel safe."

"Well, he won't be living here with me," Saba replied. "Not even if he apologizes a thousand times."

"I think he knows that," Calder said. He doubted Rahm would apologize even once. Especially since finding out his final target had made him smile. His father didn't care whether Henrik Ottosen lived or died, but he did care that an assassin had selected her own target.

"They've finished their survey of the city," Kasim said, bursting into the room. "I spoke to Omer. He said the council was overly concerned about the amount of damage from the cannon and they've retired to the tavern. I told him you were here, Inger. Omer said he'd pass that on to Charis when he has a chance. They'll be deciding what to do about Thekla Floros later, after a meal, and letting everyone know their decision in the morning."

"Thanks," Calder said. "Inger and I need to figure out where we're staying tonight. Saba, if you have room, we'd appreciate it if we could stay here, but if not, we need to head back to the ship."

"Of course, you can stay here," Saba said. "Inger can use Esma's room and Calder, you can share with Kasim."

"Thank you," Inger said. "It will save us the trouble of rowing out to the ship and then rowing back in tomorrow morning."

Calder offered to cook, and Kasim left for a few minutes, returning with a couple of fish. Cabbage and potatoes rounded out the meal, and in less than an hour, Calder set everything out on the table.

"I think we should go to the tavern and wait for word after we eat," Inger said as they sat down. "Even if they don't make a decision tonight, I can't just sit here."

"Sure." Calder handed the plate of fried fish to Saba, who took a piece and passed the plate over to Kasim. "I wouldn't mind speaking to the Master Shipbuilder and seeing how the repairs to the *Fair Winds* are going."

"I heard that Nomiki thinks it's a straightforward repair," Kasim said. "And that she already has both the material and the workers to do it."

"That's excellent news," Calder replied. "I'm doubly glad that we brought a captain and crew for her." The new crew of the *Fair Winds* was staying on the *Pathfinder* for tonight and would be ferried to shore tomorrow.

They finished their meal, and while Inger and Kasim washed up, Calder joined Saba in the sitting room.

"Are you worried that Rahm will come back?" he asked her. "He would never hurt you, Esma, or Kasim."

Saba sighed. "It just feels so unfinished. I trust what you've told me about him, but I think I need to hear it from him. I need him to tell me in person that he lied to me for all those years." She turned to him. "How is your mother handling it?"

"She cut ties with Rahm years ago," Calder said. "For her, learning what he is and what he's done is more a validation of suspicions she's had for years. And honestly, I think she is just too busy right now to spend much time dwelling on it." He shrugged.

"Then that's what I should do," Saba said. "Stay busy. Inger and Kasim are finished. Shall we see if there's any news?"

There was a small crowd in front of one of the dockside taverns. Saba led the way to Omer, who stood in front of the door.

"Is there news?" she asked.

"Aye," Omer said. "Calder Rahmson, the Arressan Council has agreed to let you keep the ship the *Pathfinder*. They asked me to request that you meet with them in the morning so the papers transferring ownership to you can be drawn up."

"I'll be happy to meet with them," Calder said. He'd expected this, but as he'd said before, he didn't really want the ship. He'd talk to Esma. Maybe they could share ownership and the profits from trading. After all, now that Rahm was gone, he had no idea how Saba would support her family.

"Inger Lund," Omer said. "The council would like your help in persuading the Fair Seas Treaty Alliance to sell ship building timber." Omer looked at Calder. "They might ask for your help as well."

Calder grinned. "That means they've made a decision about Floros."

"It does." Omer nodded. "Thekla Floros admitted to her part in the attack against Zelesso."

"She admitted it?" Calder was surprised. "Why?"

"Apparently she was angry at being detained," Omer said. "In her anger she said that she hoped Fihaldo Pinho attacked Messanos, just as they had planned the attack on Zelesso. By her own admission, she is a traitor."

"What is the penalty?" Calder asked. The Three imprisoned criminals for years, but sometimes restitution was also demanded.

"Death," Omer said. "The council does not have any leeway in the sentence, just in how it is carried out."

"Can we speak to the council?" Inger asked. She met Calder's eyes. "Charis won't like having no choice in the sentence."

"I am sorry," Omer replied. "Council is still deliberating the manner of carrying out Floros's sentence. Calder, please come back in the morning for your appointment."

"I'll be here," Calder said. He stepped away from the entrance to the tavern. He didn't feel relief, exactly. Execution was extremely harsh, though Floros had betrayed the country she should have been serving. It did mean that Floros would never again be a threat.

The group was sombre as they made their way through the streets back to Saba's house.

PIA GLANCED AWAY for a moment to rest her eyes, that was all. But when she looked back up at the rigging, Rahm was gone.

Where was he? She Concentrated, hoping to see him amongst the sails and ropes above her.

"Lose something?" a voice whispered in her ear. She whirled around and was face to face with the assassin.

"I saw you and the other one," Rahm said. "Gustav. You're not incredibly good at hiding what you're doing."

Pia shrugged. "We were told to keep watch," she said. "To see where you go."

"Why am I still up there?" he asked. "If you know I'm on

board. Is everyone scared of me?"

"Shouldn't we be?" Pia asked. "You kill people all the time. What's one more to you?"

"I don't do that anymore," Rahm said, but his grin didn't reassure Pia. Or make her feel safe.

"It's only been a few days since Ottosen died," Pia said. "I'm not sure you can be confident that you won't kill anyone else."

He scowled. "It was different without my token," he said. "It . . . bothered me." His face brightened. "But then I thought about what a huge favour I did for you." He leaned in closer. "One less task for you. Do you want to know what happened at the end?"

Pia glared at him. She wanted to know that Ottosen was afraid, that he begged for his life, that he felt terror knowing that he was about to die and that there was nothing he could do to stop it. Instead, she drew in a breath. "You're still up there because Gustav and I told Dagrun Lund that you hated the cold." His eyes narrowed for a moment, and she knew he was angry. Then, he smiled.

"They're letting me stay," he said. "They *are* afraid."

"We're being cautious."

Pia looked over Rahm's shoulder. Dagrun stood behind him, her hands on her hips. Rahm slowly turned around to face her, and Pia edged closer to Dagrun.

"Intelligencer," Rahm said.

"Resolute," Dagrun replied. "The captain of this ship is aware that you are both a thief and a stowaway. She has the right to throw you overboard."

"But you talked her out of it," Rahm said. "Because what would my son say when he learned that you had a part in his father's death."

"We came up with a solution," Dagrun said. "One you need to agree to. But remember, the other option is always available."

"I'm listening," Rahm replied.

"You can stay on this ship," Dagrun said. "And work your passage off. Until we reach Lavais Port, you will work aloft and will not eat with the crew, since you have your stolen rations. While we stop at Lavais Port, you will remain on board, in the hold. Once we're back under sail, you can bunk and eat with the crew until our next destination."

"Why can't I come in from the cold now?" Rahm asked.

"Because we are carrying a captain and crew for the newly built ship," Dagrun said. "I do not want you mingling with them."

"You don't trust them," Rahm said.

"I don't trust *you*," Dagrun replied. "We will set you ashore at a place that is convenient for us. If you behave, Calder and I might stop in to see you next time we pass by."

"You're setting me ashore on Strongrock," Rahm said with a laugh. "I believe Margit Ansdottir's *Vassan* is there. What makes you think I'll stay there?"

"I am hoping that you will promise to remain there for a few years," Dagrun said. "I know that you are an accomplished liar, but *I will know* if you lie to me about this. Think about it. I'll be back in an hour for your decision."

Dagrun left, and Pia Concentrated on Rahm.

He would do it; she could tell. He would, in good faith, promise to stay on Strongrock. Whether he could keep that promise was a different matter.

"I have an hour," Rahm said, turning to her. "I would dearly appreciate a cup of hot tea."

"Why would I get you that?" Pia asked.

"Because I did a task that you now don't have to," he replied. "Besides, if you stand there watching me for the next hour, I will tell you about Henrik Ottosen's death. Your choice."

For a moment, Pia's feet were rooted to the deck. Wind whipped around her, but she barely noticed. She desperately wanted to know that Ottosen had seen Rahm, had understood what it meant and that he'd been terrified at the end. But she was afraid that knowing would change her.

"Right after we arrived in town and parted ways," Rahm said.

Pia sprinted away from him, his laugh chasing her until she was inside.

NADEZ EXITED THE feeding centre and headed towards the river. That was the last warehouse, and unless Rahm was stealing food from someone who hadn't reported it, she had to conclude that he wasn't in the city.

The system Lauma had put in place was pretty stringent: only people who were registered would receive a meal. It was a fairness measure to ensure that no one received extra rations, but it was also effective at finding out who had newly arrived in the city.

Nadez used Key Bridge to cross the river. The Hall was just ahead, and she debated heading somewhere else, anywhere else, to have a few hours away from her duties.

She sighed. The combination of never having quite enough to eat and having far too much to do drained her energy. But they were close to the end now. Hopefully, the worst was behind them.

A few warm days had chased most of the ice from the harbour. The Frozen Pass wouldn't be open yet, but the *Tazeyar* had survived the winter. Captain Eklund was getting it ready to sail north, taking Noak and Thorben with him. If they were hindered by ice, the Byholters would use their ice boat and return home, stopping along the coasts of Nordmere and Byholt and delivering some of the new food supplies.

Any little evidence of success should give desperate people some hope.

Instead of going to her office, Nadez turned a corner and made her way towards Lauma's.

No matter how much work was waiting for the Master Intelligencer, the Intcrim Grand Freeholder always seemed to have more.

"Are you busy?" Nadez asked as she entered Lauma's offices.

"Always," the other woman called out. "But come in anyway. I can even offer you tea."

"Thank you." Nadez sat down across from Lauma and gratefully took the mug held out to her. "I didn't look. Did the *Tazeyar* set sail yet?"

"An hour ago," Lauma said. "I made tea to celebrate." She picked up her own mug and took a sip. "Any news of my former husband?"

"No." Nadez cradled the cup in her hands, enjoying the warmth. "No one at any of the feeding centres has seen him, and there have been no reports of food thefts. He could have gone back along the road. The merchant, Pavil Barda, would have food on hand."

"I can't see him going back that way," Lauma said. "I still think he would try to see me if he was in the city."

"Maybe he went north?" Nadez suggested.

"Rahm hates the cold," Lauma replied. "That was his excuse for being away in the Sapphire Sea for most of our marriage. I think he managed to get on board the *Atlaine*."

Steps crossed the floor of the outer office, and someone knocked. A guard poked his head into the office.

"There's news from Clan Ottosen," the guard said. "They've asked to meet with you."

"Are they here now?" Lauma asked.

The guard nodded. "I hope you don't mind. I saw the Master Intelligencer arrive earlier, so I thought it would be all right to have them come in."

"Yes," Lauma said. "That's fine. We'll meet them in the outer office." The guard left, and Lauma met Nadez's eyes and shrugged. "I guess they've decided who inherits the Clan Freeholdership." She got to her feet. "Shall we see who it is?"

Nadez nodded and got to her feet slowly. She needed a moment to compose herself. Whoever it was most likely had murdered Rein, and she needed to keep her disgust and anger at bay.

Tessan Ottosen stood nervously by the door, looking like she wanted to run away. An older man Nadez recognized as Freeholder Olvir Jarvi stood beside her, a hand on her arm. A younger man wandered around the office; Jarvi's son if she wasn't mistaken.

"Tessan," Lauma said. "How good to see you. And Freeholder Jarvi, I welcome both you and your son Konsta."

"It's Clan Freeholder Jarvi now," Olvir said. "As I'm sure you've guessed."

"Tessan Ottosen," Lauma said. "You must make a formal declaration. I will have someone write it up and send it to you for your signature."

"Yes, just do it," Tessan said. "Olvir . . ." she glanced at him. "Clan Freeholder Jarvi has been kind enough to provide a home for me and my children for however long we need one. So you can send the document to him, and he will make sure I get it."

"I still need you to say it," Lauma said gently.

"I, Tessan Ottosen, as the widow of Clan Freeholder Henrik Ottosen, give up any claim either I or my children might have to the Clan Freeholdership that my husband held."

"Thank you." Lauma turned to Olvir. "You will need to sign the document as well."

"Good," Olvir said, stepping over to Lauma. "I am also making

Konsta my heir."

"I'll add that to the document," Lauma said. "Congratulations to you. I look forward to working with you next time the council meets."

Tessan sidled over to Nadez, pulled something from her pocket, and shoved it at her. "Rein found this," she whispered. "It's safer with you." She quickly went back to stand by the door.

Olvir looked at Lauma. "Is that all? I was expecting something more."

Nadez closed her fist around a piece of paper. Whatever it was, Tessan had obviously kept it from Olvir, which meant she was taking a risk giving it to Nadez.

"That is all until the next council meeting," Lauma said. "That is where you and your heir will formally be presented to the other Clan Freeholders."

"But I'm Clan Freeholder now?"

"Unofficially, yes," Lauma said. "I will have someone send you the documents for yours and Tessan's signatures."

"Good," Olvir said. "I'll be expecting them." He turned and guided Tessan out of the room, his son following.

Once they were gone, Nadez let out the breath she'd been holding.

"Tessan Ottosen is doing this under duress," she said.

"Yes," Lauma agreed. "She's also doing this to try to save her children."

"You don't think it will," Nadez said. "Save them. You think that Olvir Jarvi will murder them too."

Lauma sighed. "I think that Tessan knew exactly who she was marrying," she said. "Including how he inherited the Clan Freeholdership. Unfortunately, she may not be the only one to pay for that decision."

"He won't kill them right away," Nadez replied. "It would be far too suspicious."

"No, he won't kill them right away," Lauma agreed. "Sadly, there are many ways that children can die as they grow older."

"Tessan gave me this," Nadez said, holding out her hand. "Said that Rein found it and that it was safer with me."

She carefully unrolled the balled-up piece of paper and spread it out on top of the desk.

"It's a letter to Henrik Ottosen," she said and frowned. "From

Valda Skala." She peered at the script. *"Clan Freeholder,"* she read. *"I regret to inform you that I have no information regarding any "secret" children. Perhaps if you were more specific, I could help you, but your request was so vague that I cannot answer with specifics. Regards, Valda Skala."* Nadez sucked in a breath. "Ottosen must have meant Pia and Frida."

"At least Valda refused to give him any information," Lauma said. "And Tessan is right that this is better in your hands. Bad enough that Ottosen had some questions. I would not want a man like Olvir Jarvi to learn about potential rivals."

"But why not simply destroy it?" Nadez asked. "Why risk giving me the letter?"

"I suspect Tessan will want something in return," Lauma replied. "No doubt we'll find out sooner or later."

GUSTAV EDGED AWAY from the crowd that had gathered to greet the *Atlaine.*

Berna was there of course, along with Kaja. After a brief conversation, Berna turned and led Dagrun through the crowd towards the shipbuilding office. The captain and crew for the new ship were still being ferried to shore, so he had time to get what he needed.

"I'm heading straight to Solvig's warehouse to see Frida," Pia said from his side. "What are you planning? And don't say *nothing.*"

"Did you use your Trait on me?" he asked. "That's not very nice." But he grinned. Obviously, Pia hadn't told anyone that he was going to do something without permission. Which meant she might help him. "Come on, you need to get some supplies."

Pia gave him a long look before she nodded. "I'll help you."

"Thanks." Gustav led the way to the dining hall. With most people trying to find out news from Tarklee, it was empty.

They stepped into the kitchen. Gustav had his pack with him. There wasn't much in it: at least, not yet. He pulled out his waterskin along with a second one he'd found on the ship and filled them from the barrel. Pia filled hers after him.

He paused in front of the food stores. This felt like stealing even though he would be due a share if he stayed in Lavais Port. Pia lifted the lid of a large pot.

"This," she said. "Cooked beans and barley." She grabbed a

crock from a nearby shelf and spooned the mixture into it. Once it was full, she wrapped a waxed cloth over it and tied it tight with string. "Are you doing this or not?" Pia asked.

"Doing it," Gustav replied. He filled a second crock and bundled them both into his pack. He hefted it onto his back.

"I need to get back to the ship," he said. "Unnoticed."

"That will be impossible," Pia said.

"Rahm did it," he replied. "Somehow he got on board without anyone noticing him."

"Or he threatened to kill anyone who told that they saw him," Pia replied. "Come on. It's not about not being seen, it's about who *remembers* seeing you."

Gustav followed her back out to the dock. Half a dozen sailors were stepping out of an iceboat.

"Hey," Pia called to the man in the back of the boat. "We left some gear on board. Can you take us back out to the ship?"

"Get in," the man said. "I have one last group to pick up. Mind, you'll need to be quick about getting your gear and getting back to the boat."

"Sure." Pia climbed into the iceboat, and in minutes they were heading towards the *Atlaine*. "Are you part of the crew for the new ship?" Pia asked the man. She signalled for Gustav to be quiet and keep his head down.

"Yep," the man replied. "And feeling lucky about it. Never crewed a brand new ship afore."

Gustav tuned out the conversation and stared out at the *Atlaine* as they drew closer. He was nervous. Ever since he'd found out that Rahm had stowed away and had been allowed to stay, he'd been thinking about this. Thinking about how to stay on the ship and travel to the Sapphire Sea.

He was hoping that bringing his own food would make Dagrun and Captain Demer go easy on him. And that it allowed him to be undetected until they were far enough from Lavais Port that they couldn't turn around or send him home in a dinghy.

When they reached the *Atlaine*, he followed Pia up the rope ladder to the deck.

"I'll make sure that sailor doesn't miss you on the way back to port," Pia said. "Find a place inside to hide. You don't want to be stuck in the cold like Rahm."

"I already have a spot picked out," Gustav replied. "Besides, I don't know how to crew a ship like this."

"Good luck." Pia nodded and left.

He watched her join the people waiting to board the ice boat. A few minutes later, the boat was headed back to shore. Careful not to be seen, Gustav made his way to the hold.

It was empty now that the crew for the new ship was gone and the *Atlaine*'s crew was busy getting ready to sail.

He'd left a blanket in one of the topmost hammocks, so he climbed up and settled in, pulling the blanket over his head. His plan was to stay where he was—unnoticed—as long as he could.

"I won't tell," said a voice to his left, and Gustav froze. "If you promise to share whatever food you brought on board."

Gustav lifted the blanket and peered out. Across the hold, in another top hammock, Rahm stared at him.

"Sure," Gustav replied, wondering how he'd missed the fact that he wasn't alone. "I'll be happy to share." He wasn't about to refuse a Resolute.

"Don't worry," Rahm said. "I'm crewing, so I won't be here that much, but I want the extra rations."

"All right," Gustav said. Rahm nodded, and Gustav drew the blanket over him again.

Despite Rahm's words, Gustav was worried. No one on this ship even knew he was here. A murderer, an assassin, could drop him overboard, and he would disappear without a trace. Nobody would even miss him until the *Atlaine* returned to Lavais Port and Pia searched for him. He could be weeks dead by the time he was even missed.

What had seemed like such an adventure now felt foolishly dangerous. He stayed as still as possible. An hour later, the ship rolled and started to move. He heard Rahm jump down from his hammock.

"I'll take my share now," he called out from directly below Gustav.

Gustav drew back the blanket and lowered his pack down.

"Done," Rahm said. "I hope you aren't hiding anything from me."

When Gustav pulled his pack back up it was noticeably lighter.

"Everything I brought is in the pack," Gustav said. He pulled the blanket back over him and looked in his pack. One crock and one water skin remained.

Rahm rustled around for a moment and then the hold was silent.

Gustav took a deep breath and clutched his pack to his chest. Right now, being put in a dinghy and rowing it back to Lavais Port didn't seem like such a terrible thing.

"IT'S TIME TO GO." Calder stood by the front door of Saba's house.

"I'm ready," Inger said, joining him. "Saba is staying here."

"All right." He opened the door and stepped out into the street. "Any idea what they will do to Floros?" The Three didn't execute anyone, not even murderers, but he supposed that a country who allowed the suicide assassins to operate had a different view on life and death.

"No," Inger said. "I can't imagine what it was like to argue about which is the best way to kill someone."

"Me either."

They walked in silence until they reached the tavern. Omer was waiting at the open door.

"There you are," Omer said. "The council just now asked for you. Follow me."

He led them into the tavern. Like most drinking establishments, this one could have done with a thorough cleaning. Smoke stains shadowed the hearth in the centre of the room and very little sunlight penetrated the grimy windows.

The Arressan Council stood near the bar where a pot of tea had been set out.

"Inger, Calder," Charis said as he came towards them. "Good. Let's get this done, and then we can all go back home."

"We have drawn up documents that name you as the owner of the *Pathfinder*," Jurgus said as he approached them.

"I'd like to add Esma and Kasim to that document," Calder said. He took the papers that Jurgus held out to him.

Charis grinned at Jurgus. "I told you he didn't want the ship." He looked at Calder. "Now I wonder why I didn't realize that you would name your siblings as co-owners. Nilus, can you take care of that?" Charis took the papers from Calder and handed them to the older man.

"Thank you," Calder said. "I think the next thing to deal with is the council's request for timber for shipbuilding. I will advise my mother to sell to you, but I have no authority to force her to."

"I can only do the same," Inger said. "As the Merchant Adventurers representative in Messanos, I can only advise and then do my best to make the transactions go as smoothly as possible."

"Understood," Jurgus said. "None of us expects more than that." He sighed. "I formally request permission to bring Thekla Floros back on board the *Pathfinder*. We would like to carry out her sentence in Messanos."

"Permission granted," Calder replied.

"Thank you." Jurgus hesitated. "It is Floros's wish to die in her own home, and we have agreed to allow it."

"And the method?" Calder asked.

"One she chose herself," Charis said. "Poison. We will have a healer on hand to help her through the process, and most of the council will bear witness."

"Everyone except me will attend," Audra said. She was staring out a dirty window. "Because I am the only friend she has left on this council."

"She must be executed," Nilus said. "You voted for an automatic death sentence for traitors. At Floros's insistence, I might add. You can't suddenly change your mind about the law because it affects someone you call a friend." He handed the papers back to Calder. "I never voted for any of this, but it must be done."

"We could change the law," Audra said. "If we wanted to."

"I *will not*," Jurgus said. "I voted for it as well, and I still believe it to be the right thing to do. Nilus and Charis have both sided with me on not re-opening that discussion."

"I hate this law," Nilus said. "But changing it now in order to save a council member would send a terrible message to the people of Arressa. We can look at it in a year or two, but not right now. And not for Floros."

Calder met Inger's eyes. "If that is all you need from us, we should go. I'll have the ship ready to sail early this afternoon."

"Thank you," Charis said.

"It sounds like Thekla Floros was caught in a trap she created," Calder said to Inger once they were back outside. "No doubt the treason law was meant for people opposing her and Pinho."

"People like Charis," Inger said. "That's who they would have targeted with that law. And because of that, I can't even feel sorry for her."

"Same here," Calder replied. He was fairly sure Floros didn't want their sympathy anyway.

CHAPTER 12

P IA ENTERED THE shipbuilding office. She'd Concentrated on the weather: a storm was brewing, so she needed to leave right away. In case she didn't make it to Solvig's before the storm hit, she was picking up a tent from the supply room.

No one had questioned her about Gustav when she'd left the ship, and now she wanted to leave Lavais Port before someone here asked about him. She hadn't had to lie, and she didn't want to.

"Pia, there you are."

Pia's heart sank when Kaja paused in the hallway near the main office.

"Are you coming to give your briefing about Rahm?" Kaja asked.

"Can I do it another day?" Pia replied. "I need to see Frida. If I don't leave now, I'll be stuck here until the storm is over. I left Solvig's warehouse with Rahm, so she's probably really worried about me."

"Of course," Kaja said. "Dagrun's report was very detailed, so I'm sure Berna can wait a couple of days."

"Thanks," Pia said. "I'm just grabbing a tent because a storm will hit by nightfall. Just in case I get caught in it."

"I won't keep you then," Kaja replied. "Have a safe trip, and I'll see you in a few days." She looked around. "Do you know where Gustav is?"

"I haven't seen him in a while," Pia lied. "Maybe he's checking on the new ship's progress. Has it been named yet?"

"Not yet," Kaja said. "Janni and Jarri wanted to wait for the captain and crew before deciding what to call it. I'm sure I'll find Gustav somewhere around here."

Pia made her way to the supply room as fast as she could. She didn't want to run into anyone else and have to answer more questions about Gustav. She had *not* wanted to lie to anyone, let alone a fellow Intelligencer, especially not for something she didn't even think Gustav should be doing.

But he'd asked for her help, not her opinion, and she'd hoped to be on her way to Solvig's warehouse by the time anyone missed him.

With a tent tied to her pack, she ducked out a back door and set off on foot across the island.

Enough snow had melted over the past few days that it was easy walking for the first half of her trip. Then the weather turned: the sky darkened, and the wind picked up. Half an hour later, snow started to fall in a steady stream of fat, wet flakes. With swirling snow making it hard for her to see more than a few feet in front of her, she Concentrated on keeping her feet on the correct path.

"Pia!"

Pia snapped out of her fog of Concentration. Frida was running towards her. Her little sister threw herself into her arms, and she hugged her tight.

"I was so worried when you left with that man," Frida said. "He was dangerous, wasn't he?"

"Yes," Pia said, stepping out of her sister's embrace. "Which is why I wanted him away from here."

"Is he gone for good?"

"I hope so," Pia replied. Rahm was Dagrun Lund's problem now, and that actually gave her comfort. She didn't think Rahm could keep secrets from Dagrun for long, and Pia knew how dangerous secrets could be.

"There's Solvig," Frida said, pointing at the figure standing in the door to the warehouse. "Come on, she won't be happy about letting the warm air out."

"It's good you're here, Pia," Solvig said. She stepped aside so Pia and Frida could enter the warehouse before closing the door tight against the storm.

"I'm glad I'm here too." Pia walked a few paces into the warehouse. There was only a single rack of dried fish left, and there wasn't a fire in the large space. "Have you been all right on your own?"

"Aye. I'm used to wintering with just a few folk," Solvig said. "And Frida here is better company than the fishermen I usually spend the winter with."

"Solvig's teaching me so many things," Frida said. "I can already fix a fishing net, and next she's going to show me how to make one."

"That sounds like a really useful skill," Pia said.

"In the spring, I'll use it to catch fish all by myself," Frida said. "Then I'll be able to do everything: make a net, catch fish, dry it, and then cook it.

"What about cleaning it?" Pia asked.

"Oh, I'll do that too," Frida replied. "Although I don't much like it."

"Me neither." Pia shifted her pack to one shoulder. "The storm is going to get worse. Is there anything you need me to do? Is there enough wood?"

"We should have enough," Solvig said. "Come on. It will be very cosy in my little apartment but having the one fire saves on firewood." She led the way to her living quarters.

"Here," Pia said, handing her coat to Frida. "Why don't you hang this up for me? It needs to dry off."

"It's good that you came back," Solvig said quietly. "Frida was afraid. She kept saying that Hakon was dangerous. As if I couldn't see that with my own eyes."

"He's an assassin," Pia said.

"He told you that?"

"I didn't learn that until later," Pia said. "Gustav and I met him in Setberg. We could tell he was dangerous, so there wasn't really a choice: we made a deal with him. He would make the pirates leave Nurmi in exchange for Intelligencers doing him a favour in Lavais Port."

"Not a man I'd like to bargain with," Solvig replied, and Pia shivered.

She'd spent days with Rahm, and the more she knew about him, the more she agreed with Solvig. The bargain she and

Gustav made with Rahm might have been the only time someone got the better deal, although Rahm had felt that the price he'd paid was small, compared to what he received.

"All done," Frida said.

"Come and sit," Solvig said. "I'll make tea and Pia, you can tell us the news."

Pia sat down, and for a moment she just watched Solvig putter about the kitchen. Then she took a deep breath.

"Henrik Ottosen is dead."

Frida's head came up, and she stared at Pia, her face pale. "Is he really dead?" she asked. "We can go home if we want to?"

"He's really dead," Pia repeated. "And we can go wherever we want to now." At least she hoped they could. She wasn't going to tell Frida about Nadez Norup's revelation. That they had a claim to the Clan Freeholdership. The fewer people who knew about that, the better. She didn't even like that *she* knew.

"Ottosen was the one you were running from." Solvig set the tea down on the table. "Knew you were getting away from someone."

"Was he murdered?" Frida asked in a soft voice. "Did he make the wrong person mad and they killed him?"

"Yes," Pia replied. "That's exactly what happened." There was no need to share that it was the head of the suicide assassins who was angered, or that the man she knew as Hakon was a Resolute who had killed Ottosen.

"He wasn't a very nice man," Frida said.

"No, he wasn't," Pia agreed.

DAG WIPED AWAY the sweat that was cooling on her brow.

"You are getting much better," Rafael said from her side. "I only had to correct two of your calls."

"It's still harrowing," she said. "And I'm not sure that will ever change." They were through the Teeth with an hour of daylight left, which meant they wouldn't arrive at Strongrock until well after dark.

"I don't know about *harrowing*," Rafael said. "But if you get complacent, the chances are greater that you'll make a mistake. One that could cost lives."

"I don't think complacent is going to happen any time soon. I'm going to head to the mess for some tea, want to join me?"

"Thanks, but no. I need to check in with the captain."

Tea in hand, Dag was wondering if she should drink it in the mess or take it up on deck when her Trait triggered. She closed her eyes, and when she opened them, her gaze fell on Rahm. She made her way over to him.

"Do you spend much time in here?" she asked. The itch between her shoulder blades intensified when he turned to look at her.

"Just getting some water," he replied with a smirk. "Can't have me fall out of the rigging because I'm faint with dehydration."

"What are you hiding?" she asked, and his eyes narrowed. "That you weren't hiding the last time we spoke. What happened in Lavais Port?"

"I didn't set foot off the ship," he said. "And as per your order, I stayed in my berth, in the hold, the whole time we were at anchor."

Her Trait twitched again. So, it had something to do with where he'd been. "It's not too late to throw you overboard," she said. "What will I find when I check your berth?"

"It's not my fault," Rahm said. "Remember that."

"We'll see." She set her untouched tea on an empty table and exited the mess. She made her way to the hold and stood looking at the hammocks that were strung up above.

Her eyes immediately settled on a hammock high up in a far corner. The hammock moved as whoever was in it shifted.

"Come out now," she called out. "Your pact with Rahm is over." A couple of sailors peered out at her from their own hammocks, but the one she was staring at stilled.

"I know you came on board at Lavais Port," Dag said. "The captain will not be happy if I need to bring her down here."

"Are we through the Teeth?"

"Why does it matter?" Dag asked. A face peered over the edge of the hammock. "Gustav?"

"You can't send me back if we're through the Teeth," he said. He rolled and flipped out of the hammock, hanging from it before letting go and dropping to the deck.

"Says who?" Dag replied. "Captain Demer makes the decision on what to do with a stowaway, and she might decide otherwise."

"She let Rahm stay," Gustav said. "When he stowed away."

"And we're dropping him off at Strongrock Island," she said.

"Where the captain might decide she should leave both stowaways. You're taking a big chance. Why?"

"I want to see the Sapphire Sea," Gustav replied.

She stared at him until he dropped his eyes to the deck. "I expected more from an Intelligencer," she said. "Come on. You need to explain yourself to the captain."

He followed her up to the wheel deck.

"Captain Demer," Dag said. "We have another stowaway."

"Gustav!" Darya said. "How did you even get on board? I saw you leave this ship in Lavais Port."

"I'm sorry," Gustav said, and Dag thought he finally looked sorry. "I said I forgot something in order to get back on board, and then I hid."

Dag scratched between her shoulder blades. "You will make things much worse for yourself unless you tell us the whole truth," she said. She shook her head. He knew he couldn't hide anything from her, so why was he trying?

Gustav sighed. "Pia helped me. But it wasn't her fault, it was mine. It was my idea. She said she'd make sure nobody questioned why I wasn't on the boat going back to shore."

"How did Rahm find out?" she asked. Darya raised a brow, and Dag rolled her eyes.

"He was there when I hid in the hold," Gustav said.

"What was in it for him?" Dag asked. "Rahm didn't tell anyone you were here, and he's not the type to do favours for anyone who is not family." And even then, he couldn't be counted on.

"I had to share my food and water with him," Gustav said.

"Where did *you* get that food and water," Darya asked. "It wasn't stolen from this ship because Cook increased security after the first theft."

"It's my rations from Lavais Port," Gustav said. "I figured it's what I would have eaten if I was there so . . ."

"Berna doesn't know about this," Dag said. "No one at Lavais Port gave you permission."

Gustav shook his head. "I don't really report to Berna," he said.

"You do report to Nadez," Dag said. "And she specifically said that you could not come to the Sapphire Sea." She sighed. "This is very serious. Captain Demer, what should we do with this stowaway?"

"Gustav, go below and wait for my decision," Darya said.

After a nervous glance at Dag, Gustav left.

"He has to come with us," Darya said. "There's no other option, so you need to help me figure out how to discipline him."

"I am very sorry," Dag said. "I'll speak to Nadez when we return to Tarklee. Gustav and Pia have been working independently, and they have been remarkably effective. I think they forgot that they don't make all the decisions." She paused. "And the rest of us forgot that they are not fully trained."

"It's something all of us who lead people struggle with," Darya replied. "Pia and Gustav need more discipline, but it must be done without smothering their ability to act independently."

"Yes," Dag replied. "I just didn't think any of that was my responsibility. But I am the more senior Intelligencer on board." She sighed. "As for discipline, I think for the rest of the day, if it's all right with you, I would like Rahm to teach Gustav how to do some work on this ship." She looked above at the rigging. "Maybe not something too dangerous? I don't want Gustav getting hurt."

Darya grinned. "The hold needs a very good cleaning now that it's empty. I will have Rafael assign that to Rahm and Gustav."

"Thank you," Dag replied.

The mess was almost empty when she returned to grab another mug of tea. She sat down at an empty table.

She didn't think Nadez had thought about Pia and Gustav's need for more training either: they'd just put the two of them to work and assumed that they knew how to act. And the pair had done so well that it had been easy to forget that they were young and undisciplined and only half-trained.

They both needed more supervision. She snorted. She probably did too. It was less than a year since she'd had her first assignment.

NADEZ STOOD BEHIND Lauma's chair. It wasn't a full council; there was still too much ice on the Pale Sea for the northern Clan Freeholders to travel. Lauma was the sole representative for Byholt. Melker Skala and Liina Nowack held more than fifty percent of the land in Swyford, so they were a majority, if a vote was needed. All of the Nordmerian Clan Freeholders were here: Saulia Holt and her uncle, Karl Seppa, Daina Heikki, and the new one, the one she thought of as the murderer, Olvir Jarvi.

Nordmere had asked for the meeting, so she wondered if they'd met with Jarvi first. Was he going to work with or against Saulia and her uncle?

"I wish to formally acknowledge Olvir Jarvi," Lauma said. "As the new Nordmere Clan Freeholder. He holds twenty percent of the land in Nordmere. Clan Freeholder Jarvi, do you wish to say anything?"

"It's good to be part of this council," Jarvi said. "And I hope to build productive working relationships with each one of you."

"Congratulations," Heikki said, and the rest of them echoed her, although Lauma didn't think anyone looked particularly happy.

"Now that we've acknowledged our newest council member," Lauma said, "I declare this council valid. We have a majority for each country present, so any decisions we make will be binding." She leaned over the table. "Are there any objections?" She paused for a moment, but no one spoke up. "All right. Clan Freeholder Seppa, you asked for this meeting. Please explain."

"Winter is almost over," he said. "It's time to hold an election for a real Grand Freeholder."

Nadez suppressed the urge to roll her eyes. Lauma's title may have been interim, but she'd been the best Grand Freeholder in Nadez's memory.

"I agree," Lauma replied. "I have no problem with that. Once the Frozen Pass opens, we will have two more ships, in addition to the *Atlaine*, that can sail to the Sapphire Sea and return with food. The spring growing season will be in full swing in the south in a few weeks. We are very close to being out of the crisis."

"You're not going to argue?" Seppa asked.

"You sound disappointed," Lauma replied. "I have been very clear that this was temporary and that I only assumed the role because I knew how important it was that it be done by someone competent and compassionate."

"You took that position over objections," Heikki said.

"It was a compromise agreed to by every country," Lauma said. "There were no objections when I assumed the role—a role I never wanted. Any objections were raised later, when we made changes to the way the Grand Freeholder is elected."

"Giving you the ability to veto anyone you don't like," Heikki said.

"So that *no* country is forced to be governed by someone they think will harm their people," Lauma replied.

"I was in favour of that change," Skala said. "At first reluctantly, but I've thought about it a lot over this past winter. I think that if the wrong Swyford Clan Freeholder had been Grand Freeholder, we would have had chaos and starvation and most likely rebellions that some of us at this table might not have survived. I thank Lauma Strauskas for her stewardship; for getting us to the other side of a disaster that was created by the greed and selfishness of one of us." Skala looked directly at Nadez. "My grandmother Valda has been telling me about some of the terrible things that happened in the past when Grand Freeholders did everything for themselves and nothing for anyone else. I, for one, will be looking for compassion in the next candidates."

"Thank you, Clan Freeholder Skala," Lauma said. "The Treaty dictates that the next Grand Freeholder will be from Swyford. I suggest we task Clan Freeholders Skala and Heikki to consult with their peers and submit candidates for consideration. Agreed?"

"Skala and I agree on behalf of Swyford," Heikki said.

"I agree," Saulia said.

"As do I," Seppa added. "That's a majority for Nordmere."

"I agree as well," Jarvi said. "I would also like to know how soon we can meet for the vote."

"I think the vote could be held about a month from now," Skala said. "It may be spring in the south, but the north will still have travel difficulties for some weeks."

"As I understand it," Jarvi said. "Clan Freeholder Strauskas is the only one required from Byholt."

"Do you think it appropriate for me to exclude my fellow Clan Freeholders?" Lauma asked. "Would you think the same if Nordmere excluded you?"

"I hold too much land for them to ignore me," Jarvi said.

"Just because I hold the majority of land does not mean I don't need or heed the advice of my peers," Lauma said. "We will see what one month brings. If we can hold the vote then, we will. But if I cannot consult with my fellow Byholt Clan Freeholders, I will not be voting."

"That seems fair," Saulia said before Jarvi could respond.

"Uncle?" Seppa nodded. "Nordmere agrees," Saulia finished.

Jarvi scowled at Saulia, but he didn't say anything else. Nadez watched him as the group filed out of the room.

"Should we warn Saulia about Olvir Jarvi?" she asked Lauma once they were alone.

"I have no doubt that Saulia knows exactly who and what Jarvi is," Lauma replied. "In fact, I wouldn't be surprised if she makes an alliance with Clan Jarvi."

"An alliance? With a murderer?" Nadez was shocked. "Why? And how?"

"An alliance with the *clan*," Lauma replied. "Because Olvir is dangerous. As you said, he has committed murder with no penalty and a great benefit. It does seem to be a family tradition, and he might think he could do it again. As to how, I expect it could be by means of the Holt family tradition: through marriage. Olvir Jarvi has more than one son."

"I suppose the trick will be to pick one she trusts," Nadez replied.

"If Saulia doesn't already know which, if any, she can trust, then no one can help her," Lauma said.

"Dag is due back soon," Calder said to Inger. She was waiting for her turn to climb down into a dinghy for the short row to Messanos. Charis and the rest of the council, as well as Thekla Floros, were already on shore.

"I'll start sourcing food," Inger replied. "For both the *Atlaine* and the *Pathfinder*. I wish I could stay on board. I really don't want to be in the city during the execution." She sighed and turned to him. "But I know you have things to do."

Calder grunted. His *things to do* included trying to find out where Pinho was. The first place he planned on looking was Strongrock because if Pinho was there, it meant he had a ship and men to help him start his campaign all over.

"Take care," Inger said. She hugged him and climbed over the gunwale.

"You too," Calder said. He watched the dinghy until it was halfway to the dock before he went sternward to the wheel.

"Are we ready to sail?" Esma asked. She was standing beside the wheel with First Mate Nataniel.

"We are," Calder said. "Nataniel, can you take us out? Make a course to Strongrock Island."

"Aye, Captain," Nataniel replied. He called out an order to haul the anchor, and Calder edged out of the way, Esma trailing him.

"It's a lot different from sailing the *Hakon*," she said.

"The basics are the same," Calder replied. "You need wind in the sails and enough draught that you don't run aground. But the crew needs directions. Watch Nataniel and Luiza as much as you can," he continued, referring to the Second Mate. "That's if you want to learn."

"Of course, I do," Esma replied. "You're sharing this ship, so I need to be able to take care of it. Even if I never actually captain it, I need to know enough to hire a good one. Besides." She grinned at him. "I am not letting Kasim be better at this than me."

"I told you that I'd give it to you outright if you want," Calder said.

"I'm not ready for that," Esma replied. "It's a much bigger responsibility than I expected. All these people making a living and a life on board. I don't know enough to not make bad decisions, but I do know that a bad decision at sea can be deadly to everyone on board."

"See?" Calder said. "You've already learned two of the most important lessons. That a captain can be a danger to everyone on board and that you need to be able to recognize when you don't know enough." He stared at the quickly receding city. "I'm going below to get out of everyone's way. Come find me if you notice anything wrong."

"You're assuming I will know," Esma replied.

"You'll know if someone isn't following orders," he said. "Even though you might not be able to tell if the orders themselves are a danger."

During the trip to and from Zelesso, he'd gotten a bit of a feel for who on the crew could be trusted and who was careless, but that was with him captaining the ship.

He needed to be able to trust his First and Second Mates, and the crew needed to obey them. Which meant Calder couldn't stay on deck and watch.

"I'll come find you if that happens," Esma said.

"Thank you." Calder headed down to the captain's cabin. When he'd boarded the ship, he'd searched all of the cabins for anything that might have information about Fihaldo Pinho and especially any unknown allies. He hadn't seen anything in the few minutes he'd had with the documents in the captain's cabin, but now that he had some time, he was hoping to make a more thorough search.

Most recently, the Arressan Council had been using the cabin. Chairs ringed the table, and empty mugs had been set on a tray near the door. He dragged the chairs away from the table and lined them up along the walls.

Papers and maps had been stacked on a side table, and Calder moved the whole pile onto the main table. Standing, he went through them one by one, reading every word, trying to decipher every note.

At the end, he had a large stack of papers that looked unimportant and four papers, including one map, that he thought might help him uncover at least some of Pinho's secrets.

He stared at the map of the Sapphire Sea. Cryptic notes dotted the coastline, mostly in Arressan and Pilalian. He was certain that one spot was where Rahm's token had been hidden, but whether the rest held dangerous people or goods, he didn't know.

And if Pinho was dead, did any of this matter? He hadn't heard anything about the man that made him think his allies would continue to be a threat without him.

Dag would be able to figure it out, but who knew when he'd see her next? It was possible the *Atlaine* would sail into Messanos, fill her hold, and sail back out before he returned from this search.

The light was failing, and instead of lighting a lamp, he put the papers away and headed up to the deck.

He paused on the way up as a thought crossed his mind. Thekla Floros would be dead now. Even if he didn't find Pinho, the Arressan Council was safer from any future meddling by him.

He stepped out on deck to a spectacular sunset.

CHAPTER 13

GUSTAV LEANED OUT over the bow. Strongrock Island, a place that, until now, had only been a point on a map, was straight ahead, although he couldn't see it yet.

"Did Cook say you could leave the mess?"

He turned to find Dagrun Lund coming towards him.

"He did," Gustav replied. "I finished my duties quickly and don't have to be back until the evening meal."

"Good." She stopped beside him and stared out towards the island. It was late afternoon, and they were heading for the beach with two abandoned fishing huts. She was assuming they were still abandoned since there was a fairly dense forest between them and the settlement.

"Are we going ashore?" he asked. Not that he thought he would be allowed to leave the ship, but if someone was going ashore and coming back, there would be more time to look at the island. If he could finish his kitchen duties, that is.

"We haven't decided yet," Dagrun said. "That's what I'm here to figure out."

"Oh, you're using your Trait."

"I am," Dagrun replied. "Trying to see if there are any Hidden dangers. Tell me about the pirates that were in Nurmi."

"Oh." He paused trying to remember. "There were eight or nine of them, and their captain was a woman named Ursa Ozlinch."

179

"I know Ursa," Dagrun said. "She's not a sailor but probably has a weak Keeper Trait that makes people look to her for leadership. Who else?"

"A sailor named Benil," Gustav said. "He likes to drink. And he's not very bright. With a few mugs of ale, I was able to convince him to show me the promise to pay note. He kept complaining about the cold. And losing their ship. He seemed to regret following Ursa instead of staying with the rest of the pirates and the ship."

"Do you think any of the others felt the same about her?" Dagrun asked.

"Probably," Gustav replied. "If he would tell that to a stranger, I have to think he would have said it to at least some of the other pirates."

"I agree. Which means Ursa, if she's on Strongrock, is not in charge."

"Rahm would probably know," Gustav said. "He's the one who convinced the pirates to leave Nurmi."

"Getting the truth from Rahm is a challenge," she said. "But let's ask him."

"You want me to come?" he asked, not able to keep the surprise out of his voice. "I thought you were angry at me."

"I am," Dagrun said. "But that doesn't mean I won't use you. You and Pia made a deal with Rahm, and as far as I can tell, everyone delivered on their promises. That might make Rahm trust you." She grimaced. "As far as he trusts anyone. Besides, I think he's more likely to truthfully answer questions about his part of your bargain with you there."

She left the gunwale, and he followed her to the middle of the ship. She stopped beside the mast and peered up.

"Rahm," she called. "Come down. We need to talk."

"Not without the captain's orders," came the reply.

Dagrun shook her head. "I'll be right back."

Dagrun left, and Gustav stared up. Rahm sat on a spar, his feet dangling in air. He waved at him. Gustav frowned and didn't return the wave. He didn't really want to talk to the Pilalian. He might not be an assassin any more, but he was still dangerous.

Dagrun returned with Captain Demer.

"Are you a strong swimmer?" the captain called. "It's not too late for me to throw you overboard. Come down now."

"Aye, Captain." A few seconds later, Rahm dropped to the deck. "What do we need to talk about?"

"Answer their questions truthfully, and that's an order," Captain Demer said before leaving them.

"The pirates in Nurmi," Dagrun said. "How did you get them to leave?"

"I told them that I'd kill them all if they didn't," Rahm replied.

"Would you have?" Gustav asked. "That wasn't part of our bargain."

Rahm smiled, and Gustav suppressed a shiver. "You didn't specify that they had to live." He shrugged. "They agreed to leave, but only after I killed one of them so they knew I wasn't making an idle threat."

"Were they coming here to Strongrock?" Dagrun asked.

"Probably," Rahm replied. "None of them have much imagination, and they didn't have a ship. Even if they did have a ship, Ursa Ozlinch is no captain, no matter what she calls herself."

"Did the rest of them have the skills to sail ice boats from Nurmi to Strongrock?" Dagrun asked.

"Maybe," Rahm replied. "Or maybe they died trying. Not my problem."

"Is anything?" Gustav asked. "Is there anything you actually care about?"

"His family," Dagrun replied. "Isn't that right, Rahm? Although you now have two families who are disappointed with you."

Rahm scowled but didn't reply.

"What do you know about Steen?" Dagrun asked.

"Now that is a good question," Rahm said. "Much more useful to know about him than Ursa."

"Why is that?" Dagrun asked.

"Ursa's power came from Ansdottir," Rahm replied. "And she was always one to follow orders. Steen's not much for orders unless he's giving them."

"But he's not very smart," Dagrun said, and Rahm laughed.

"You've met Steen," he said.

"Yes. I know that he's angry and dangerous."

"Which is why Ursa Ozlinch is not an issue," Rahm said. "If she made it to Strongrock, she's not alive now."

"You think Steen would have killed her."

"He's one to hold a grudge," Rahm said. "And not one to hold his temper."

"You're not afraid of him," Gustav said. "Even though he might have dozens of pirates taking orders from him."

"You don't know anything about pirates," Rahm replied. "Their survival requires them to follow the person most likely to keep them alive. Ansdottir was good at that until she got too greedy and thought making a deal with Tarmo Holt was a way to get rich. Until then, Strongrock was a safe harbour with an inn and a fully stocked tavern. The way Ansdottir targeted ships was smart too. Never taking more than one from any single country in a season meant that the losses were small enough to not provoke retaliation."

"Then she made her deal with Tarmo Holt," Dagrun said. "And Fihaldo Pinho saw an opportunity. And he forced you to put it in motion."

"*Yes.*" One word but said with such anger that Gustav took a half step back.

An order was shouted, and Rahm turned to look across the water.

"If that's all," Rahm said. "I will go and gather my few belongings. We are about to arrive at Strongrock."

"One last thing," Dagrun said. "Should anyone come ashore with you?"

"No," Rahm said. "But next time you pass by, feel free to visit." He sighed and looked away. "I would especially like to see any of my children."

"I'll let Calder know," Dagrun replied.

Rahm nodded and left.

"He actually does care for his family," Gustav said. "I wasn't sure he was even capable of caring for anyone other than himself."

"He's been shaped by his token," Dagrun said, and he thought she sounded a little sad. "You know Berna, Yakop, and Calder a little, and I've met Esma and Kasim. Perhaps, without that token, Rahm would have been more like them."

"You think it's too late for him to change," Gustav said.

"I think *he* thinks it's too late for him to change," she replied. "Which means he won't even try." She turned to him. "But that answers my question. No one else is going ashore."

PIA STEPPED OUT of the warehouse. The wind from the south was warm, and the sky was clear. Even the weak early spring sun would be enough to melt the ice in the small harbour.

"Be time to take the runners off the boats soon," Solvig said from a perch near the dock. She held a fishing pole rather than a net, which Pia took to mean she was whiling away the time rather than desperate to catch their supper.

"I guess we made it to spring then," Pia said. She stopped beside Solvig and sighed.

"I guess we did," Solvig repeated. "Largely due to you and your fellow Intelligencers."

"And Lauma Strauskas," Pia said. She and Gustav had done some important things over the winter, but her last few actions, helping Rahm get to Tarklee and letting Gustav stow away on the *Atlaine*, made her feel guilty.

"Lauma Strauskas was the right Grand Freeholder at the right time," Solvig said. "But she was there because Intelligencers made it possible for her to be there."

"I suppose." Pia sighed again.

"You wanna talk about it?" Solvig asked. "I know something's bothering you."

Pia looked over at her, but the older woman was staring at her fishing line.

"I'm just bored," Pia said. "I've spent the past few months doing things that helped the Three get to this point, and now all I have to do is wait for plants to grow." Even though the ice was melting, it would be another few weeks before anything grew, let alone anything they could eat.

"Just say you don't want to talk," Solvig said. "Instead of giving me a partially true excuse. I know you're bored. But that's not what's bothering you."

Pia hesitated. What if Solvig didn't understand about Ottosen? What if she told her to leave and to take Frida with her?

She blew out a breath. A few months ago, she would have welcomed that choice; now she worried that taking care of her sister meant that she could no longer be an Intelligencer. Not that she felt she deserved that. But she trusted Solvig with her sister, which meant she should tell Solvig the truth.

"I told you that the man you know as Hakon is an assassin." Solvig nodded, so Pia continued. "His real name is Rahm, and he's the one who murdered Henrik Ottosen. I knew he was going to do it, and I *wanted* Ottosen dead. That's one reason why I helped him get to Tarklee."

"He's an assassin, and Ottosen was his target?" Solvig asked. "Yes."

"Someone else wanted Ottosen dead," Solvig said. "Enough to hire an assassin to do it. I don't see any of this as your fault."

"But I helped him," Pia replied.

"We both knew he was dangerous, which is the other reason why you helped get him away from here." Solvig paused. "Rahm. Any relation to Calder Rahmson?"

"Yes," Pia said. "Rahm is Calder's father."

"Does he know what his father is?"

Pia nodded. She didn't need to tell her that Calder had named Ottosen as Rahm's target.

"I doubt you could have stopped a man like that from doing what he did," Solvig said. "Since his own son wasn't able to."

"How do you know Calder tried to stop him?" Pia asked. It was something she'd never thought about partly because she knew that until his token was Unmade, Rahm had no choice. He had to kill or suffer.

"Wouldn't you?" Solvig asked. "And as far as helping him, would it have changed anything if you hadn't?"

"Not about Ottosen," Pia said. "But other people might have been hurt." Like Pavil Barda. She'd been able to convince him to take them to Tarklee in his wagon. Rahm might have killed Pavil and taken his horse and wagon anyway.

"Sounds like there were no good choices," Solvig said. "You did what you could so things didn't get worse. As far as *wanting* Ottosen dead, wanting something isn't a crime. And a man like Henrik Ottosen obviously had more than you wanting him dead."

"Yes." Pia still felt partly to blame, but at least Solvig didn't hate her.

"What else?" Solvig asked. "The Rahm situation was sorted out in Tarklee. You were worried what I would think, not what Intelligencers would do. Now you're worried about them again."

"I helped Gustav stow away on the *Atlaine*," she said. "It was heading through the Teeth to the Sapphire Sea."

Solvig whooped. "That's where he got to," she said with a laugh. "Off on an adventure." She turned to Pia. "And I ask again, would anything have changed if you hadn't helped?"

"He might have been caught," Pia said.

"And he would have been in trouble without having the adventure," Solvig replied. "No one will blame you for anything Gustav does." She chuckled. "Knowing the lad, probably no one will really blame *him*. My guess is he'll make himself useful in some way that makes everyone forget he wasn't supposed to be there. So stop worrying about your part in it. Do you think Gustav is worrying about the consequences?"

"No," Pia said. "He'll just try to do his best to make things better."

"Exactly," Solvig said. She got to her feet. "No luck fishing today." She grinned at Pia. "Leastways no luck catching dinner. Salt fish stew is already on the stove, but I think I'll add a few of those Pilalian spices to it. Should be ready in an hour."

"All right." Pia stared out across the water. She felt as though a weight had been lifted off her shoulders.

She'd been holding herself responsible for Frida for so long—*Ottosen* had been holding her responsible by threatening her little sister unless Pia did what he wanted—that she'd believed that she was responsible for everything. Even things that other people decided to do.

Solvig was right: nothing she had done had changed the outcomes of either situation. Ottosen would still have been assassinated by Rahm, and Gustav would have tried to stow away on the *Atlaine*.

Now she just had to convince Nadez.

"YOU BOTH ARE really bringing the crew along," Calder said. Nataniel was at the wheel, and Luiza stood off to one side, the spyglass in her hands.

"They're eager," Nataniel said. "With so many ships lost, sailors understand that there aren't likely to be many opportunities to work this summer."

"Are they really fine waiting for their pay until we've delivered our first shipment?" When Charis had told him the arrangement, he'd been both relieved and worried.

"The crew understands that you are not a regular trader,"

Luiza said. "And are without a large enough stake to both buy goods and pay their wages straight away."

"It still feels wrong," Calder replied. "But I have no other choice. Esma and I have discussed it, and any profits we see this summer will be split with the crew."

"Like pirates?" Nataniel asked with a laugh.

"I suppose so," Calder replied. "It seems fair, doesn't it?"

"Aye," Luiza replied. "It does. Look." She put the spyglass to her eye. "Strongrock is in sight, Sir."

"Good. This side of the island shouldn't be inhabited, but I'd like to confirm that. Stay well offshore until dark. There's a small beach with a couple of buildings we need to check. It's possible Pinho and his men have made that their base, rather than heading directly to the settlement and a possible conflict with the pirates."

"Yes, Sir," Nataniel said. He called out a few orders, and Calder nodded and headed to the bow where Esma stood staring out at the island.

"I told Nataniel and Luiza that we plan on sharing the profits with the crew," he said.

"Good." She looked over her shoulder at him. "I hate the thought that we can't pay them until we start to trade. They're even sailing us here," she waved a hand toward Strongrock, "with no expectation of pay."

"Let's hope Inger is able to find us goods that we can afford," he said. He'd captained trading ships before, but he'd never been the one who had to pay to fill the hold. He didn't want this, nor could he stay on board. His duty was to the Fair Seas Treaty Alliance and the Three.

"Nataniel and Luiza are doing well," Calder said. "I am worried that he's not quite ready to take over as Captain, but maybe another few weeks will convince me."

"I like both of them," Esma said. "But I have no ability to either captain the ship or know who is capable of that role."

"No," Calder said. "But you are part owner. Having an owner on board makes a difference with the crew and when dealing with traders."

"Sure, so traders know they can take advantage of me."

"Some will," Calder replied. "It's a very short-term strategy, especially when there are so few ships available to buy and ship their goods. Just keep track of who dealt fairly when you were new, and who did not. My advice is to always be honest even with those you can't trust. Eventually, honest tradespeople will search you out."

"That's the long-term strategy?" Esma asked. "Let people take advantage of me so others know I can be trusted? Sounds expensive."

"Learning is always going to cost something," Calder said. "The trick is to figure out what you can afford to pay. In my mind, losing coin and gaining a reputation for trading fairly is the better plan. Remember, on board a ship there are very few secrets: the crew sees pretty much everything that's going on, including how you are dealing with traders. If you want to attract and keep an honest crew, you need them to know that you are honest."

"My mother would agree with you," Esma said.

"So would mine," Calder replied. "It's our father who would not."

"What are we going to do if Pinho is on Strongrock?" Esma asked.

Calder sighed. "Probably nothing. I hate to leave him there with access to a ship, but this is a trading ship and we do not represent any country. Any action we took against Pinho would see us labelled as pirates: we can't afford that. My goal is to find out if he's there and try to determine if the pirates are now working with him."

"You think they will be," Esma said. "And that he'll have use of a ship again."

"I don't know. Pinho betrayed Margit Ansdottir. The *Vassan* was *her* ship. Some of the pirates might not like the way that plays out." He shrugged. "It depends on whether any one of the pirates is willing to fight Pinho for control. All we can do right now is try to find out what's happening."

CHAPTER 14

LAUMA HAD BEEN right. Nadez reread the note from Valda Skala before tearing it up.

Saulia Holt had met in secret with Dren Jarvi, Olvir's youngest son. Nadez had no idea how Valda knew about it, but she didn't doubt the truth of it. Just as she knew about Pia and Frida, something Nadez was still grateful the older woman had kept from Ottosen.

She knocked on the door to Lauma's office and peeked in.

"News about Saulia," she said.

"Come in," Lauma replied. "Which son did she choose?"

"Dren." Nadez sat across from Lauma who nodded.

"That's who I would have suggested." Lauma grinned. "If anyone had asked me. He's the youngest, not even twenty, and as the fifth child, he has very little chance of being anything other than a part of his brother's household."

"Will Saulia be able to manage him?" Nadez asked. "Won't he work against her with his father?"

"I'm sure they've come to an agreement," Lauma replied. "He hasn't distinguished himself as either too compliant or too rebellious with his father. Nor have I heard that he has a cruel streak like his oldest brother Konsta. People I've spoken with about that family seem to think it's because Dren is dull."

"But you don't."

Lauma shrugged. "He did well in his studies. It's possible he's smart enough to not cause any trouble because he knows the consequences could be painful for him. Or perhaps the rest of his brothers compete for attention and Dren is simply outmatched and overlooked. Either way, Saulia could do worse."

"You don't think he will betray Saulia to his father?"

"I suspect Dren will be grateful to be out of his father's house and married to a Clan Freeholder," Lauma said. "One that, with her uncle, holds more power than Olvir Jarvi does."

"It does seem to legitimize Olvir's position as Clan Freeholder," Nadez said.

"He *is* Clan Freeholder," Lauma replied. "Unless you can prove he killed Rein Chebek, he will keep the title."

"I haven't given up," Nadez replied. "But there are so few leads." Not one servant who used to work for Henrik Ottosen had been willing to talk to her. Even Valda Skala had declined, making Nadez wonder if Olvir was a threat to everyone.

"Tessan Ottosen is due here in a few minutes," Lauma said, surprising Nadez. "She wants to discuss something with me. Perhaps she will talk to you."

"Do you know what she wants?" Nadez asked. "I've been asking her to see me for days. Sometimes she doesn't even reply."

"I have an idea why she's coming," Lauma said, and she smiled sadly.

There was a sound in the outside office. Nadez peered out to see a guard enter, followed by Tessan and her three children.

"Tessan Ottosen to see the Grand Freeholder," the guard said.

Lauma rose and went to stand in the doorway to her office. "Thank you. Tessan, I hope you don't mind if the Master Intelligencer joins us? I understand you have not been able to find time to speak with her about Rein Chebek."

Tessan looked like she was about to cry, run away, or maybe both. Then her shoulders drooped, and she looked defeated.

"I won't say anything against my Clan Freeholder," she said.

"You don't have to say anything you are not comfortable saying," Lauma replied. She sent a pointed look Nadez's way. "Come and sit. Your children should be safe enough in the outer office."

Nadez moved over to allow Tessan to sit in the chair next to the door.

The woman sighed and fidgeted for a moment before clasping

her hands and staring at them. "My children are not safe anywhere," she finally said. "That's what I need to talk to you about." She looked over at Nadez before settling her gaze on Lauma. "I ask for your help in making them safer than they are now."

"I see," Lauma replied. "The Master Intelligencer and I have our theories about what happened to your husband and to Rein. Nadez?"

"I can't do anything without witnesses," Nadez replied. "And proof."

"Henrik's fate was almost expected," Tessan said. "At least by me. As for poor Rein, I don't know anything; although, like you, I have a theory. But solving these killings will not help me or my children."

"What will?" Lauma asked.

"I ask that you foster them," Tessan said. "Take them north to Byholt and let them live. Maybe Sigurd can be a logger, or maybe they'll all become sailors. Anything that allows them to grow up."

"What about you?" Nadez asked. This was the plea of a desperate mother.

"I don't matter," Tessan said. "My only purpose right now is to protect my children. And I know that I can't protect them. Certainly not in Nordmere and probably not in Swyford. So that leaves Byholt. Lauma Strauskas is the most powerful Freeholder in Byholt. If she can't protect them, no one can." She looked over at Nadez. "You know I've done my best to keep other children safe. I ask that you both do the same for mine."

Nadez nodded: this was why Tessan had given her Valda's letter, rather than simply destroying it. This was the favour she wanted.

Lauma closed her eyes. When she opened them, she too looked at Nadez. "Tessan needs to know the truth about her husband's death," she said. "While we both appreciate the risks she took to keep those other children safe, I will not let her hand her own children to me unless she does."

Nadez nodded. "It's your secret."

"We know who killed Henrik," Lauma said. "It was a Resolute."

"Oh. I assumed it was the suicide assassins."

"It was on behalf of them," Lauma said. She glanced at Nadez.

"And the Resolute is my former husband. I thought you should know that before you trust me with your children's safety."

"Your former husband is a Resolute?" After a moment, Tessan smiled and relaxed for the first time since she'd arrive in the office. "Then Byholt, under your care, will be the safest place for them."

"It's not something I want known," Lauma said.

"Oh, don't worry," Tessan said. "I won't tell anyone. Does that mean you will foster my children?"

"I will," Lauma replied. "We'll need to wait until the ships are sailing again though. I'll send word when I'm ready."

"Thank you." Tessan stood up. "Thank you. I had nowhere else to turn."

"I will do my best for them," Lauma replied.

It took Tessan a few minutes to gather her children. Once they were gone, Nadez met Lauma's eyes.

"She will talk about Rahm," she said.

"Of course," Lauma replied. "But only to Olvir, and only in order to make sure he is afraid to try to harm her children in Byholt." She smiled. "Rahm has a use." Her smile faded. "Let's hope it's enough to keep these children safe."

"And Tessan?" Nadez asked. "She didn't ask for refuge for herself. What will happen to her?"

"Nothing good," Lauma replied. "If she's lucky, without Ottosen's children to worry about, she may be able to make an alliance with a man who will protect her. Although any alliance will not favour her." Lauma sighed. "My guess is that she will not live very long after she sends her children to Byholt."

"Another murder at the hands of Olvir?" Nadez asked. She was starting to hate the man; though, Lauma seemed to think this was all business as usual for Clan Freeholders. Had it always been this bloodthirsty?

"Or she might decide to take matters into her own hands," Lauma said. "If she thinks that her death will help save her children."

"And we can do nothing to help."

"Tessan admitted that she was expecting this," Lauma replied. "She knew who and what Henrik Ottosen was before she married him, and that marriage was to help her family. Unfortunately, Clan Ottosen absorbed Tessan's family, and there are none left who are independent enough to help her."

"It seems drastic," Nadez replied. "And so very wrong."

"I keep forgetting that you are not on the inside," Lauma replied. "Most Clan Freeholders gain power through either murder or marriage. I am an exception."

"Saulia Holt inherited," Nadez replied.

"Because Tarmo and Asla were murdered," Lauma reminded her. "Not by someone from the Fair Seas Treaty Alliance, but neither of them died of natural causes."

"It's surprising that anyone wants to become Clan Freeholder," Nadez replied.

She hoped Olvir Jarvi never found out about Pia and Frida: that Ottosen's death and Valda's willingness to keep the secret meant that the Engen girls were safe.

No wonder Pia was terrified by the thought. It could be a death sentence even for the most prepared.

"ARE YOU SURE we can spare a dinghy?" Dag asked Darya. The captain had already told Rahm to take one of the three small boats, but Dag worried that they might need them all later.

"Three are not enough to save us all if we start sinking," Darya said. "If that's what you're worried about." She smiled to soften her answer.

"I wasn't," Dag replied. "But now I wonder if I should be."

"It takes a lot to sink a ship like this," Darya said. "And usually a long time. Long enough to get us closer to land. I would rather not risk even one single sailor on the task of rowing Rahm ashore. We have no idea what is happening on Strongrock, and I won't risk a sailor not being able to return to the ship."

"I'll do it." Gustav stepped away from the gunwale. "Rahm likes me. Well, he likes me as much as he likes anyone. I'm used to rowing, so it shouldn't take me very long to get back here."

"He'll make you row there," Dag said. "Which means your back will be to the island the whole way. It doesn't seem safe."

"Captain Demer?" Gustav said. "It's a chance to keep the dinghy. If anything happens, I'll abandon the boat and swim back."

Darya met Dag's eyes. "Gustav is not part of my crew," she said. "That is your decision. I would prefer to not lose the dinghy, but I will only agree if you feel it's absolutely safe."

"No," Dag said to Gustav. "And that's an order. You may think you've been forgiven for stowing away on the *Atlaine*, but you haven't been. Not by me. Don't make things worse by disregarding a direct order."

"I won't," Gustav said. He sighed. "I have duties in the kitchen." He slowly walked away.

Once he had gone below, Darya laughed. "He's going to do something, isn't he?"

"He better not," Dag replied. She really hoped he didn't try to go ashore. Strongrock was not safe in the best of times and now, with Rahm setting foot on it? She thought it would be even more dangerous.

Darya called a few orders, and the anchor was released. It was almost dusk, and they were less than a mile offshore. The pirate settlement was northwest, just past the beach with the abandoned fishing huts. Though the beach looked deserted, Dag still worried that someone might be here. She'd walked along this coast. There was a path through the forest making it easy to get here on foot.

"I'll see Rahm off," she said to Darya.

"And make sure Gustav doesn't get in the dinghy with him?"

"Yes." Dag headed to the bow where Rafael was getting a dinghy ready to launch. Rahm stood to one side, his eyes on the island in front of them.

"Have you spent much time on Strongrock?" she asked him.

"More than I ever wanted to," he said. "That was before Ansdottir was captain here. She arrived just as I was leaving."

"That's why you were able to double-cross her for Pinho," Dag said. "She knew you as a pirate."

Rahm shrugged. "She trusted the wrong person."

"You, she trusted you."

"Yes. No one should trust me. I certainly don't trust anyone else."

"It sounds lonely," Dag said, suddenly sad for him. If what Rahm had told Gustav was true, he'd been forced into a life of an assassin incredibly young, and his token had meant there had been no way out. Her Trait activated as something Hidden was uncovered. "That's why you have two families."

He turned to look at her. "It didn't help though," he said. "I had to lie to everyone. I always told myself that it was to protect them, but really it was to protect myself."

The dinghy was lowered over the side.

"We're ready," Rafael called.

"Will you be all right?" Dag asked.

"Don't worry about me." Rahm flashed a grin. "I'm always all right."

"Gustav wanted to go with you," she said. "I told him no. If he somehow ends up in the dinghy, you are to bring him back."

"I already told him I'd toss him overboard," Rahm said. "The very last thing I want is to worry about him."

"Would you?" she asked. "Worry about him?"

Rahm sighed. "I wouldn't want to, but I have children his age."

"Kasim and Berna," Dag replied. "Calder wants them all to meet. Maybe he can bring all your children here for a visit?"

"Why would he do that?"

"They deserve the chance to ask you questions," Dag said. "Though I'm not sure you would tell them the truth. I'm not sure you even know what the truth is."

"I would like to see them." He turned to her. "I would appreciate it if you asked Calder to do that."

"I will," Dag said. "As long as it's safe for them here."

"I'll know that in a few hours," Rahm said. He nodded, hoisted his pack onto his back, and headed for the dinghy.

Dag leaned over to make sure Gustav was nowhere in sight. Rahm settled in at the oars and started rowing.

"Do you think he'll survive the night?" Rafael asked when he joined her at the gunwale.

The dinghy headed straight towards the beach and though Rahm faced the ship, she didn't see him look her way.

"Rahm is hard to kill," she said. She hoped that was still true, despite the loss of his token.

CHAPTER 15

AFTER THE SUN went down, no lights were visible on shore.

Calder had the ship sail a little closer to the beach. The two structures had an air of disuse. The door to one of the buildings was open—the school, he thought—and it looked like part of the roof had collapsed. It didn't mean no one was there, but he thought that if anyone was, they were not part of the main group of pirates.

"It looks abandoned," Calder said to Nataniel. "So we don't need to go ashore. It's time to see what's happening in the main settlement. We'll sail with lights until I give the signal to douse them."

"Aye, Sir." Nataniel called out an order before spinning the wheel. In response, the ship started to arc back out to sea.

"Is it safe to sail without lights?" Esma asked him as she followed him to the bow.

"Safe enough," he replied. "I've sailed around this spit of land in the dark before." As long as they didn't run into the *Vassan*, they should fine. He wasn't sure what he was hoping would happen. He wanted to know if Pinho was here, on Strongrock, and in charge of the pirates, but he wasn't actually prepared to send anyone ashore to find out.

There was no sign of a dinghy at the next beach: the one that had been here had been used by the pirates who had been abandoned by Tarmo Holt.

"Lights out!" he called. The point was just ahead.

His focus narrowed as his Trait triggered. He grinned when he recognized the ship: Luck was working tonight.

"We need to slow down and signal," Calder called to Nataniel as he hurried towards him. "That's the *Atlaine*." A lit lamp was handed to him, and Calder headed to the bow. Orders were called, and sailors scrambled to shorten the sails. The ship started to slow a moment later.

He swung the lamp back and forth, before shuttering it and unshuttering it, trying to replicate an Intelligencer code. There was a response from the *Atlaine*: a lamp swung back and forth.

The *Pathfinder* barely moved as it waited for the other ship to come alongside.

"Dag!" he called out. He could see her in the bow of the *Atlaine*, and she waved at him. "Come aboard!" She nodded, and he hurried back to the wheel.

"Drop anchor," Calder said. "And keep an eye out for their dinghy."

"Was that your Trait?" Esma asked when she joined him. "It seems awfully Lucky that we meet up with the *Atlaine* just before getting to the pirates."

"Yes," Calder replied. "That's Luck. Hopefully Dag has information on Pinho's whereabouts." It was what he was trying to find out, but he knew his Trait didn't always give him what he wanted.

He stared at the beach while he waited for Dag. There was still no sign of life on shore.

The *Atlaine* came about and launched a dinghy. Dag sat in the bow, and Rafael was at the tiller. Two sailors were rowing, and Calder grinned when he recognized one of them as Jaak.

Dag climbed over the gunwale first and stepped directly into his arms.

"Why am I not surprised to find you with a ship?" she said. He shrugged and kissed her.

"It's an interesting story," Esma said. "Dagrun, it's nice to see you again."

"You too, Esma," Dag replied.

"Jaak, Rafael," Calder said. "Welcome aboard the *Pathfinder*. And Gustav. I did not expect to see you." The younger Intelligencer grinned, and Dag rolled her eyes.

"I'll tell you all about it," Dag said. "I assume there's a cabin where we can talk?"

"This way. Esma, please ask Nataniel to join us," Calder said. "You need to come too."

He led the way to the captain's cabin. Once the door was closed, Dag walked back into his arms.

"Gustav stowed away," she said. "In Lavais Port. And we just left your father on Strongrock."

"What?" Calder was shocked. "How? Never mind. I know how. He is single-minded and hard to stop. Ottosen?"

Dag nodded, stepping away from Calder. "Rahm made it to Tarklee before I did," she said. "After stopping in Lavais Port where his token was Unmade." She turned to look at Gustav. "I thought you might want to ask Gustav about that. He and Pia made a bargain with Rahm."

"I hope Pia lived too?" he asked. Gustav nodded, and he relaxed. "But that means there is no longer a way to control Rahm, which is a very good thing."

There was a knock on the door, and Esma entered, followed by Nataniel.

"Gustav is just filling me in on what our father has been up to." Calder turned back to Gustav. "What about this bargain?"

"We," Gustav said. "I mean, me and Pia, found Rahm in Setberg. He said his name was Hakon and that he'd come from Nurmi. We realized that he was lying, and then he figured out that we were Intelligencers. He knew about Jarri: that he Unmakes things."

"I told him," Calder said. "He asked for your help?"

"He wanted to trade," Gustav said. "And we didn't think it a good idea to refuse. We told him that pirates were causing trouble in Nurmi and that if he could get them out of town, we'd take him to Jarri."

"Ursa Ozlinch and her group," Dag said. "They left when Rahm told them to. He thinks that if she returned to Strongrock that Steen would have killed her."

"So, Rahm's token was Unmade," Calder said. "What about Ottosen?"

"Rahm took the road to Tarklee," Dag said.

Gustav looked at the deck, which made Calder wonder if he had helped his father.

"I gave him Ottosen's name," Calder said. "On behalf of someone even Rahm wouldn't dare betray. My father would have completed this task no matter who helped him."

"That's what I thought," Gustav said. "Pia helped him get to Tarklee, but I know she feels bad about it. I mean, she hated Ottosen, but she didn't really want him dead."

Dag gave him a look, and Calder knew that Pia had indeed wanted Ottosen dead. And after what the Clan Freeholder had done to her and her sister, he couldn't blame her. At least she hadn't tried to kill him herself.

"If you know my father killed Ottosen," he said to Dag. "Why is he not locked up in Tarklee? Did my mother let him go?"

"He stowed away on the *Atlaine*," Dag said. "We found him before arriving in Lavais Port. There was no time to send him back and really, I doubt there's a jail that will hold him for long." She shrugged. "He no longer can be hired as an assassin, and he agreed to stay on Strongrock for a couple of years."

"You just set him ashore now?" Strongrock was as good a place as any for his father. "We think Pinho might already be there. This used to be one of his ships. His flagship was destroyed, and a third was damaged and captured. My fear is that he will end up in charge of both the pirates and the *Vassan*."

"Which means Pinho will still be a threat," Esma said.

"He'll have a base where he can regroup and rebuild," Calder added. "He has resources in Pilalia if he can get access to them, including plenty of coin to make promises to pirates with."

Dag and Rafael exchanged a look. "Rafael wondered if your father would live through the night," she said. "Maybe he won't."

"Where did he go ashore?" Calder asked.

"Close to the abandoned huts on the other side of the settlement," Dag replied. "We didn't want anyone to see him arrive. We kept the *Atlaine* dark when we sailed past the harbour, and we didn't hear any alarms."

He blew out a breath, surprised to find that he was relieved. "Then he has all the advantage he needs." He shrugged. "If Rahm survives, it will be because Pinho does not. And we will be in the same situation as Pia. Hoping someone is dead but not wanting it to be us who kills them."

"And our father will have dealt another death," Esma said.

NADEZ HURRIED THROUGH the streets and across Key Bridge to the warehouse feeding station.

Unlike when she'd been followed and then directed to a warehouse where she could find some of the stolen food, this time she'd been sent a message.

The message had been cryptic: someone had important information for the Master Intelligencer, and if she didn't show up before dark, the person would leave.

She assumed it was food: what else was so important? Had Valda Skala told a second person to return stolen food? Is that why the method of informing her was so different?

She slowed as she approached the warehouse. It was in a fairly prosperous part of town, which seemed unusual for the type of message she'd received. The other food had been returned to warehouses in the poorest neighbourhoods.

"Master Intelligencer," the man at the door said. "You're wanted in the back corner."

Nadez nodded and headed in the direction he'd pointed. The corner was dark, but when she was halfway there, a hooded figure stepped out into the light.

"I need your help," the man said when she stopped in front of him.

There was movement in the shadow, and she took a step back. But it wasn't anything dangerous. A child of about six looked up at her with tear-stained cheeks. The child, a boy, turned, and a second one, identical, joined him.

"You'll take care of them?" the man asked.

"Yes. Do they know what their Traits do?" It was the only reason why the children would be given to her. "Are you their father?"

"A relative," the man said. "And that's all I'm going to say. Karlis and Kaspars." He indicated the children. "Know who I am, but they've been asked not to tell." He looked away and his shoulders drooped. "No one knows what they can do." He turned and faced her. "We have an idea, they have an idea, but *knowing* might have been dangerous for them."

"I see. And their circumstances have changed recently," she said. These children had to have been under Henrik Ottosen's protection. Was Olvir Jarvi threatening them?

The man frowned. "Can you take them or not?"

"I can take them," she said. "But I can't promise that they will become Intelligencers. I will only train them if they have the right temperament."

"But you'll keep them safe?"

"I will do my best," Nadez replied.

The man turned and knelt down in front of the boys. He gathered them in his arms, and they buried their faces and sobbed.

He rose and sighed before stepping away from them.

"They will always be loved," he said to Nadez. "But we can't keep them safe."

"I understand," Nadez said.

With one last look at the twins, the man walked across the warehouse and out the door.

She turned her attention to the children, who cried quietly.

"I will do my best for you," she said. "Come on. Have you eaten?"

"Not hungry," one boy said.

"We'll get you something anyway," Nadez replied. She ushered the children to the front and had the man in charge put a few spoonful of stew in bowls for them. She didn't want to leave the warehouse so soon after the twin's father had, and she was certain that he was their father.

Silent, they sat at a table. One of the boys picked up the spoon, but he didn't actually eat the food.

When she felt that enough time had passed, Nadez returned the uneaten food: it hadn't been touched and even if it had been, it was precious enough that it would be reheated and given out to someone else.

With a boy holding onto each hand, she walked them back to the Hall. She'd keep them in her apartment for tonight and figure out what to do with them in the morning.

During the walk back to the Hall, she wondered how many other children were in danger because there was a new Clan Freeholder.

She couldn't remember the last time a new Clan Freeholder had been determined by some means other than inheriting. Lauma, maybe, when she'd bought her way into her Clan Freeholdership. Although as Lauma had pointed out, both Ottosen and Saulia Holt had inherited when murders had been committed. Had bloodshed always been part of Clan Freehold successions? She hated to admit that in the past she might not have paid much attention to the deaths of children, or faithful employees like Rein Chebek.

CHAPTER 16

GUSTAV STARED AT Strongrock Island. He desperately wanted to set foot on the island, but he knew there was little chance of that.

He sighed and headed back to the wheel where Calder Rahmson and Dagrun Lund were huddled.

"We shouldn't leave without knowing for certain," Dagrun said. "There's too much at stake."

"It's dangerous," Calder replied.

"Of course it is," Dagrun said. "But we need to know. The Three remain in immediate danger if Pinho controls Strongrock."

"And only in distant danger if our father does." That was Esma, Calder's sister. "The same can be said of Arressa."

"I don't like it," Calder replied.

"Neither do I," Dagrun said. "But it has to be done."

"We must be careful," Calder said. "Too many on that island know who we are. Including Pinho."

"I'll go," Gustav said, stepping closer. The other three stared at him. "Rahm trusts me as much as he trusts anyone, and no one else will know who I am. And my Trait should help."

Dagrun frowned before she sighed. "It might work. Gustav has the sailing skills to make it here in a sailboat if anyone asks."

Calder stared at him. "It will be dangerous."

"I know." Gustav didn't remind them that he and Pia had been walking into and out of dangerous situations all winter.

"Tonight," Dagrun said. "While it's still dark." She looked at

Calder. "I have to go. My Trait will keep us both hidden, and I won't let anyone see *me*. If we come across any pirates, Gustav will approach them."

"If you're sure," Calder said. "Gustav, you will do exactly what Dag tells you."

"I promise," Gustav said, doing his best to keep his excitement out of his voice. He was going to Strongrock!

"We mean it," Dagrun said, staring at him. "I'll go ashore with you and take you along the path to the edge of the settlement. At that point, *I* will decide if you go any further. If it looks too dangerous, we will return to the ship. Do you understand?"

"I understand." Gustav nodded.

"All right," Dagrun said. "Meet me in the captain's cabin in an hour. I'll have people there who can fill you in on what we know about Strongrock, the pirates, and Pinho and his men."

"Jaak should go ashore too," Calder said. "If he's willing. I don't like the idea of having only one person who can row."

"I'll ask him," Dagrun said. "I need him to talk to Gustav anyway."

"Why Jaak?" Gustav asked. He'd talked to the sailor and knew he'd been with Calder and Dagrun for a long time, but he thought he was just part of the crew.

"Because Jaak grew up on Strongrock," Dagrun replied. "He used to be a pirate. Now find something to eat, or a tea, and be back in an hour."

"Will do." Gustav turned and headed for the mess. Jaak had grown up a pirate. He'd probably sailed under Margit Ansdottir. He must have some stories to tell.

He found a warm pot of tea and sat at a table, slowly sipping tea while he tried to tamp down his excitement. He was going to set foot on Strongrock Island!

"I MIGHT NEED another horse and wagon just for ferrying Intelligencers along the road," Pavil said to Pia. He pulled on the reins, and his horse and wagon came to a stop. "Maybe set one up here so you don't always have to walk to my place."

Here was the edge of Tarklee. It was mid-morning, and the streets were busy.

Pia jumped down from the wagon. "That's actually a good idea," she said. She'd mention it to Nadez. At least she hoped she had a chance to talk to Nadez about plans for Intelligencers.

"It would cost something to keep a horse and wagon here in town," Pavil said. "Someone needs to look after them and drive the wagon, but it would make travel along the road faster."

"It would," Pia said. "You'd have to charge people for the trip. I'm sure the Intelligencers would be steady customers."

"Need more'n just you," Pavel said. "But it might be worth a try."

"I think so too," Pia said. "Thank you again." She waved and headed off towards the centre of the city. The closer she got to the Hall, the more nervous she became.

Solvig hadn't blamed her for her actions, but Nadez might. Especially helping Gustav stow away on the *Atlaine*.

So, she was here to confess. And to be truthful, it seemed like a better option than returning to Lavais Port and being asked about Gustav's whereabouts. She didn't want to lie, not to Berna and not to her fellow Intelligencers. She'd decided that her best option was to come to Tarklee and confess to Nadez what she'd done.

At least this way she'd know immediately if the Master Intelligencer wanted her to quit.

The streets she walked through were calm, and everyone she passed seemed reasonably content.

The Hall was quiet as well. She showed her patch to the single guard at the entrance and headed directly to the Master Intelligencer's office.

The door to the outer office was open, so she entered.

"How do we figure out what they can do?" someone asked.

"I have no idea." That was Nadez. "We might have to wait for Dagrun to return."

"We know," a child said, and surprised, Pia leaned into Nadez's office.

The Master Intelligencer sat at her desk, Lauma Strauskas standing at her side. Both women were staring at two children who sat across from Nadez.

Lauma spotted her first. "Pia, you're back. Not more bad news, I hope?"

"No," she said. "The captain and crew were delivered safely to Lavais Port. I visited my sister and then came back here as Nadez requested."

"I'm glad you're here," Nadez said. "I don't like all my Intelligencers in one place. Pia, meet our newest potential recruits, Kaspars and Karlis."

Two heads turned to her. "Hi," Pia said. The boys, obviously twins, blinked and turned back to face Nadez. Pia's stomach dropped: she knew who these boys were. Ottosen had tried to keep them a secret, but rumours and whispers about twins had always caught her attention.

"We were just discussing what to do with them," Lauma said.

"They need supervision," Nadez said. "But we don't know what their Traits are, so we can't leave them with just anyone." She sighed. "And none of the teachers are in Tarklee."

"I'll take them," Pia said. It would give her a chance to be useful, and to make Nadez realize that she needed her.

"Are you sure?" Nadez asked.

"Yes. I can show them the dining hall, and I know where the extra clothing is kept. Do they have a room?"

"They are far too young to be on their own," Lauma said. "Nadez, they will need to stay with you until you can find someone to look after them."

"We're not babies," one boy said. "We can look after ourselves. And we can do things."

Pia's smile was sad. She recognized the fear behind the need to not be a burden. "I'd like to know what you can do," she said. She met Nadez's eyes. "If I spend time with them, I can probably get enough information to figure out their Traits."

"That would be very helpful," Nadez said. "Bring them back here at the end of the day. Lauma is right, they are far too young to be left on their own." She paused. "Was there something else you wanted to speak to me about?"

"It can wait," Pia said. "Come on, Karlis and Kaspars. Let's get you a change of clothes." The twins followed her into the outer office. "Wait here a minute," she said before stepping back into Nadez's office.

Lauma and Nadez looked at her expectantly.

"I know who they are," Pia said quietly. "The children of one of Ottosen's guards."

"Really?" Nadez asked. "How would these children be a threat to the new Clan Freeholder?"

"It's possible that simply being of interest to Ottosen puts them in danger," Lauma said. She turned to Nadez. "Jarvi might not have any idea that the children have Traits. It could be about loyalty."

"Then why deliver just the children and not try to save the whole family?" Nadez asked.

"Because with you, being trained as Intelligencers, they will be protected in a way they would not be if their whole family tried to escape," Lauma said. She sighed. "I hope word gets out that we're willing to help them all."

"I'm sure it will," Pia said. "People talk. That's how I know about these boys."

"I hope so," Nadez replied. She looked directly at Pia. "I had no idea Clan Freeholder succession was so dangerous. Especially for children."

"It can be dangerous for everyone," Lauma said.

"I see that now," Nadez said. "Thank you, Pia. I'll see you and the boys back here later."

Pia nodded and ducked out of the room. The twins were staring at her with wide eyes, and she knew they'd overheard the conversation.

"I won't tell anyone else," she said to them. "I promise."

"Why should we trust you?" one boy asked.

Pia shrugged. "You shouldn't. I certainly didn't trust anyone when I ended up in Ottosen's household. What you *can* trust is what you learn and what you can do. And starting today, you have a chance at both."

She ushered them out the door and then led the way to the dining hall. She had to assume they would never trust her. But she still had to figure out what their Traits were.

DAG OPENED THE door. Gustav stood outside the captain's cabin looking a little nervous. He grinned, and she stepped aside so he could enter.

"Jaak," she said as she re-joined the group around the table. "I think you know Gustav?"

"Sure," Jaak said.

Gustav filled the empty space between Calder and Darya. Esma was on Darya's other side, then Jaak, Dag, and Calder.

A map of Strongrock Island was on the table. Dag pointed to the beach where they were anchored. "Here's where we are now," she said. "Jaak will stay with the dinghy." She traced a line along the coast. "I'll take Gustav along the path to the square. We know from reports that the inn has been damaged by fire, but we can't assume no one is there."

"If it has a roof," Jaak said. "Someone'll be using it."

"Calder confirmed that no one is using the school or the bunkhouse," Dag said. "And they have roofs." She turned to Gustav. "Jaak grew up on this other beach, along with more children who had been found alone in Tarklee. There was a woman who looked after them until Margit Ansdottir brought them here."

"It was better than starving," Jaak said. "But I didn't like being a pirate."

"The pump is in the square," Calder said. "It's the main source of water for the settlement. It might be guarded, depending on who has control of the island."

"Which we have to assume is Pinho," Dag said. "If there is a guard at the pump, Gustav, that's as far as you need to go. Use your Trait and see if you can get the guard to tell you who's in charge. I'll be watching, so if you get into trouble, signal, and I'll create a diversion. Then you get out of there." She looked at him, and he nodded.

"I'll make this signal." He flashed the Intelligencer distress signal. "And if they are restraining my hands, I'll do this." He nodded his head back and forth.

"If they try to restrain your hands, I will have already created a diversion," Dag said. "And I will make the decision on whether you leave the path, is that clear?" There were so many things that could go wrong. She had to trust her Trait to uncover any Hidden dangers.

"Are you sure you don't want Luck with you?" Calder asked. Dag shook her head. "It's too unpredictable," she replied. "Besides, if we get caught and Rahm is in charge, we might need you and Esma to bargain for our safe return." She didn't actually expect them to be needed: Rahm wanted his family to visit. Keeping Dag prisoner might get Calder onto the island but would ensure that his other children would stay away.

"Are we ready?" Dag looked around the room. Five heads nodded at her. "Let's go."

Darya led the way up to the deck. The dinghy had already been lowered on the side of the ship away from shore.

Jaak and Gustav both climbed down into the dinghy. Dag shared a look with Calder before going over the gunwale. She sat in the bow while Gustav settled at the oars and Jaak sat in the stern, his hand on the tiller. With a few strokes, Gustav had the dinghy out of the shadow of the ship. The beach ahead was dark and deserted. Dag stared intently at the shore, but nothing triggered her Trait.

A dozen minutes later, sand scraped the bottom of the boat. Dag jumped into the gentle surf and pulled the dinghy up onto the beach. Jaak joined her while Gustav stowed the oars.

"If we're not back in two hours, head back to the ship," Dag said, leaning close to Jaak's ear.

"Sure," he replied. With the dinghy's painter in hand, he sat down with his back to the boat and almost disappeared in the shadow of the prow.

"Come on." Dag grabbed Gustav's sleeve and led him up the beach to the path. She paused before stepping into the woods. Faint moonlight bathed where the beach met the path. She didn't see any evidence of recent visitors: the sand was windswept and there were no footprints in the dirt of the path. It looked like no one had been here since the last rain.

"We will be moving slowly," she said to Gustav. "It will take a while to get to the square. Stay close, pay attention to where I step and to my hand signals. Do not trip or bump into me. Understand?"

"Yes," Gustav replied. "I'll do my best."

"Fair enough." She couldn't ask for more, really, but she had no idea if Gustav's best would be good enough. Her Trait should help hide them both, as long as they were quiet, but he was from an island port and had then moved to Tarklee. She had no idea if he had any experience walking quietly on a trail. And what was worse, she could almost feel his nervous excitement.

But despite being only half-trained, he had proven to be incredibly resourceful even back when they were both staying in Joosep's safe house.

It took them twenty minutes to reach the square. She knelt behind a bush, and with Gustav crouching at her back, she peered out.

And frowned. The pump was not being guarded. What did that

mean? The itch between her shoulder blades suddenly blossomed as her Trait was triggered. Before she could figure out where the danger was, Gustav lurched to his feet and practically stepped over her to enter the square.

CHAPTER 17

GUSTAV DID HIS best not to step on Dagrun. He stumbled away from her towards the square, making as much noise as he could.

He hadn't seen anyone, but he'd smelled urine and had just reacted. This was what he'd been told to do: interact with whoever was guarding the pump in the square. It just so happened the guard was taking a piss almost on top of them.

"Heya," Gustav called out, trying to force Charisma into his words. "You hear the news?"

The guard stepped out of the woods and stared at him. "Where did you come from?"

"I've been hiding out," Gustav said and shrugged. "Didn't want to get in the middle of anything. Not my fight, you hear?"

"Aye, I hear," the other man said. "Too many captains and not enough ships. Alls I want is what we had. A tavern with ale, a captain who was smart, and a hammock in the hold."

"And plenty to go around," Gustav said. "How many captains are there? Two? Three? Four? And really, Ursa's never been a sailor."

"That's what I've always said," the pirate replied. "She was a good tavern keep though. Steen didn't have to string her up."

"It's a miracle she made it back here," Gustav said. "That is not a fun trip. All the way from Swyford in those little sailboats. Never been so cold. Any word on the *Vassan* heading to the Sapphire Sea? Sure would like to be warm again."

"You came from Swyford too, huh?" the pirate asked him. He stared at him for a few moments. "Where did you say you've been?"

"Down the beach aways," Gustav replied. "You ever know a sailor named Jaak?"

The pirate spit. "Heard he turned traitor. What about him?"

"Well, before he turned traitor, he told me about the beach where he grew up. There's a couple of cabins and some good fishing there."

"Never been there," the pirate said. "But yeah, Jaak grew up along there. I've heard nothing about when the *Vassan* will sail. We still have too many captains."

"Thought only Steen was left," Gustav said. "On account of Ursa being gone."

"A new one showed up," the pirate said. "A Pilalian. Trying to buy our loyalty with promises. Says he needs the *Vassan* so he can get coin and bring it back. Me? I want to see the coin first. I agree with Steen on that account."

"Can't blame you," Gustav said. He put his hands behind his back and did his best to signal that information to Dagrun. And that was his task done. Pinho was here. All he had to do now was sneak away from this pirate and head back to Dagrun.

Suddenly, shouts came from the direction of the tavern.

"What's that all about?" Gustav asked.

"That can only be trouble." The pirate looked at him for a moment. "I need to see what's going on. And you're coming with me."

Before Gustav could react, the pirate grabbed his arm and started pulling him towards the tavern. Just as he was wondering whether he should break free, another pirate joined them.

"Who's this?" the new pirate asked. He seized Gustav's other arm, trapping him between them.

"A friend of Jaak's," the guard replied. "Nils, what's happened?"

"Nothing Steen can't handle," Nils replied. He stared at Gustav. "A friend of a traitor is a traitor."

With his arms restrained, Gustav didn't have a chance to signal Dagrun while he was led towards the tavern. He kept his head lowered even as he tried to get a feel for his surroundings.

They passed the burned-out inn, and just ahead a fire lit up the night sky. Would Dagrun have a chance to create a diversion? That had been the plan, but what if she'd been taken prisoner as well?

The tavern was a dark shadow against the brightness of the fire. Nils shoved him into the shadowed wall.

"Keep him here while I let Steen know we found a traitor," he said and headed towards the fire and the increasing shouts and cries ahead.

"You heard him," the pirate said. "Don't move." He pushed Gustav's chest up against the wooden wall, forcing his head to one side. Gustav stared at the side of his captor's face.

The shouts were louder now and seemed angrier. Sounds of fighting reached them—grunts and thuds and then a scream— and Gustav's pirate guard looked unsure.

"The new captain has his own men, doesn't he?" Gustav asked. Even if he had no ship, Gustav doubted that Pinho had come here alone. His guard glared at him and then seemed to make a decision.

He thrust Gustav ahead of him, out from behind the building and into the light.

Off balance, Gustav fell to his hands and knees.

And that saved him.

Something flew through the air above him, striking his guard. A soft groan escaped him and then he slid to the ground, half on top of Gustav. He twisted around and pushed the man off him. A knife was buried in one eye and the other stared up at the night sky.

Panicked, Gustav slithered out from under the dead pirate and crawled back around the side of the tavern.

Breathing heavily and staying low, he peered out at chaos.

Half a dozen men stood back-to-back, swords and clubs raised in defence. A couple of pirates ran at them with their own weapons raised. There was a furious scuffle, and then one of the attackers fell back, clutching a bleeding arm. The other attacker was felled and lay still on the ground. The small group of defenders shifted, and Gustav saw a sword dripping with what had to be blood.

He sucked in a breath, waiting for another attack, but the rest of the pirates took a step back. One man at the back swung his arms wide, and the pirates formed a large circle with the defenders inside.

"One of you killed Pinho," a man in the centre of the defenders yelled. "Which one of you did it? We only want him."

"It wasn't one of us," the pirate who had made the arm motion said. He walked through the crowd and stopped, facing Pinho's man. "And if it was, I will deal with him."

"Will you, Steen? It leaves you as the only captain," the first man said. "We all heard how you treated Ursa Ozlinch. Why wouldn't we think you dealt with Fihaldo Pinho in the same way?"

"Ursa Ozlinch was a traitor to pirates," Steen replied. "And was tried by pirates. Her death was justice. Pinho's death was not."

"And yet he's dead just the same," the man replied. "And none of you will ever see the coin he promised."

"A promise doesn't feed a hungry man," Steen said. "Or buy a barrel of ale." Steen made a hand signal, and the circle of pirates closed in on Pinho's men. "Anyone who wishes to join us, put down your weapons and become a Strongrock pirate."

"And if we don't?"

Something flew past Gustav, and a second later, Steen stumbled and fell. The crowd of pirates rippled, many of them looking over their shoulders.

Gustav recognized Nils, who leaned over Steen. "Steen's dead!" he yelled.

"It wasn't us," Pinho's man called out. "It came from over there." He pointed in Gustav's direction.

Gustav froze for a moment, before he started backing away from the tavern wall.

As soon as he was out of the fire light, he turned and started running back towards the pump.

Someone grabbed him and pulled him into the ruins of the inn.

"Shh," someone said into his ear. "We need to be quiet."

He looked over his shoulder to find Rahm grinning at him. Gustav widened his eyes but didn't make a sound.

"Secure the ship!" someone called as they ran past the inn. "To the *Vassan*!"

A dozen other people ran past, and now Gustav worried about Dagrun.

"She's safe," Rahm whispered in his ear. "And soon the pirates will mostly be out at sea, and we'll be safe too."

Gustav did his best to calm his racing heart. He didn't need Pia's Concentration to figure out that Rahm had just killed at least one—and probably two—men.

The assassin might be safe, but Gustav wasn't sure he was.

As soon as the pirate grabbed Gustav, Dag rose to her feet.

When the second pirate arrived, she hunched down, hiding in the bushes. The plan had been to create a diversion if Gustav had trouble, but they had assumed a single pirate would be watching the pump. With two pirates holding Gustav, she needed to figure out a new plan.

One that did not include leaving him behind.

She watched them lead Gustav along the path towards the tavern. Once they were out of sight, she crept out of her hiding place and followed. When she reached the remains of the inn, the itch started between her shoulder blades.

She ducked low and headed into the ruins, crawling across the broken and charred floor, testing it before she put her weight on it. The itch intensified when she reached a gap where the floor had fallen into the cellar below. A tiny movement allowed her to home in on a slightly darker shadow below her. Before she could decide what to do, the shadow moved, and a head turned towards her.

"I can hear you breathing," a voice she recognized whispered. "Don't come any closer."

"Rahm?" Dag wasn't sure if she should be relieved or worried. What was he doing hiding out here? Of course. Rahm had started whatever trouble was happening at the inn.

"Go away," Rahm replied.

"I have to get Gustav," Dag said. If he'd been hiding here for a while, he would have seen the pirates take him past. "You know I can't leave without him."

"I'll get him," Rahm said after a moment, and Dag could almost feel his sigh. "You will only make things worse."

"Let me know what I can do," Dag said. She didn't like leaving Gustav's life in Rahm's hands, but she had no idea what he'd started at the inn.

"I already told you," Rahm said. "Go away."

"I'll wait near the pump," Dag said. "If you're not there by dawn, I will assume the worst."

"You're worried about me," Rahm said. "How touching. Now go. I won't be long."

Dag backtracked and made her way out of the inn. Once back at the square, she found a hiding place that allowed her to watch the path that led from the settlement.

The noises and shouts from the inn subsided for a few minutes before suddenly rising again. Had Rahm caused that by rescuing Gustav, or had something else happened?

Gustav had signalled that Pinho was on Strongrock. Was he fighting with the pirates? Had Rahm somehow started a fight between Pinho and Steen? Her Trait activated and then she knew.

That was why Rahm was hiding: he had started a fight between Pinho and the pirates, who were probably being led by Steen. What had he said about Steen? That he was one to hold a grudge and not hold his temper.

So a fight between them would be likely and what was even more likely was that one of them wouldn't survive. Which would benefit Rahm.

Dag didn't think the former Resolute would leave the outcome up to chance: he would make sure one of them died. And since Pinho had stolen his token and caused him harm, she would bet that he was already dead and the fighting was over who was to blame.

Shouts came closer and she heard the sounds of people running. The path from the tavern was crowded with pirates rushing towards the square.

She held her breath, but they weren't looking for intruders. Instead, she heard calls for the *Vassan,* and then fifteen or twenty pirates ran past her heading to the dock.

A few moments later she heard splashing alongside grunts and curses. Dag made her way to the edge of the dock: moonlight showed three dinghies rowing towards the *Vassan.*

She edged into a shadow to watch in case stragglers—either pirates or Pinho's men—followed the main group.

Two figures appeared on the path. Dag closed her eyes in relief: Gustav was in front, running, with Rahm right behind him. After making sure no one was following them, she stepped out from her hiding place.

She met them at the pump, and Gustav launched himself into her arms.

"I'm sorry," he said. "I didn't mean to get taken."

She hugged him. "That was not your fault," she said.

"Are they gone?" Rahm asked.

"About twenty left," Dag replied. She stepped back, looking to see if Gustav had been injured. "In three dinghies."

"I'm not hurt," Gustav said. "Thanks to Rahm."

"Yes," Dag replied. Looking past Gustav, she met Rahm's gaze. "Thank you."

"You owe me a favour," Rahm said.

"I do," she agreed. "But that's not why you did this."

Rahm shrugged. "I like him. And he kept his part of a bargain. You'd be surprised how many people don't."

"Like Pinho," Dag said. "Whose death started all of this." She waved a hand at the square.

Rahm shrugged again. "I had a plan."

"Steen's dead too," Gustav said. "Tonight, someone threw a knife and killed him."

"Someone?" Dag asked, looking at Rahm.

"Also part of my plan," Rahm said. "Although I had to move that part up in order to save Gustav. For you."

"You offered," Dag reminded him. "But I am grateful." She turned to Gustav. "Come on, Jaak will be worried, and we need to warn the ships about the *Vassan*."

"Don't worry about the *Vassan*," Rahm said. "Without a captain, they won't go far."

"Because the other potential captains are dead. Pinho," Dag said, and Rahm nodded. "And Steen." Another nod. The threat he posed to the Three died with Pinho. She should be relieved, and part of her was. But she didn't like that even without his token, Rahm was still killing.

"Ursa is dead too," Gustav said. "Steen killed her."

"Now that anyone looking to be the captain of the pirates is dead," Dag said, "why wait out here?"

"It's very dangerous to *want* to be captain of pirates," Rahm replied. "I don't yet know who I can trust."

"But if they ask you to lead," she replied. "They'll discipline themselves."

"That is usually how it happens," Rahm agreed. "Now go back to your ship. And tell my son and daughter that I look forward to a visit in three months or so."

"I will do that." Dag turned toward the square.

"Good luck," Gustav said behind her, and Rahm chuckled.

"Luck is my son's Trait. I count on skill and knowledge."

Gustav silently followed her all the way back to the beach. Jaak and the dinghy were still there, and she let out a breath she hadn't realized she was holding. It felt like they'd been gone far longer than two hours.

"He probably has a bit of Luck, doesn't he?" Gustav asked quietly.

"Probably," Dag replied. She stepped out onto the beach and waved. Jaak waved back, and she headed his way. They'd gotten the information they needed. It was time to set sail for Messanos and fill the hold with food.

CHAPTER 18

NADEZ SET THE report on top of the others she'd already read and picked up the next one. She was halfway through Joosep's notes detailing the Intelligencer instructors, and she still had no idea where to find any of them.

Apparently keeping instructors' identities secret had included not mentioning where any of them had come from. Which meant that she had no idea where to look.

She scanned the paper and then set that one aside as well.

There was a knock on her door, and grateful for the interruption, she looked up to find Pia leaning against the doorframe.

"Oh, you're back. Bring them in." The twins were the reason she was trying to find instructors.

Pia ushered Karlis and Kaspars into her office, and the boys sat in the chairs.

"Did you figure out their Traits?" Nadez asked.

"She did not," one of the boys said. "We told her."

Pia shrugged. "I asked them. But I did Concentrate to confirm what they told me. Karlis is Creative and Kaspars is Uncreative."

"I draw pictures," one boy said, and Nadez assumed that was Karlis. "My brother is bad at that."

"I see," Nadez replied. She raised her eyebrows at Pia.

"From what I can tell," Pia said. "Karlis tackles issues in ways other people don't. Kaspars is particularly good at following directions." She shrugged. "Whether one or both of them would be good Intelligencers? I don't know."

"They can't be trained if I can't find any instructors." Nadez gestured to the papers on her desk. "Joosep didn't leave a record of where any of them came from, so I have no idea where to start looking."

"Can I take a look?" Pia asked. "If I have enough information, I might be able to use my Trait and find some connections."

"I would be grateful," Nadez said. "I'll take the boys, and if you have time right now, feel free to look through anything in here that might help."

"I have nothing but time," Pia said.

"Excellent. Kaspars, Karlis, you're coming with me. I need to see Lauma and then we'll find something to eat."

She herded the children into the outer office.

"Can I talk to you first?" Pia asked.

"Yes. Stay here, boys." She stepped back into her office.

Pia stared at the floor. "I helped Gustav stow away on the *Atlaine*."

"What?" Nadez asked. "He stowed away? How?"

"We both got off the ship at Lavais Port," Pia said. "But Gustav collected food and water. They were rations he would have eaten had he stayed, so it wasn't stealing. Not really. Then he asked for my help getting back on the ship." She sighed. "And I helped him. I know I shouldn't have, but I did. I'll understand if you think this means I'm not fit to be an Intelligencer. Especially since I helped Rahm get to Tarklee."

"Rahm's actions were neither your fault nor your responsibility," Nadez said. "I thought you understood that? And as for not being an Intelligencer, that is your decision, always, but I do not want you to quit. I need you—the Three needs you—just as Gustav is also needed. Though both of you will be reprimanded." Gustav had asked for permission to go, and he'd been refused. She would need to find a proper way to discipline him for that.

"Are you sure?"

"Yes. So, Gustav is on his way to the Sapphire Sea. I hope he can be useful. To be honest, this confirms that finding instructors is long overdue. Half-trained intelligencers like the two of you— no matter how effective you've been during this crisis—need to complete your training. Take a look through Joosep's notes, and then tomorrow morning, let me know if you've found anything that will help me track down any instructors. After that, the twins will be your responsibility for the rest of the day. Think of it as part of your punishment.

"I will," Pia said. "And I'll find something in here if it takes me all night."

"Good, see you in the morning." Nadez grinned as she left her office. At least she didn't have to watch the twins tomorrow. She knew Intelligencers accepted young children into training— Calder had been six when he'd arrived—but she hadn't had to deal with what that meant. Children that young needed constant supervision, and she had no one available who could do that. Pia had to be temporary: she was neither through her own training nor an adult.

Nadez sighed as she stepped outside.

She'd been working in a crisis for so long that even she expected to be able to do everything. But with so many things that needed to be done, there was no way she could manage it all by herself.

It was time to rebuild both the Intelligencer organization and the training school. And changes would be made. No more secrecy for one: no matter how well-intentioned Joosep's decision to hide the identities of Intelligencers, students, and instructors was, it had crippled them when he and his knowledge were lost.

It was up to her to make sure that didn't happen again.

She sighed again. But she needed to find key people before she could do that.

CALDER KEPT AN eye on the empty beach until the dinghy was alongside the *Pathfinder*. Dag climbed over the gunwale, but Gustav and Jaak stayed in the dinghy.

"We ran into some trouble," Dag said, hugging him. "Rahm sends his regards."

"But everyone is all right?" he asked. He relaxed when Dag nodded against his chest. "What did my father do this time?"

"He saved Gustav from the pirates," Dag replied. She stepped out of his arms. "But that was after he started some sort of conflict on Strongrock." She paused. "One that ended up with both Pinho and Steen dead."

"Leaving my father in control." Calder wasn't surprised. He was also relieved. As much as Rahm hadn't been the best father, he was all he had.

"Not quite yet," Dag said. "But he expects that he soon will be. He would like you and Esma to visit in about three months."

"When he'll be the captain of the pirates," Calder said. "Will he stay on the island?"

"For now," Dag replied. "I think there's a better chance of that if you visit him. But right now, the only thing we need to worry about is getting food to the Three."

"That would be nice," he said. "To only worry about that." He sighed. "I have to stay with the *Pathfinder* until I have a competent captain that I trust."

"Ask Darya to sail her," Dag replied. "If you think Rafael can manage the *Atlaine*." She sighed and ran a hand through her hair. "It's not like we know who will end up owning the *Atlaine* anyway."

"That is a very good idea," Calder said. "I'll ask her when we return to Messanos. That will give me a chance to discuss it with Esma and Nataniel."

"All right," Dag said. "I'm taking Jaak and Gustav on the *Atlaine,* but we'll see you in Messanos."

They shared another hug and a quick kiss before Dag climbed back over the gunwale. Twenty minutes later he watched the *Atlaine*'s sails unfurl as the ship prepared to sail.

Calder found Esma and Nataniel at the wheel.

"We'll be following the *Atlaine* to Messanos," he said. "We can get copies of the ownership documents for the *Pathfinder* made while we're there. I want you and Kasim to have documented proof that you are owners."

"I don't know how we can ever thank you," Esma said. "Now that our father is on Strongrock, I have no idea how we would survive otherwise."

"You can thank me by being a fair trader," he said. "And by being good to the people you employ." He'd been on enough ships to know that some owners and captains made life harder than it had to be for the people who crewed for them.

Calder turned to Nataniel. "Haul anchor. Unless you want to let the *Atlaine* get way ahead of us."

"I think we can beat them to Messanos," Nataniel said. "If you are all right with us trying."

"Why not?" Calder smiled. "Let's race them to Messanos."

CHAPTER 19

PIA SNAPPED AWAKE, and for a moment, she was confused. She lifted her head and realized she had fallen asleep at Nadez's desk. Papers were scattered across the desktop in front of her.

She'd drooled on one of them. She wiped that paper against her trousers and was happy that it wasn't too smudged.

She'd been looking for clues that would help find instructors and had obviously dozed off.

The lamp was still burning, but the dawn light coming in through the window was brighter, so she turned down the wick and extinguished the flame.

She hadn't found anything before falling asleep. She shuffled a page in front of her and leaned over it. No matter how she'd Concentrated, nothing in Joosep's notes had added up to anything.

But *something* must be there: by all accounts Joosep had been secretive and had guarded the identities of staff and students fiercely, but these lists that Nadez had found detailed everything else about them. Ages, areas of expertise, even the dates when they'd arrived at the Hall.

But there were no mentions of families: no spouses or children, not even any Clan affiliations, and that was something that Joosep would have *had* to know in order to trust them.

But where did he keep that information? Based on the copious notes about everything else, she had to believe it was somewhere.

If he'd somehow hidden the details in his notes, she hadn't been able to figure it out. She grabbed a page that described one of her instructors. There was no name listed, but Pia knew her as Instructor Ula. For two years Ula had taught Pia, but she had no idea where the woman had grown up or whether she had a family. She reread the notes, looking for anything that seemed odd.

She closed her eyes and Concentrated, and memories of a particular class surfaced. Ula had been talking about the White Wood and how it was the major source of timber for shipbuilding. Then she'd described how the woods smelled after it rained.

Pia opened her eyes. Ula was probably from Byholt and had spent at least some of her early years in the far north. Lauma was from Cutterstown; she might even know her family.

Pia studied the paper that contained information about Ula. Something here had triggered her Trait. Halfway down the page she saw it. A small detail that she'd thought nothing of before. The list of Ula's skills included woodcraft and tree identification: two things she would have learned while growing up near the largest forest in the Three.

Pia pulled another page of notes towards her. This was for someone she didn't know, a man who mainly taught self-defence and weaponry. But his list of other skills included riding and caring for horses. The Hall kept horses for training purposes, but most horses were in Swyford. She would bet that's where this instructor was from. Nadez might know the name of a weapons instructor who was also a horseman. There couldn't be that many, especially when they could guess his age because they knew when he had arrived at the Hall.

She was getting excited. Byholt wouldn't be easily accessible until the Pale Sea thawed, but she could take the road to Swyford herself.

"Have you been here all night?"

Pia looked up to find Nadez standing in the doorway, the twins hovering behind her.

"I found it," Pia said. "The clues Joosep left in the notes." She waved a hand over a stack of papers. "I know the countries, and in some cases the areas where these instructors spent time."

Nadez sat down across from her. "That is excellent. All I needed was a starting point. What were the clues? I might be able to figure out the rest."

Pia took a paper from the pile. "It's here," she pointed out. "The last two skills listed are related to where the instructor grew up. Or at least, where they spent enough time to learn specific local talents."

"This is very helpful," Nadez said. "Thank you. I almost hate to task you with looking after the twins, but they need someone, and you're the only one here."

"That's all right," Pia replied. "I'm just glad I could help." As far as she was concerned, it didn't make up for her transgressions no matter what Nadez said. But it did make her feel useful, like she was a contributing Intelligencer.

Pia got to her feet and stretched. "I'm famished. Even if the twins have eaten, they are coming to the dining hall with me."

"Take them on a tour afterwards," Nadez said.

"I will." Smiling, Pia left the office, rounded up the two boys, and ignored their protests as she led the way to the dining hall.

NADEZ SAT ACROSS from Lauma and set the list of instructors in front of her. She hadn't been able to name all of them, but along with the one Pia knew, she had enough to start with.

"Do you know any of these people?" she asked. "I need to get the school up and running again, and I think a couple of these instructors came from northern Byholt."

"I recognize two of them," Lauma said. "When I go home, I will ask them to return to their duties here; although, I can't guarantee they will want to."

"Asking is all you can do," Nadez replied. "Do you expect to be leaving soon? Are the Clan Freeholders forcing the vote?" Nadez knew it was going to happen, but she didn't feel ready for a new Grand Freeholder.

"No," Lauma replied. "But I am hopeful that the sea will be free of ice soon, and I admit that I am tired of all of this responsibility. Swyford has made their choice for Grand Freeholder, am I am feeling much more confident about the transition."

"Is it Skala?" Nadez asked. He was her choice mostly because she'd come to appreciate the wisdom and insight of his grandmother.

"Yes," Lauma said. "I do need to talk to my fellow Byholter Clan Freeholders, but I am inclined to approve him."

"I think he's a decent choice," Nadez replied. "And far better than Timonis. So, three years of Skala and then it's Byholt's turn to supply the Grand Freeholder. Would you take on that role again?"

"Not me. Maybe Yakop will be interested."

"Or Berna," Nadez said. "She's been managing things in Lavais Port very well. In three years, she will still be young, but if given the right opportunities between now and then, she could be ready."

"I'll think about that and talk to her and Yakop about it," Lauma said. "Getting her back home to stay will be impossible now anyway. But it's a dangerous thing, to be a young woman in politics."

"I plan on her having allies," Nadez replied. "I want both Calder and Dagrun here, in Tarklee. At least until we settle the school and decide how Intelligencers move forward."

"Are you thinking of stepping down too?"

"Not yet," Nadez replied. "But I won't ever be able to step down if I never train someone to replace me."

"Something many people forget," Lauma replied.

A guard knocked and entered.

"Ships have been spotted," he said. "They're entering the harbour."

"What ships?" Nadez asked. It was far too soon for Dagrun to return. Unless they'd run into trouble.

"I've been told they are log haulers," the guard replied. "I don't know more."

"Thank you," Lauma said. "That is exceptionally good news. The ice on the Pale Sea must have retreated."

"That's a relief," Nadez said. "That both log haulers survived."

"I was worried we would lose one or both," Lauma said.

"Let's go greet them," Nadez said. She led the way out of Lauma's office.

A crowd had gathered at the edge of the dock, and Nadez and Lauma stood at the back.

"More than anything else, I feel that this means we made it to spring," Lauma said. "I wasn't sure we would."

"Neither was I," Nadez replied. They still had a ways to go: the Frozen Pass might not open for a few weeks yet, and the north wouldn't see any plants for a while, but at least they could distribute the food they did have.

Most importantly, she had hope that they'd seen the end of so much disruptive Clan Freeholder deceptions. Not that she expected them to stop scheming, but she did think they would focus on each other and not try to destroy the Alliance or threaten the Three in other ways.

At least for now, until shipping was back to some semblance of normal.

EPILOGUE

"IT'S GOOD TO see so many ships in the harbour," Dag said. She and Calder were standing on the main dock looking out across Tarklee Harbour. The *Atlaine* and the *Pathfinder* were both anchored just off shore alongside the new ship, the *Sea Hope*. Last night the *Oakhaven* and *Tove's Folly* had arrived with Clan Freeholders from both north and south. Including Freeholder Timonis, who Lauma had promised to deal with today, on her last day as Interim Grand Freeholder.

"And good to know that we don't have to leave on any of them," Calder said. He put his arm around her shoulder and pulled her to him. "We might get a chance to spend more than a few days together in the same place."

"I'm counting on it," Dag replied. She'd arrived on the *Atlaine* a few days before Calder and the *Pathfinder*. Darya Demer would captain the *Pathfinder* and her less-seasoned crew for the rest of the season while Rafael took over the *Atlaine*. "Nadez said we can use Joosep's old safe house for as long as we want."

"It will be nice to have some real privacy," Calder replied.

"As long as we don't tell too many people where we are," Dag replied. They'd been using her and Inger's old apartment for the past few nights, and it seemed like the entire city knew they were there.

She sighed. "We should go see how Timonis is faring." She stepped out of his arms, grabbed his hand, and tugged him towards the Hall.

By the time they arrived at the council meeting room, Clan Freeholders were already leaving.

"It's done?" Dag asked Kaja.

"Just now," the other Intelligencer replied. "It went as expected. Only Timonis seemed surprised that he was being sanctioned for treason. There was no agreement on a jail sentence, but he has been permanently stripped of his holdings. Everything except the Lavais shipyards—which will be held and managed by the Grand Freeholder on behalf of the Three—will be divided between the remaining Swyford Clan Freeholders."

"And the new Grand Freeholder agreed?" Calder asked.

"He did." Kaja grinned. "He now holds the majority of Swyford, and he can blame everything on Lauma."

"Good." Dag nodded to Saulia Holt as she left the meeting room. "Clan Freeholder."

"Intelligencer," Saulia said. She stopped. "I owe you my gratitude. All of you, along with Lauma Strauskas. The events my parents put into action would have been devastating for the city. I'm sorry I didn't really see that until it was too late. I hope we can work together in the future."

"I hope for that as well," Dag replied. No doubt Saulia was also grateful that her father's treasonous acts weren't raised and her own Clan Freeholdership challenged. She smiled and slipped past Saulia into the meeting room. Perhaps this would keep the rest of the Clan Freeholders in line until shipping recovered completely.

Pia and Gustav were collecting water glasses from the tables. Lauma sat at the head table with Clan Freeholder Melker Skala. Nadez stood to off one side. The Byholt contingent was the only one left.

"I need to talk to Yakop and Berna," Calder said. "We need to decide where and when to meet for our visit to Rahm. The next two months will go by quickly."

"I'll be with Nadez," Dag replied. She paused at an empty table, and Nadez joined her.

"I'm glad you're here," Nadez said. "After he's finished with Lauma, Grand Freeholder Melker Skala wants to talk to me about the Intelligencers. I want both you and Calder here as well since we've already made some decisions."

"So we have." She glanced at Pia and Gustav. "Which one will be assisting you? Gustav?"

Nadez grinned. "Between a new Grand Freeholder and reopening the training facility, there is a lot of paperwork. Gustav *hates* paperwork. His transgression was the worst."

"Then I'll take Pia," Dag replied. "Unless you want to send her out to look for more instructors?"

"Until we get more students, the two instructors we found will do for now," Nadez said. "Once word gets out that the training facility is operating again, I suspect people will come to us if they want to teach again. Look, I think they're done."

Lauma stood up and glanced over at the Byholters. "I'll be in town for the next week or so," she said to Skala. "In case I'm needed for anything. Otherwise, I wish you good luck as the Grand Freeholder."

"Thank you for all you've done," Skala said. "I think the Alliance is stronger and more aligned than it has been for decades."

"I wouldn't expect that to last if I were you," Lauma said. "Nadez? Your turn."

Dag and Nadez crossed to the head table where Calder joined them.

"Nadez, you're not quitting on me, are you?" Skala asked. "My grandmother speaks highly of you, and we need stability right now."

"Not yet," Nadez replied. "But eventually I will be splitting the Master Intelligencer role into two: Calder will manage Intelligencers working in the field, and Dagrun will handle the more political aspects of the job along with the training facility."

The three of them had agreed that more than one person should shoulder the burden. Decisions would likely be better with more than one opinion.

"What about you?" Skala asked.

"I might retire then," Nadez replied.

"I'll recruit you to teach," Dag said quickly.

"Take your time deciding," Skala said. "We still have much to do. Can I meet with the three of you tomorrow afternoon?"

"That will be fine," Nadez said. She stepped away from the table, and Dag and Calder followed her.

"Teach what?" Nadez asked.

"Clan Freeholder history," Dag replied, with a grin.

THE END

AUTHOR BIOGRAPHY

Jane Glatt loves that along with creating original worlds, writing fantasy allows her to indulge her curiosity about an eclectic group of subjects. So far she's researched synaesthesia, medieval guilds, tidal rivers, cities atop bridges, pirates and privateers, plants used for healing, and the history of spying. For that last one she blames a visit to the International Spy Museum (yes, it's a real place), in Washington, D.C.

For news on Jane's future releases visit her website http://janeglatt.com/index.html and sign up for her newsletter

www.ingramcontent.com/pod-product-compliance
Lightning Source LLC
Chambersburg PA
CBHW030327030726
47499CB00003B/679